THE WAR REMAINS

— • —

THE BARBER BROTHERS' NEXT ADVENTURE

JASON B. BAKER

GREER

B O O K S

THE WAR REMAINS

ALSO BY

"This writer has a future in the genre."

-RON SCHWAB, Bestselling author of Coldsmith, *Old Dogs*, *The Accidental Sheriff*, and other classic Western novels.

The Barber Brothers' Adventures

The Ace's Bounty

The War Remains

The Legacy Stand

Barber Brothers' Adventures Prequel

The Sheriff's Pursuit

The Vengeance of Reed Caine

Red Canyon Reckoning

River's Fortune

Sins of Santa Fe

Narrative Non-Fiction

Chicago To Appomattox: The 39th Illinois Infantry In The Civil War

Learn more about Jason and his books, and sign up for future updates at JasonBakerAuthor.com

True peace is not merely the absence of war, it is the presence of justice.

-Jane Addams

CONTENTS

PROLOGUE

—◦—

Iron County, Missouri - Early morning, September 27, 1864

D awn's first light crept over the landscape, casting long shadows between the trees. Captain Elijah Barber, leading a small contingent of his Union cavalry company, surveyed the dense growth with a grim determination. Only the droning hum of locusts, the awakening chorus of birds, and the creaking of saddle leather from the anxious soldiers behind him broke the silence.

"We know you're in there," Elijah called out, addressing the hidden Confederate guerrillas. Silence followed, the forest holding its breath. Elijah's blue uniform, stained and worn, bore the marks of countless skirmishes. Around him, his men adjusted their gear, the brass buttons of their coats glinting in the emerging sunlight, and rifles at the ready.

"What's the plan, sir?" Elijah's sole remaining lieutenant asked.

Elijah turned from the darkened woods to his lieutenant and then to his first sergeant and younger brother, Moses. "We advance with caution," he decided. He dismounted with a fluid grace, handing his reins to a private. "A handful of us on foot will flush them out while the rest surround them." Elijah directed Moses and his lieutenant in opposite directions away from himself, then ordered his still-mounted men to move into position outside the stand of trees. "I'll go up the middle. Once it starts, keep those repeaters firing and make us look like more than we are."

"I'd like to join, sir." Corporal William Jones dismounted and stepped forward, his presence and purpose unmistakable despite his blood-soaked bandage. Only three days prior, he had taken a rifle butt to the head while trying to stop a ruthless deserter from escaping—a deserter who had killed one of their own.

Elijah studied Jones, a comrade who had grown up alongside him and his brother Moses. He had promised Jones's father Talbot, the sheriff and father figure of their youth, that he'd watch over him during the war. Now, even after being viciously attacked by their escaped prisoner, the corporal was volunteering for a fight that Elijah wanted to keep him out of in his condition. But the determination in Jones's eyes left little room for refusal, and he noticed Moses nodding in agreement.

"Very well," Elijah relented. "Stay close to me." As William took his place by his side, Elijah felt the weight of his promise to the sheriff, a burden heavier than any rifle. In his heart, he wrestled with the weight of failing to bring William home safely, a fear that mingled with the relentless drive to complete their mission.

Elijah watched the mounted men ride off to prepare their ambush, then turned his attention back to the looming woods. "You've got our man, and we want him back."

The reply quickly came this time. "And we want ours back."

Elijah indeed held prisoners from this band of guerrillas and bushwhackers, but he couldn't afford to release them. "No can do," he called back.

A heavy silence hung in the air. Then, a voice spoke up, ominous and unforgiving. "Then we'll hang him as we done with the others."

Elijah clenched his jaw, and he could see Moses's eyes narrow. For weeks, they had been pursuing this elusive group, all while dealing with the relentless approach of Confederate regulars. Just a week ago, they had stumbled upon a grim sight: a few local loyalists hanging from the trees, not even soldiers—innocents who had dared to stand by the Union.

"You'd only be doing me a favor," Elijah replied. "He's a deserter, a bounty jumper. He killed one of our own to escape. He's not coming back to fight you."

"Perhaps we should let them handle it for us, Captain," the lieutenant suggested.

"Might be the prudent choice," Moses added.

Elijah contemplated their words and then returned his attention to the dark woods. He yearned to bring this deserter and murderer to justice after the havoc he had wreaked on their company amid the horrors of war. He was committed to this course of action, and the rest of his company was already in position.

The guerrilla leader's voice called out again. "He says he's one of us now. Claims he's on our side."

Elijah shook his head at the mention of the man whose actions had added this dangerous game of cat and mouse to what was already a dangerous situation with General Price's force advancing toward them. Without a word, Elijah chambered a round into his Spencer carbine and began advancing. Startled, his men followed suit, fanning out as Elijah gestured. He peered into the woods, leveled the rifle against his shoulder, and squeezed the trigger.

The air erupted with gunfire, a sudden and violent outburst that shattered the stillness. Elijah heard rifles crack alongside him as balls snapped past him, tearing through leaves, trees, and men. Gunpowder smoke filled the air, stinging Elijah's eyes as he dashed through the underbrush. The sharp reports of gunfire were deafening; each shot adding to the mix of fear and adrenaline. As the skirmish unfolded, Elijah saw the figure of the murdering deserter, hands bound, dart from cover to cover.

Elijah stopped and turned, shouting over the noise. "I see him, Will. Stay with me." Elijah dashed in the direction the prisoner was running, and when he appeared from behind a tree, he clubbed him in the back with his rifle. "I got him," he yelled. As he pulled the deserter to his feet, he did not see William alongside him, and a sickening grin covered the prisoner's face.

"Looks like we can make a trade after all," a voice shouted over the din of battle. Two haggard-looking young men stood no more than twenty yards away, one of them holding onto William with a revolver to his head. "Let him go, and we'll let the corporal live," the gunman yelled over the noise.

Elijah hesitated, his eyes darting between the captive he held and the men holding one of his own. They almost looked as if they could be brothers, even though one was tall and lean, the other short and stocky. They shared a look of roughness and brutality that Elijah could sense but not describe.

"You're the one who killed my friend to escape!" William shouted to Elijah's prisoner.

"Tried to kill you too," the prisoner shouted back.

As Elijah shook the man and told him to be quiet, he heard Moses yelling. He saw his brother dragging the lieutenant toward cover. "We gotta go, Eli! Reb cavalry is crashing in from the east." Recalling his promise to bring William home safely, and all the death of the previous week, he reluctantly pushed the deserter back toward the men holding William captive.

The deserter dashed into the thicket, and the gunmen shoved William back toward Elijah, but a chilling smirk soon came to the captor's face. "No, don't!" Elijah's voice tore through the noise, but in a cruel, fleeting moment, the man pulled the trigger, shooting William in the back. The other assailant fired at Elijah, the bullet whistling past him before they vanished into the forest. Elijah, driven by a surge of rage, emptied the remaining shots in his carbine, each bullet missing its mark.

Rushing forward, Elijah cradled Corporal Jones in his arms. William's wide-open eyes were empty of life as Elijah's hand pulled away from the young man's neck, soaked in blood. Nearby, a bullet kicked up a spray of dirt, and the distant sound of enemy cavalry grew louder, approaching from the only direction his men weren't covering.

With trembling hands, Elijah dragged William's lifeless body, his mind a whirlwind of guilt, sorrow, and disgust. He reached his bugler, his voice breaking as he commanded, "Sound the retreat." The haunting notes of the call resonated through the air.

As Elijah and Moses worked to gather their men and retreat, Moses caught a glimpse of William's body. Clenching his jaw, he fought back the anguish, his voice strained. "Killed him after you let him go?"

His eyes were haunted and distant. Elijah gave a faint nod, and memories of him, Moses, and William growing up in Illinois flooded back to him. The faces of the men responsible for this atrocity were now etched into his memory, their features seared into his mind. Without another word, he turned his focus to leading their battered unit to safety, each step fueled by a silent vow to seek justice for William and the senseless violence they had endured.

Return to Rockville

— ◦ —

Greencastle, Indiana - Immediately following the events of "The Ace's Bounty."

Sheriff Owen Cartwright, a sturdy man in his late forties with a grizzled beard and sharp eyes that had seen more than their share of trouble, leaned against a wooden rail of the Putnam County courthouse. He fixed his stare on the two men standing before him: Jack and Miles Crenshaw. They were notorious even beyond the county's borders, but he had to release them today.

Jack, the elder of the two, stood with a cocky tilt to his hat, his lips twisted. He was the taller and leaner of the pair, with dark, unruly hair that hung just over his eyes. His brother Miles, slightly shorter but stockier, shared the same air of arrogance, his eyes darting around the room with a restless energy.

Sheriff Cartwright cleared his throat, the sound echoing in the empty courtroom. "Boys," he started, "the circuit judge has been through twice now. No witness, no case, though." He paused, his eyes narrowing. "But don't think this means you're innocent."

Jack snickered, leaning back casually. "Well, Sheriff, justice is on our side today."

Miles chimed in, his voice laced with mockery. "Yeah, we're just two misunderstood souls, ain't we, Jack?" He looked at his brother, smiling at his approving grin.

The sheriff's jaw tightened, his hands clenched at his sides. "I had to sell your horses to cover your keep," he spat. "The county can't afford to feed the likes of you, and I'm tired of lookin' at ya."

The brothers exchanged a look. They collected their meager belongings, a couple of worn saddlebags Cartwright had tossed on the ground, and strolled toward the door, their boots echoing on the wooden floor.

"Guns and belts?" Jack spun on his boot heels and raised an eyebrow.

"Yeah," Miles added. "We ain't been convicted, you can't keep our belongings."

Cartwright bristled and stormed off to the adjacent sheriff's office, and the brothers followed him inside. He reached into a desk drawer, produced two gun belts, and checked the chambers were both empty before tossing them at the brothers' feet. With a grin, Jack picked them both up, handing one to his brother and strapping on the other.

Sheriff Cartwright followed them to the doorway, watching with a scowl as they made their way across the dusty street to the livery. He felt a churn in his stomach as he saw them shake a pile of coins from the saddle bags, buying back their horses with likely stolen money.

As they mounted up, Jack tipped his hat. "Thanks for the hospitality, Sheriff. Maybe we'll drop by again sometime."

Sheriff Cartwright spat. "I see ya in my county again, and I'll kill ya myself."

Miles laughed, a harsh, grating sound, as he spurred his horse into a trot. "Not very lawman of you, Sheriff."

Sheriff Cartwright watched them ride out of town. These men were trouble. He knew this wasn't the last he'd hear of the Crenshaw brothers.

———

JACK AND MILES returned to Rockville just before dusk. The ride from Greencastle, one county over, had been uneventful, a welcome change after their recent ordeal. The absence of rescue during their incarceration puzzled them. Still, they surmised it had been their boss's doing that the vital witness never appeared.

The setting sun cast a warm glow on Rockville's dusty streets and boardwalks. The scent of horse and leather mingled with the evening breeze, carrying faint whispers of the town's daily life winding down.

As they moved through town, the charred remains of the old grocery caught their attention. Workers were still clearing the debris.

"Looks like Frank lost his patience," Jack remarked.

Miles chuckled, smiling at his older brother. "Couldn't wait any longer for her to sell, I reckon."

They rode past the sheriff's office, where a sign announcing an ordinance banning the wearing of firearms inside the town's limits was posted.

"Since when?" Miles wondered aloud.

"Maybe it's smart on Frank's part. Make sure we're the only guns on the street." Jack dismounted and scanned the quiet streets. A few locals were lighting lamps or closing shops, but something seemed different.

The brothers exchanged knowing glances as they walked toward the tavern. "Something's off," Miles whispered.

"Sure is," Jack agreed.

At the Rockville Inn and Tavern, they observed the unusual calm as their meal was served without the usual camaraderie or recognition. Jack noticed all the nervous eyes on their revolvers.

"Don't see Frank or Charlie. . . or anyone familiar," Miles said.

Midway through his meal, Jack paused and surveyed the room. "I don't like it." He resumed eating. "Hurry up and finish."

As they prepared to leave, a tavern employee approached their table. "Gentleman," he began nervously, "perhaps you are new to town, but there's a ban on carrying firearms. Now, I don't mean to cause any trouble personally, but the Sheriff—"

"How long has that been a law?" Jack interrupted.

"Where is everyone?" Miles added.

"Well, sir, ever since we got the town back," the tavern employee answered. "Not that long, I guess." He then turned to Miles. "And where is who?"

"Dammit, man, you know who he means," Jack spat. He stood from the table and got in the employee's face.

"All dead, hanged, or run out," replied the employee. "Frank included." He swallowed hard and stepped back.

Jack's expression darkened. "That so?"

The employee just nodded. "Will that be all then?" He stuttered.

Jack placed a toothpick in his mouth. "I 'spose so." He tossed a couple of coins on the table, not bothering to see if it was enough. "C'mon, Miles."

After mounting up, they continued down the thoroughfare toward the west end of town. Reaching the saloon, they saw a new sign calling it The Marshal House. Next door was the now completed grocery and mercantile, with Mary Adams, not Frank Tucker, listed as proprietor.

Jack eyed at a young boy trying to catch fireflies in a jar out front. "When did they change the name of the saloon, lad?"

The boy eagerly offered the information. "Right after some U.S. Marshals came in and saved our town. There was a fire, and one of them saved me. I got to ride his horse!" The boy adopted a stern look. "They made all the bad men go away."

Jack bent forward in the saddle and eyed him. "What bad men would that be?"

"The ones who robbed a bank and then the train and made everyone in town scared." The boy admired his jar of fireflies for a moment, holding them up to Jack, who smiled. "My uncle said Mr. Tucker did wrong by those marshals when they were all soldiers together and that justice always catches up to you."

Jack laughed, but it was void of any emotion. "Well, don't that sound like a lot of excitement?" He turned to Miles. "You hear that? A train robbery and justice from doin' wrong in the war."

Miles raised an eyebrow, smiling at the boy. "And horse rides."

Mary Adams walked outside and saw her son talking to the strange men. She ushered him inside and then inspected them. "Can I help you, gentlemen?"

"Ma'am." Jack touched the brim of his hat. "Ya'll sell digging tools?" he asked.

She tilted her head. "We've got some shovels and spades."

Jack gestured from Miles to the door with his finger. "Go on, get us one 'a them spades, Miles. A lamp and oil if they got that, too." He eyed his brother. "And anything else we're presently out of."

Miles dismounted and followed Mary Adams inside, and Jack put in a plug of tobacco as he gazed down the street.

"Hope you don't plan on staying." George Adams appeared at the saloon's door, a shotgun leaning against the frame.

"Evenin,' George." Jack spit into the dirt and adjusted himself in his saddle. "Looks like we missed quite a time. Good to see you brave enough to live in town again, though." Jack pointed at the shotgun. "Careful now. Sheriff says there's a ban on firearms." Jack turned back toward the sheriff's office, where the deputy stepped outside, watching the interaction. When Jack tapped the brim of his dirty gray hat, the deputy began to walk down the street toward them.

"Consider yourself lucky you missed it all," George said. He stepped out onto the boardwalk. "We hanged Charlie and a handful of others. Got a letter just the other day, too. Your boss skedaddled off toward St. Louis but didn't get much farther."

Jack twisted his face and spit again. "I guess we have no choice but to find work elsewhere." He glanced up to check the deputy's progress and saw the older sheriff following behind. "Sheriff Miller found his spine, did he?" George gave no response.

Miles emerged from the store, tossing a box of revolver cartridges to Jack, and then secured the spade and lantern with his things.

"Banned guns but not the ammo, huh, George?" Jack opened the box of .36 caliber paper cartridges and removed six before tossing the box back to Miles.

Miles mounted, and George Adams spoke. "If I ever see you again—"

"Yeah, yeah. You'll kill us," Jack interjected. "Sheriff in Greenville said the same." He flipped open the chamber of his Griswold revolver and began loading the cartridges, watching Miles start to do the same. "And you, George? Did you fight alongside these brave marshals to take the town back? Kill a few of my friends?"

Deputy Thomas Owens was now close enough to the men to speak without shouting. "Everything alright, George?" He stopped suddenly and stared. "My God, is that Jack Crenshaw?"

George took a step forward, holding a hand to the deputy while glaring at Jack. "You're damn right I did, Jack."

Jack shook his head and clicked his tongue. "I figured as much." Then, in one smooth motion, he snapped the chamber shut, cocked the hammer, pointed it at George Adams, and pulled the trigger.

The bark of the revolver shocked everyone but Jack. Mary's face drained of color, her eyes widening in shock and disbelief. Her mouth opened slightly, a silent scream forming as her hands trembled violently at her sides. Her breaths came in short, sharp gasps, each a struggle as she stared at the growing crimson stain on her brother's shirt.

Deputy Owens ran forward, pulling his weapon, and Jack turned in the saddle, resting his right hand on his left arm, and pulled the trigger again, the deputy falling to the ground.

"What in the hell?" Sheriff Lawrence Miller yelled, struggling to pull his weapon as he approached the scene.

"All yours, Miles." Jack turned his horse from the carnage with a clinical detachment and heard the report of his brother's gun as he stopped just short of the boardwalk before the mercantile. Mary's horror morphed into fierce protectiveness as she pulled her son closer, her body shielding him.

The boy stuck his head around his mother's back and stared at Jack. "You can never get *all* the bad guys," Jack said. He saw the boy's eyes move to the shotgun near his uncle. "Don't try to be a hero, boy." Jack's voice dropped to a chilling whisper. "They often end up just like your uncle there—cold and forgotten." His smile was a cruel slash in the dimming light, a predator amusing himself with his prey's fear.

Jack holstered the revolver, tugged on his reins, and kicked his horse. He cantered off to the west without a second glimpse at what he had done, and Miles scanned the street before catching up.

"Where to, Jack?" Miles asked.

"The cabin first," he replied. "We'll dig up the money they hopefully didn't find to stake our travels."

"Where are we headed? Back home?"

Jack nodded and gazed upon the horizon as they rode out. "I reckon it's time to claim what's mine," he mused.

OMAHA

Nebraska Territory - Late May 1866

As the first fingers of dawn stretched across the boundless prairie, the land stirred with the promise of a new day. Tall, wild grasses swayed like waves in an emerald sea, propelled by a gentle yet insistent breeze. The half-light of the early morning set the dew aglitter, each drop a tiny prism on the earth's rich mane, sparkling in the burgeoning sunlight.

A fierce orange bled into the sky on the darkened horizon, signaling the sun's slow ascent. Ahead, the burgeoning town stood defiant, its wooden and brick edifices marking the current boundary of civilization. Smoke wafted from chimneys, trailing off towards the endless, untamed prairie—for the moment, still wild.

The frantic pounding of hoofbeats startled a covey of pheasants from their cover, but Elijah Barber paid no heed to their raucous calls. He drove his horse, Bear, on, hugging the animal's form, their bodies moving as one. He glanced over his shoulder, searching for a sign of his pursuer, but found only the empty trail.

"He hasn't given up," Elijah muttered, more to himself than to Bear. He eased the horse's pace with a gentle pull on the reins. The black-dappled buckskin's breath came in heavy bursts. Elijah eyed the horizon, now painted in shades of purple, and then the well-trodden path leading into the town's pulsing center. The supply route, beaten and packed down, was the lifeline of the burgeoning railroad, a behemoth that spanned east to west, taming the wilds with bands of iron and steam.

But it was also a glaring trail to those who might seek him out—a path where trouble could find its mark. With a resolute nod to the untamed surroundings, Elijah made his decision. He steered Bear off the path of progress, forging into the wilderness again.

Soon after, the sound of an approaching rider filled the air—a rhythmic, pounding cadence that grew louder each second. A boisterous yell cut through the morning quiet, and Moses Barber crested a nearby rise. Astride his sorrel, Copper, Moses's grin was wide as he closed the distance, his hand mimicking a gun in a jestful challenge.

Elijah shook his head in amusement, urging Bear on with a nudge of his heels. Omaha lay ahead, a crude but developing town dropped down on the prairie's edge. Today's wager was straightforward: the morning's loser would have to accomplish the day's most demanding chores at the livery.

ELIJAH AND MOSES stormed into Omaha, their horses' hooves thundering on the hardened earth, announcing their arrival. Approaching downtown's bustle, they slowed Bear and Copper to a walk, where untamed prairie met the steady march of civilization. The city buzzed with the energy of early risers and the relentless hum of burgeoning industry.

The streets of Omaha thrummed with the vigor of progress, pushing against the tranquil prairies surrounding it. New buildings, a testament to the town's rapid growth, jutted out among the older wooden structures, their presence a bold declaration of the dawn of a new era.

Reaching Douglas Street, they dismounted, giving their weary animals a rest. Around them, bright-eyed merchants displayed their wares. At the same time, the rhythmic song of the blacksmith's hammer punctuated the air, accompanying the sounds of boots on the boardwalks. They passed a newly erected brick building, one of the town's few, housing a billiards saloon on the ground floor, with the offices of the *Omaha Daily Herald* above.

"Paper says they'll have the grading out to a hundred miles by next month," Moses mused.

Elijah glanced toward the newspaper office and then back at Moses. "Taken up reading the news now?"

Moses returned a look of feigned indignation. "A businessman has got to stay informed in this changin' world," he said, grinning as Elijah rolled his eyes.

"You just like that they did a story on what we did and our choosing to stick around." Elijah had not been a fan of the paper's dramatization of their pursuit of Frank Tucker and hailing them as heroes turned local businessmen.

"Did wonders for business though, didn't it?" Moses retorted.

Just a year ago, they were entangled in a losing battle to revive their Illinois farm, a struggle intensified by their wartime absence and the loss of their parents. The conflict had robbed them of comrades, leaving peace as elusive as the prosperity they sought. Yet when duty called again, in the form of a U.S. Marshal seeking skilled cavalrymen to pursue outlaws, they reluctantly accepted.

Now, Omaha was home. They had arrived just after the first rails of the Union Pacific had been laid in Omaha, initiating the westward rail expansion. A mere decade and a half ago, this land was teeming with tall prairie grass and wildlife dotted with a few settlements and Native American tribes. But by 1860, it had swelled to two thousand residents, then soon breached ten thousand inhabitants.

The brothers made their way to *Omaha Livery Stage & Freight*, a business they now co-owned as they worked toward owning it outright. The bounty from capturing Frank Tucker the previous summer had provided a generous start, but they were far from wealthy. Each day, however, marked a step away from their past, an ascent marked by persistence and hard work.

At the livery, activity buzzed like a beehive: horses to shoe, carriages to mend, wagons to load, and a steady stream of patrons to deal with. Elijah embraced the work with a quiet enthusiasm, leaving no room for dwelling on the war's shadows or the previous year's bloodshed. This labor carried an honesty that lightened the spirit.

Moses, ever the social weaver, managed clients with ease, his laughter and stories mingling with the noise of the business. Each brother had found their niche in a world striving to define itself.

Omaha, burgeoning with dreamers and rail workers, saw the Barbers' destinies intertwine with the town's vigorous heartbeat. Talk of statehood rippled through the streets, and amidst this clamor, they found something akin to home. Elijah often reflected on the stark contrast between the past battlefields and the livery's relative peace. It was a change he welcomed, yet the echoes of their past were sometimes unavoidable.

"Mornin,' Mr. Barber," greeted a regular customer, tipping his hat to Elijah. "Only recently heard about your exploits last summer. Town's safer with you 'round."

Elijah offered a modest nod. "Just doin' what's right, sir."

Late in the day, Patrick Hennessey, the sentinel of the business, appeared with a ledger in hand. He was a strong-willed man of about sixty who reminded both brothers of their father. The man had profound respect in the community and was full of wisdom from a lifetime around horses and stables. He was a robust and barrel-chested man whose graying hair was always neatly combed.

He exchanged meaningful words with Elijah, a firm pat on the shoulder conveying mutual respect. Nodding at Moses, who was completing the day's transactions, Hennessey allowed himself a rare grin.

"You boys are holdin' your own," he rasped. His voice weathered by the years as much as his face. "Just make sure this place stands strong after it's all yours."

"We'll keep it sturdy, right, Mo?" Elijah replied.

"Like Grant's army," Moses confirmed, thumbs hooked in his suspenders.

Hennessey chuckled. "You know, boys," his voice was tinged with sorrow, "I always thought one of *my* boys would take over this place. Lost John in the war, and Patrick. . . well, the drink caught up to him. And Maggie, my girl, has the spirit of a stallion, and her brothers had her in ridin' britches more than dresses, but this world's not kind to women with dreams beyond their kitchens."

"Ya know, Mr. Hennessey, Eli and I had our bacon saved by just that type 'a woman last summer. She'd have them ridin' britches underneath a skirt and get bad fellers lookin' one way, then pull on 'em."

Elijah scratched his chin and turned away, not wanting to get into a debate about the domestic expectations of the man he was trying to buy a business from.

Patrick Hennessey eyed Moses with a raised eyebrow, then laughed softly. "Well, Moses, I woulda liked to have seen that." The man waved and was on his way as Elijah shook his head at Moses.

"What?" Moses got back to his work. "I liked her."

Later, as nightfall cloaked Omaha, a sharp knock at the office door shattered the tranquility.

Moses arched an eyebrow. "Well shucks, Eli, I was all set to kick off my Friday evening at the Steamboat Saloon."

Elijah, at the door, frowned. "Business first," he muttered, opening the door. "If you need a rental, the hostler can—"

In the doorway stood two stoic men, badges gleaming on their chests, guns holstered at their sides. Elijah assessed them, then heard Moses's boots behind him.

"Gentlemen," said the younger man, emotionless. The older one just grunted.

Moses grinned. "Must be good this time if you *both* are here to try and recruit us." The grin fell from his face when neither man shifted their expression.

Elijah eyed them. "What is it?"

The younger man took a deep breath. "You said to come only if we really needed you. . ."

There was a heaviness in the air, and Elijah felt a familiar tension in his stomach, reminiscent of the unease before a skirmish. His face hardened as he turned to the older man, who spoke.

"They're just across the river."

BEIN' READY

— • —

The four men sat around a dusty table in the central office of Hennessey's Livery and Freight. A single oil lamp cast elongated shadows on the walls lined with faded maps and ledgers. Elijah puffed on his pipe, taking in the news the two lawmen had brought.

"So what, you came to recruit us to go after them?" Elijah left the pipe in the corner of his mouth as he spoke, eyeing the men.

The older man held up a hand. "That ain't what this is," he said, his voice gruff. A tall, rugged man around fifty, Douglas County Sheriff Thomas Carter had a weather-beaten face, sharp, gray eyes, and a permanently furrowed brow just below salt and pepper hair. His physical strength was as impressive as his commanding demeanor. Missing only the mustache, he reminded Elijah of their old mentor, Talbot Jones, and the thought saddened him a bit.

"Good," Elijah responded. He nodded at Moses, who returned the gesture. "Because we ain't—"

"We need you to help ensure we're ready, though," the other man interrupted. Omaha City Marshal John Hawkins was ten years the sheriff's junior, with a stocky build and air of authority that came naturally to him. His thin, sandy brown hair, cropped short in a no-nonsense style, and face adorned with a neatly trimmed beard made Elijah think he could be Moses's twin were the hair red. Elijah assumed Moses would say he favored the sheriff minus twenty years of aging.

Moses spoke up. "What does bein' ready look like?"

"Well, you read the papers," Marshal Hawkins said with exasperation. Moses gave a wink to Elijah, who rolled his eyes. "They knocked off that bank in St Joseph six months ago in broad daylight. Then they hit that Hannibal and St. Joseph Train three months later, making off with railroad payroll, supplies, and even weapons. Now they've been hitting stagecoaches guerilla style all along the river, moving north. None of those places was ready, and lawmen and innocent folks alike are dead on top of the robberies."

Elijah removed the pipe from his mouth and eyed Sheriff Carter. "And what makes you think they're in Council Bluffs?"

The sheriff had been chewing on a cigar as they spoke but now struck a match on the side of the table and lit it. "Sheriff in Pottawattamie County sent me a wire this afternoon. That Mexican horse trader that comes to town now and then claims he saw 'em." He shook out the match and exhaled a cloud of smoke. "Few other folks have said they spotted a group that fits 'The Shadow Commander's' outfit. Marshal Service hasn't had any luck yet. They think it's Nate Morrow but can't prove it. I guess the railroad has considered bringing in the Pinkertons. But for now, he's in the wind, and it's blown him here."

Elijah sat back and glanced at Moses, who had a concerned look on his face. The horse trader was likely Augusto, with whom they had done some business. *Just when I thought I could live a quiet, stable life.* He leaned his head against his fist. "You never answered Mo's question, though. What does bein' ready look like? Seems like you're askin' us to plan or lead something."

"We ain't soldiers no more, fellas," Moses said. Elijah was glad he said it, even if he sounded disappointed.

"No, but you fought this sort in the war. . ." Marshal Hawkins trailed off as if that was all the argument he needed to make. "Well, dammit, don't act like that isn't true and that you didn't roll into our town a year ago having taken down the most notorious criminal east of the Mississippi."

Sheriff Carter held a cigar before him, then used it to point at the marshal and himself. "He and I only got a handful of deputies each, and we're just askin' if you'll stand with us if the time comes." He eyed Marshal Hawkins and stuck the cigar back in his mouth. "This is why I ain't ever asked 'em for anything before; they no longer want this life."

The marshal closed his eyes and rubbed his forehead. "I get it, gentlemen. But if you're inclined to make this place your home, we'd sure appreciate it if you were willing to use your skills to defend it."

Elijah met the lawmen's eyes and then glanced at his brother. "I can't imagine they'll have the gumption to ride straight into a town this size. . ." He drifted off, thinking about his following words. "We won't join any posse to root them out or track them down, but I suppose we'll help protect the town should it somehow come to that."

The marshal and sheriff stood up, nodding their thanks. "We appreciate it, truly," Marshal Hawkins said. "Let us hope it doesn't come to that."

As the door closed behind them, Moses leaned back in his chair, a thoughtful look on his face. "Well, that's something," he mused. "Anyhow, I'm famished and could use a drink after that. Shall we?"

Elijah grabbed his bowler hat from a hook, but a familiar unease stirred. The past, it seemed, might never be left behind. He hoped this quiet life they had carved out in Omaha would not be disrupted.

ELIJAH AND MOSES stepped out into the brisk evening air of
Omaha. The transition from day to night in Omaha was like watching
two worlds converge – the industrious hum of daytime giving way to a
more relaxed, almost celebratory evening ambiance. Lanterns flickered
to life, their flames dancing on the wooden facades of buildings and
the muddy streets.

Their boots knocked on the wooden boardwalk, then crunched
into the street. The distant sound of a fiddle accompanied by a piano
drifted through the air, mingling with the raucous laughter and chatter of townsfolk enjoying their Friday night.

Moses cocked his head toward Elijah as they walked, speaking in
a low voice. "So, whatcha think about what they said? The Morrow
gang. . ."

Elijah shrugged, scanning the lively street. "Not sure what to make
of it. Omaha seems like a risky target. But, guess we better keep our
eyes open, just in case." He didn't slow as he spoke, bee-lining for the
saloon. "I got no desire for a fight, though."

As they walked, they passed storefronts with their windows aglow,
showcasing the latest goods from back East. The occasional clatter of a
passing carriage and the muffled conversations of pedestrians replaced
the industrious sounds of the day. The scent of fried food and wood
smoke wafted through the air, a tempting invitation to the many
eateries and drinking establishments dotting the town.

The Steamboat Saloon, a sturdy two-story structure with a swinging wooden sign, was a Barber favorite. Nice enough to keep out
the riff-raff but not so nice they didn't feel like they belonged. The
large windows, partially obscured by drawn curtains, emitted a soft,
inviting light, with lively piano music echoing into the street.

Inside was a harmonious blend of refinement and rustic charm.
Wooden beams supported the ceiling, while polished brass fixtures

and oil lamps cast a warm, inviting glow over the patrons. The clinking of glasses and the subdued hum of conversation created a noisy but not overwhelming atmosphere, just the way the brothers liked it.

At the back, a well-stocked bar boasted an array of bottles while tables spread across the wooden floor. Everyone, from well-dressed businessmen to local workers and even the occasional drifter, enjoyed their drinks and meals in a relaxed ambiance.

Elijah and Moses scanned the room until they caught sight of Samuel "Big Sam" Donovan. A boisterous figure with a larger-than-life presence, Big Sam sat at a table near the center of the saloon, a broad grin on his face. He raised his hand high, beckoning the brothers with an enthusiastic wave.

He stood and stuck his hand out as they arrived at the table, and Elijah winced pre-emptively. He was close to six and a half feet tall; his handshake was like a bear trap, and his frame was like an oak, solid and unyielding, a towering presence that commanded attention in any room. He was the only man Elijah knew that made him feel short, and Moses said Big Sam was the only man in Omaha he couldn't take in a fight.

"It's no good when I'm here well before the bosses." Big Sam dropped into a chair. He worked for the livery, loading and unloading freight wagons and occasionally skinning mule teams.

Moses laughed. "Ain't ours yet, Sam. I'm startin' to think Hennessey don't have any designs on retiring soon after all."

Sam waved down a waitress before turning back to the brothers. "Saw the marshal and the sheriff marching through town together on my way here," he said. "Don't see the two 'a them together very often."

"That's why we were late," Elijah began. "They came to—"

"Well, how are you boys this evenin'?" Jane, their favorite waitress, leaned a hip onto Moses's shoulder, who did not appear to mind. She had a habit of toying with Moses, drawn to his outgoing personality, muscular, rugged build, and well-groomed red beard. Elijah bit his lip, perturbed. His brother got attention that his lean, beardless frame didn't seem to command, and he was upset he had been interrupted. "Everything alright, Elijah?"

He gave a thin smile and nod, but Moses came to his rescue. "Oh, we were just havin' a less than pleasant business conversation, but nothin' to fret about. He's too serious." Moses winked at his brother.

"I'll bring out some coffee, gentlemen," Jane offered. "We've got beef and potatoes with carrots and a tasty apple pie tonight. Does that tickle your fancy?" Their unanimous nods signaled their approval, and Jane vanished into the kitchen.

Moses watched her leave, then turned to Sam and spoke in a playful tone. "Back in Illinois, I had a crush on the tavern girl, but she always had her eyes on Elijah. Times have changed." He grinned. "Now he fancies that schoolteacher, Abigail."

Elijah forced a playful laugh, trying to hide how much he didn't enjoy this conversation. It was a sore spot for him that he'd left Danville last summer without saying goodbye to the daughter of the tavern owners. Now, the schoolteacher knew she had his eye, but he was awkward around her. Watching Moses interact so easily with the fairer sex, then rib him about it, rubbed him the wrong way as the older brother.

Big Sam seemed to sense the unease at the table and changed the subject after Jane returned with coffee and the three shots of whiskey she knew they'd order. "So, Eli, you were 'bout to say somethin' about the marshal and the sheriff and why you were late?"

Elijah's eyes sparked with recognition as he finished a sip of coffee. "They came by to say they suspect Nate Morrow's gang is just opposite the river in Council Bluffs and wanted to know if we'd stand with them should it come to that."

Moses looked at Sam, raised his eyebrows, and then downed his whiskey, Sam doing the same shortly after. Elijah sipped at his and set it back down.

Big Sam shook his head. "Well, fellas, I hope you don't judge everyone from Missouri by the actions of that scoundrel."

Elijah and Moses nodded, familiar with the complexities of Missouri's divided loyalties during the war. "Missouri was a border state, Sam. We know not everyone took the same path," Elijah said.

Big Sam took a big bite off his plate of beef that had arrived, then leaned in. "It wasn't the most popular decision in my town that I joined Lincoln's Union force." He shook his head and then ate some more. "Nate Morrow, though, led guerrillas in bloody raids against both Union forces and Missourians he considered as not resisting occupation. A real devil, that one." Sam pointed at the brothers with his fork. "Got to chase General Price early on, 'fore they sent us to Tennessee and such. . . Glad they sent you fellas to protect my home."

"Nate Morrow was like Bloody Bill Anderson or Quantrill," Moses added, downing a second whiskey. "Men who didn't just fight; they terrorized. Morrow's kind left a deep scar, not just on the land but in the hearts of folks."

Elijah nodded, his gaze distant as his mind tormented him with thoughts of the guerrillas they fought in Missouri. "So now he's leading his gang on a rampage across the Midwest. And they think Omaha could be next." He sipped his whiskey some more. "Their war ain't over."

Big Sam's expression turned serious. "What's his gripe, anyhow? Bunch 'a rebs with bees in their bonnets over the war not turnin' out the way they wanted?"

Moses chuckled, but Elijah's tone was serious. "It ain't just rebs. Papers say there's one or two fellas who wore blue with him. I guess they got complaints about the war just makin' rich folks richer at the expense of those who fought and leavin' half the country in tatters."

They were quiet for a moment before Elijah continued. "Men like Morrow don't just disappear into thin air," he mused. "They're using the disarray after the war—towns struggling to rebuild, law stretched thin—perfect hunting grounds for outlaws."

Moses nodded in agreement, his expression turning grim. "That's the sad truth of it. The war might be over, but its shadows still loom over us. Folks are trying to rebuild their lives, and here are these men, preying on that vulnerability."

Elijah looked into his drink. "The war changed the face of the nation, but for some, it just changed the way they fight their battles."

They sat processing Elijah's statement, and then Big Sam spoke up. "If it comes to a fight, count me in. I may have left the war, but I didn't forget how to stand up to men like Morrow." He wiped his plate up with a biscuit and swallowed before pushing his plate away. "Whatever his grievance, killin' innocent folks ain't the way."

Elijah swirled the whiskey in his glass. "Let's hope it doesn't come to that, Sam. Omaha's been peaceful enough. Lot of good things happening here."

"I'm just glad you fellas found work here, then found me down in Kansas." Big Sam was referring to the previous fall when the brothers, brand new to working with Patrick Hennessey, had earned the man's trust by leading a contract wagon train of army supplies down to Kansas. Big Sam had just finished his service and wondered if the brothers could get him work in Omaha.

"Remember on the way back from Kansas when we had to camp out in that storm?" Moses asked, a chuckle escaping his lips. "Sam built us a shelter so sturdy, thought we'd wake up in a log cabin!"

Big Sam laughed heartily, adding, "Had to keep you boys dry. You're worthless when cold and wet, and I needed the work."

Elijah smiled at the memory. "Couldn't have made it through that night without your quick thinking, Sam."

Moses said, "I'm Glad you came back with us, Sam. The livery is all the better for it, and if trouble's now brewing, it's good to know we have people we can count on." Elijah eyed him to see if his brother was itching for a fight after all.

As the evening wore on, the brothers enjoyed the company and mingled with friends from town. Unable to keep up with Moses and Big Sam's drinking, Elijah excused himself to take the air and stepped outside. The night had deepened, and the lamps on the streets of Omaha took full effect. Leaning against a post, he lit his pipe and savored the aroma and solitude the habit afforded him. There was never a time he did it without thinking of his father or Talbot.

Elijah's thoughts often wandered to the past, to the trials and tribulations that had shaped him. The pipe in his hand wasn't just a habit but a tangible link to sweet and sorrowful memories. In these quiet moments, he grappled with the duality of his desires—for peace and the inevitable pull towards conflict that his skills and history brought. Lost in thought, he stared down the street toward the livery, trying to will their full ownership and the peace and prosperity of the town into existence.

"Elijah?" a soft voice called out, breaking his reverie. He turned, taking a moment to recognize Abigail, the schoolteacher, standing a few steps away. She was returning from supper with a friend, her delicate features illuminated by the dim streetlight. Her presence brought warmth to the cool evening air.

"Evening, Miss Abigail," Elijah greeted. He took the pipe from his mouth, suddenly conscious of his rugged appearance next to her genteel demeanor.

"I didn't expect to run into you tonight," she said, tucking a loose strand of strawberry blond hair behind her ear. Her eyes held a glimmer of interest, a subtle invitation to conversation, as she waved at her friend, who stepped away, busying herself pretending to window shop.

Elijah shifted his weight. "Just had some business to discuss with Moses and a few others over supper," he replied. His eyes met hers before drifting away.

Abigail nodded. "I heard some rumors about trouble brewing near Council Bluffs. It must be a concern for everyone in Omaha," she ventured, her tone laced with concern.

Elijah exhaled a cloud of smoke, his expression growing distant. He then waved the smoke away and tapped out the pipe with a sheepish grin. "Yeah, there's talk of the Morrow gang causing trouble. I just hope it's nothing that'll reach us here."

Her eyes softened. "Omaha has been peaceful, thanks to people like you and your brother. It would be a shame to see that peace disturbed."

"That's what we're hoping for. Just a quiet life." He toed the dirt on the boardwalk. "I don't know that Mo and I have anything to do with it, though."

Abigail smiled. "I'll be by the livery tomorrow morning. I need to rent a horse for my weekly ride in the country. It's always more enjoyable with company," she said.

Elijah, missing the implication, only nodded politely at first. "Yes, ma'am. We'll make sure you have a good horse, Abigail."

She raised her eyebrow and looked at him, then laughed.

Elijah shook his head. "And I just realized you want me to ride with you." She smiled broadly. "Well yes ma'am, that would be lovely," he said.

"I'll see you then, Elijah."

"Enjoy your evening." He tipped his hat.

As she walked away, Elijah watched her go, wondering why he was so awkward around her. Upbeat piano music from inside caught his attention, and he spied Moses swinging Jane around the dance floor. Shaking his head, he began his walk home.

A FAMILIAR SOUND

—•—

The first light of dawn had just begun to seep through the windows of the livery office when Elijah found himself lost in thought. Seated at a modest wooden desk strewn with ledgers and loose papers, he scanned the wooden wall's knots and grooves, his mind tumultuous.

Elijah's eyes lingered on the old cavalry slouch hat hanging on the wall. More than a relic, it was a tangible link to his past and soldier days. Each fray and stain on the fabric was a story, a memory of hard-fought battles and narrow escapes.

Below the hat, a sturdy trunk sat closed, its contents unseen yet not forgotten. Within lay his revolvers and the Spencer repeating rifle – tools of a life he had tried to leave behind, which now beckoned him with a whisper he hoped to ignore. He only got them out now if riding outside town, but otherwise had avoided opening that trunk since their arrival in Omaha - a silent vow to embrace a new life devoid of violence and confrontation.

Outside the office, the stable was stirring to life. The sound of hooves, the soft nickers of horses, and the distant clanging of a blacksmith's hammer provided a backdrop to Elijah's introspection. He leaned back in his chair, closing his eyes, trying to will the world to allow him and Moses the peace they sought here.

He thought about Abigail, the schoolteacher, and the awkward dance of their budding yet stilted relationship. Her smile, the way she tucked her strawberry hair behind her ear, her subtle hints – all played in his mind like a melody he couldn't quite grasp. He was more at home on the battlefield or working stables than in the intricate dance of courtship.

The office door creaked open, and Moses entered his usual exuberant self. Despite returning late the previous night, his energy seemed boundless, fueled only by a cup of coffee and his eternal optimism.

"Mornin,' Eli," Moses cheerfully greeted. His red beard appeared particularly fiery in the morning light. "You're here even earlier than usual. Dwellin' on those Morrow rumors?"

Elijah offered a noncommittal grunt, his eyes opening to fix on his brother. Moses' lack of concern over the Morrow gang was both a relief and a frustration. He envied Moses's ability to live in the moment, unburdened by the shadows that clung to Elijah like a second skin.

"Just thinking," Elijah said, his voice low. "About everything."

Moses nodded, understanding his brother's unspoken words. He sat on the trunk and patted it affectionately. "You know, Eli, sometimes I miss the sound of those repeaters." He gestured with his coffee mug out the window. But I reckon Omaha's better off with 'em in the trunk."

Elijah managed a small smile, appreciative of his brother's attempt to lighten the mood. "Let's keep it that way." He stood and gave Moses a once-over. "Thanks for puttin' on your nicer-looking sack suit," he said with a grin.

Moses laughed. "What'd Talbot always say? Our Sunday or important meeting suits were just the cleanest ones with the fewest holes?"

"Let's get to the bank, then." He eyed the slouch hat and grabbed his bowler hat off the desk. We gotta make sure our future here is as sturdy as Hennessey's old stables."

THE MORNING SUN cast a golden hue over Omaha's streets as Elijah and Moses made their way to the bank. The town was awakening to its daily rhythm; shopkeepers swept their front steps, fresh bread wafted from the bakery, and horse-drawn carriages clattered on cobblestone streets.

The First National Bank of Omaha, a bastion of financial security within the burgeoning city, was one of the finer buildings in the growing town. As the Barber brothers entered, they were greeted by polished wood, marble, and the distinct scent of wealth and prosperity. Elaborate lighting fixtures hung from the high ceiling, casting a soft glow over the ornate furnishings.

Moses whistled, his stride confident and carefree. Elijah walked with a measured pace, preoccupied with the upcoming financial transactions. Inside, the atmosphere was one of quiet efficiency, and the staff greeted them with warm smiles, acknowledging their reputation as dependable businessmen. Elijah, cautious by nature with such things, pulled out a neatly folded paper detailing their financial plans, double-checking each number and calculation.

Standing against the counter, Moses chatted with Thomas, the bank teller, whose laughter reflected the town's general ease. "Looks like you boys are well on your way to making the livery the talk of the town," Thomas commented, perusing the documents.

"We're just trying to ensure everything is in order. Can't afford missteps," Elijah said.

Moses chuckled, clapping Elijah's back. "My brother could find a cloud in every silver lining. But don't mind him, Thomas. We're doing just fine, thanks to folks like you."

Walter Bradley, the portly, well-groomed bank manager, approached from his office. "Elijah and Moses Barber, isn't it?" he greeted warmly, shaking their hands. "It's a pleasure. I hear you're making strides with Hennessey's Livery."

Elijah returned the handshake. "Good to see you, Mr. Bradley." Moses also shook his hand.

"Thomas taking care of you?" Mr. Bradley asked, gesturing toward the teller.

"Oh yessir," Moses replied. "Our only delay is Elijah's due diligence." Elijah rolled his eyes.

Mr. Bradley laughed. "Well, that's fine. It's a great undertaking, and we appreciate your trust."

After discussing future investments and business plans, Mr. Bradley shook their hands again. "Don't hesitate if you need further assistance. We appreciate your business."

"We're much obliged," Elijah responded.

"Thanks for taking a chance on us. Hope to see you soon," Moses added.

Exiting the bank, Moses glanced at Elijah. "You worry too much, brother. This town's got a good feel. We've got backers now, something we've never had before. We're right where we need to be."

Adjusting his bowler hat, Elijah shot back a look of mild annoyance. "I just wish you'd take our responsibilities at the bank seriously, Mo. And ease up on the jokes at my expense around others."

Before Moses could retort, Elijah was drawn to a heavy-laden freight wagon ambling down the street. The wagon was over-stuffed, its load teetering dangerously. Such a sight was common with the constant flux of goods to the railhead. Still, something about this wagon struck Elijah as off. He observed the drivers, who appeared nervous, casting furtive glances around. Riding nearby were rough-looking men, seeming to be providing protection.

Elijah's gaze lingered on one of the men who grinned and touched the brim of his hat as he rode past. The man's smile didn't reach his eyes, which darted around with a wariness that spoke of secrets and danger. A flicker of recognition sparked inside Elijah. Shaking off the thought, he turned his attention back to Moses, only to be interrupted by the familiar rumble of another wagon.

Big Sam, guiding his wagon with a practiced hand, pulled up beside them, wiping the sweat from his brow. "Sorry, bosses," he panted, his bulky frame casting a shadow on the street. "This load's running behind. Got held up at the river by that wagon up ahead," he motioned to the wagon Elijah had just scrutinized. "Couple of old soldiers doin' the bullwhackin,' but they weren't doin' it well."

Elijah nodded. "No trouble, Sam. These things happen," he replied. Something about the wagon still didn't sit right with him, but he decided his unease was due to his worry about the Morrow Gang and his irritation with Moses. He glanced at the loaded wagon, noting the careful stacking of crates, barrels, and sacks. "Glad you're more careful with our freight than them."

"Yeah, no worry at all," Moses added. He climbed up on the driver's box and clapped Sam on the shoulder, startling a large dog that popped its head up from the other side of the wagon seat, barking a deep, resonant warning.

The dog, Brutus, was a mix of breeds. His appearance suggested the strength of a mastiff, and his agility hinted at herding lineage. His coat was striking brindle and black, and his deep brown eyes took in the scene with an intelligence that belied his rugged appearance. Big

Sam had adopted him the previous fall after tossing his owner in the river upon witnessing the dog's mistreatment. Like his owner, Brutus appeared meaner than he was unless you crossed him.

Big Sam leaned down, whispering a few words to Brutus in a gentle tone for a man of his size. It was a side of him few got to see, where the rough exterior gave way to a kinship with the dog that had been his loyal companion through thick and thin. He sat up, patting Brutus on the head. "Easy, Brutus. You know they're friends." He turned to the Barbers, still chuckling. "Sorry 'bout that. Brutus here's a bit overprotective, but he's good as gold."

"Long as he keeps guarding our wagon loads as he guards you," Elijah remarked, eyeing Brutus, who had settled back down but kept a watchful eye on Moses.

"Sure 'nuff he does. Best companion I could ask for," Sam said. "Ain't no one getting past Brutus without him lettin' me know."

Brutus eyed Moses as Sam clicked his tongue, urging the horses forward. The wagon resumed its slow journey, the sound of hooves and wheels blending into the town's ambient noises. Moses jumped down, dusting off his pants, and as the wagon pulled away, Brutus gave a wag of his tail, showing no hard feelings.

Moses caught up with Elijah. "Oh, Eli," he said as if suddenly inspired. Elijah turned his head to indicate he was listening. "That pretty schoolteacher is gonna be comin' by for her Saturday ride. You know, I was thinking that red roan mare we got has a mane almost as striking as Abigail's hair. Wouldn't it be somethin' if you pointed that out to her? Might be the kind of sweet talk she'd appreciate, coming from a man of few words like yourself."

Elijah stopped before turning the corner to the livery. "Don't talk to me about that sort of thing in public, Mo. I'll sick that dang dog on you." He turned the corner and then turned back, his voice low. "And how do you know I'm going for a ride with her?"

Moses laughed, clearly tickled by the interaction. "Oh, we all saw you chattin' last night. If you don't tell her, I will." Elijah just shook his head, then looked up to see her approaching the livery.

Abigail stood there, the morning sun catching the highlights in her hair, turning them to shades of gold and auburn. She wore a simple yet elegant riding outfit, her posture graceful and expectant. There was a moment where Elijah caught a glimpse of what could be—a life different from the one he knew, filled with gentle mornings such as this.

Moses dashed ahead with his usual flair, breaking Elijah's daydream when he called back. "I'll tell her about the mare," Moses called behind him.

ELIJAH ENTERED THE OFFICE through a side door in the freight yard and dropped off his bank paperwork. He stared at the door that led to where Moses and Abigail would be, then exited where he'd come in and walked around to the stalls nearest the office, where Bear was waiting.

"Well, boy, I don't much care for his interfering with such things, but I 'spose he's right about that schoolteacher." He cupped a handful of grain in his hand and let Bear eat as he stroked his neck. "Be on your best behavior, and make sure I don't say anything dumb."

Elijah finished saddling Bear and began to lead him through the alley between the stables and the office building when he saw someone poke their head in his office and then back out in a hurry.

Elijah recognized him. "Marshal Hawkins?"

The marshal's eyes lit up in recognition. "There you are." He walked over, shook Elijah's hand, and regarded his saddled horse. "Headin' somewhere?"

Elijah turned toward the office. "I, uh." He paused. "Just a short ride."

"Good. We're having a meeting at the Herndon House at noon," Marshal Hawkins said. "Bring your brother. There will be conversations about how to handle this Shadow Commander business."

"The Herndon House?" Elijah's surprise came through. The opulent three-story hotel, the nicest building in Omaha, that Elijah assumed catered only to the Union Pacific bosses and the city's most prosperous. His mind briefly wandered, pondering the significance of being summoned to such an important meeting. It wasn't just the unexpected venue that surprised him but also the implicit trust and reliance on his judgment. These moments of recognition both honored and burdened him.

The marshal chuckled, seeming to sense Elijah's surprise. "Yeah, politicians and business folks called it. I reckon they don't want to get embarrassed and want to make sure we lowly lawmen don't make them look inept and such."

Elijah patted Bear on the neck, sensing the horse getting antsy for his impending ride. "I ain't a lawman, marshal."

The marshal waved his hand as he began to walk away. "Yeah, yeah. I told them you were with us, though, and we needed you. Bring an appetite; those fancy folks always order too much food."

Elijah tied Bear to a post in front of the office and entered, removing his hat as he did and smiling at Abigail when he saw her.

"Elijah," she said. "Good morning." A brightness came to her face.

"Good morning, Miss Abigail." He held his hat awkwardly in his hands and pointed to the window. "Perfect morning for a ride."

"Hey there, Eli." Moses was grinning from ear to ear. He looked from Elijah to Abigail. "I told her you suggested that red roan mare." The two brothers stared at each other until Moses broke. "Anyhow, Billy is gettin' her saddled and brought out."

"Thank you, Moses." Elijah crossed the room to the counter, staring at Moses with wide eyes Abigail couldn't see. "You're so accommodating." He lowered his voice and leaned over the desk. "Marshal wants us to meet at the Herndon House at noon."

"The Herndon House?" Moses asked, then whistled. "What on Earth does—"

Elijah held a hand up and jerked his head toward the schoolteacher. "Just be ready when I get back." He turned to Abigail. "Shall we ride?"

Abigail accepted Elijah's arm, and he guided her outside and helped her into the saddle of the awaiting roan mare. Elijah shook his head at Billy, the young hostler, who shared the same mischievous grin Moses did inside.

Hoping she was observing, he swung onto Bear with a cavalryman's practiced ease and grace before turning to Abigail and nudging Bear into the street.

"Your brother was immensely helpful this morning. He mentioned you picked out this horse for me, saying its color reminded you of my hair."

Elijah felt his cheeks flush. "The mare does complement your hair quite beautifully."

She smiled, and Elijah was thankful he navigated the discussion well enough. "So where should we ride this morning? I'd like you to choose."

Elijah hadn't thought about it but squinted toward the river. "There's a nice path that gives a great view of the river and all the commotion but is far enough away to be quiet."

"That sounds great," she said. Elijah urged Bear to pick up the pace, and Abigail and the mare followed suit.

They rode side by side, the steady clip-clop of their horses' hooves setting a rhythm against the backdrop of Omaha's waking sounds. The path Elijah had chosen meandered along the river, offering glimpses of the bustling activity at the docks and the calm, steady flow of the water. Despite the scene's tranquility, Elijah's mind was elsewhere, between the imminent meeting at the hotel and the burgeoning relationship he navigated with Abigail.

The sun climbed higher, casting a warm glow over the river, making the surface glimmer like a spread of jewels. Abigail seemed to enjoy the scenery, her eyes scanning the landscape. "It's beautiful here," she said, breaking the silence. "Omaha really is growing, isn't it?"

Elijah nodded. "It's a different place every day. Keeps us on our toes at the livery." Elijah wished he could stay in moments like this.

The conversation drifted to lighter topics, the easy chatter helping Elijah to forget his concerns. However, Abigail soon circled back to something more personal. "I overheard you talking about a meeting at the Herndon House," she said, her tone cautious. "Is everything alright?"

Elijah paused, weighing his words carefully. "It's a gathering of sorts, discussing precautions for the town's safety. It's nothing for you to worry about, though. We're just lending our experience where it's needed."

Abigail glanced at him, her expression thoughtful. "Your past. . . your time in the war, and chasing Frank Tucker. . . it must have been difficult."

Elijah cringed at the mention of his past. "It was what was needed at the time," he replied, keeping his tone even.

"I admire that," Abigail said. "Your commitment to helping others, to serving. But," she paused, searching for the right words. "After losing my brother in the war and friends of our family. . . I have five fewer loved ones in my life because of that war. I've seen enough violence to last a lifetime." She looked at him until his eyes met hers. "I would prefer not to lose anyone else I care about."

Elijah looked down momentarily, unsure how to handle such remarks but understanding her sentiments. The last thing he wanted was to bring more turmoil into her life. "I understand," he said quietly. "I'm trying to leave that life behind, too."

They rode silently for a few moments before resuming lighter, more enjoyable conversation while returning to the livery. Elijah helped Abigail down from the mare, their hands lingering for a moment longer than necessary. "Thank you for the ride, Elijah," she said. She gazed up into his eyes, then a bit further at his hat. "That hat suits you better than the one you got off the boat with Frank Tucker wearing."

"It was my pleasure," he replied. He reached up and tipped the hat as he smiled. "I'd like to agree." He was proud of how he'd handled a sweet moment and wanted his life filled with more like it.

Handing the mare's reins to Billy, Elijah tied Bear's around a post out front, intending to say goodbye to Abigail and then collect Moses for the meeting. However, a distant sound caught his attention unnoticed by Abigail and others around him, and his head jerked toward the river.

Elijah's instincts as a former soldier snapped into focus. The distant sound was unmistakable – the sharp, sporadic reports of gunfire, a sound he knew all too well. His face hardened, and the familiar weight of responsibility settled on his shoulders. He hustled Abigail toward the livery office.

"Elijah, what are you—"

She was interrupted by Moses as they entered the office. "I heard it," he exclaimed. Moses disappeared into the back as Elijah tried to guide Abigail to a seat. "Elijah, tell me what is going on."

A much more distinct burst of gunfire shattered the calm, echoing from somewhere between downtown and the open area east of the river, and Abigail shrieked, then covered her mouth.

"Billy!" Moses called out toward the stable as his boots pounded toward the office. "Get my saddle on Copper." Moses re-emerged in the office wearing his gun belt, his cheerful demeanor of earlier now gone. He moved with a soldier's efficiency, a side of him that surfaced only in moments of crisis. "Looks like we're back in it, brother." He handed Elijah his gun belt, then stuck the slouch hat on his brother's head, tossing the bowler aside. "We told 'em they could count on us."

Elijah secured the belt around his waist, checked the Colt Army 1860 revolver, and straightened the cavalry hat on his head.

The gunfire grew louder, and Elijah's trained ears knew shots were now being traded. "Hope them fool deputies aren't gettin' all shot up chargin' in there," Moses said. He held a Spencer rifle in each hand and tossed one to Elijah. "No more considering whether we'll help or not."

Elijah nodded, then turned to Abigail and knelt before her. "Billy will get you safely home. You'll be alright."

He turned and headed out the door to Bear, hearing that Abigail was following, but he did not turn back. Swinging aboard, Elijah secured his rifle in the scabbard, then turned to his brother. "You ready?"

Moses nodded. Elijah glanced at Abigail's worried eyes, then, without a word, gave Bear a kick, and the brothers were off toward the gunfire.

A NEW FRIEND

—·—

Elijah and Moses charged through downtown. The sound of gunfire ahead quickened their horses' strides as startled on-lookers stepped back, their faces full of fear. Elijah noticed a mother clutching her child, hurrying away into the nearest alley. At the same time, a shopkeeper pulled closed his store's shutters. A tense, fearful silence replaced the usual bustling sounds of the town, punctuated only by the distant gunfire.

The townsfolk's wide eyes followed the brothers, who raced to-wards the danger while the citizens scattered, desperate to escape the harrowing sounds of the battle unfolding.

Elijah leaned forward in the saddle, squinting through the haze of gun smoke ahead. Amidst the clamor of gunshots and the clatter of hooves, he caught glimpses of horses darting for cover. "I see Sheriff Carter," Elijah yelled, his voice cutting through the din. He pointed toward a stand of trees to the west. "Looks like he and the marshal are headed for cover." He eased Bear's pace, assessing the landscape's layout and the outlaws' positions. Years of battle had honed his ability to read a skirmish in moments, a skill that now surged back to the forefront of his mind. "I see three dead deputies on the trail down there."

With a quick nod, Moses gestured eastward, where three riders were charging from the river toward the sheriff and marshal. "Ambush caught 'em by surprise," he shouted back. "But charging uphill with revolvers ain't exactly a tactical genius move."

"Let's get on either side of them and force them into a decision," Elijah said. Without any further words, the brothers urged their horses southward, descending from the north to intercept the riders heading. Elijah veered to the left, not needing to look to know Moses was moving right.

Elijah drew his Spencer rifle, levering a round into the chamber as he maneuvered. Settling the rifle against his shoulder, he targeted the closest rider, who was only beginning to notice his approach. When the man pointed his revolver at Elijah, the sharp report of his rifle broke the air. Elijah's first shot missed, and he cursed being out of practice. He quickly levered in a second round and fired again, and the man fell from his horse, collapsing into the dust.

Simultaneously, Elijah heard Moses's shot ring out, his target slumping and sliding to the ground. Realizing his dire situation, the third man ceased his charge and dropped his revolver. He threw his hands up in surrender as his horse turned in a frantic circle. Elijah and Moses converged on him, Elijah holstering his rifle and drawing his revolver as they closed in.

"I'm done shootin,' mister," the man stammered. His face wore a mask of terror as he looked between the two brothers. "Where in blazes did you two even come from?"

Elijah's kept his revolver trained on the man. "Guide your horse toward those trees, where the sheriff is," he ordered, his tone leaving no room for argument. "And don't try anything."

As they escorted the captive toward the makeshift refuge, they found Sheriff Carter and Marshal Hawkins taking cover among the trees. The marshal was collecting their horses that had wandered a bit. Turning back toward Elijah and Moses, relief washed over his face when he saw the brothers. "Thank God you're here," he exclaimed. "We were sitting ducks out there."

Sheriff Carter, however, seemed less pleased, his expression sour. "Never thought it'd come to this," he muttered. He was leaning against a tree and eyed the brothers. "Relying on civilians to bail us out." He glanced toward the dead deputies on the trail.

Moses dismounted, keeping a watchful eye on the surroundings. "You ever see civilians shoot like that? Looks like we got here just in time," he said.

Elijah stared at Moses, trying to tell him now wasn't the time. "What happened?"

Marshal Hawkins pointed to the three deputies. "We had one of my deputies and both of the Sheriff's checking on things around the river, then riding the trail up into town, ensuring everything was alright. Tom and I were headed down to chat with them and let them know about the meeting later, and we came out of the trees right when five fellas rode up and started shooting at them."

"Five?" Elijah raised an eyebrow.

"We only counted three. Two off to meet their maker and this sorry fella right here." Moses reached up and pulled the prisoner down to the ground before reaching into a saddle bag for some rope to bind his hands.

"Two fellas rode off when we started shootin' back," Sheriff Carter said in a labored voice. He pushed himself off the tree and began to hobble toward the men.

Elijah then noticed the dark red stain high on his pants, which was growing. "You're shot, Sheriff."

Marshal Hawkins spun around. "Jesus, Tom, you didn't say anything."

The ornery old sheriff waved them all off. "I'll be fine." The weakness in his voice and paleness of his face said otherwise, however, as he found another tree to support him. Marshal Hawkins gave the brothers a worried look as they watched the stain grow.

Marshal Hawkins eyed the bound man, sitting on the ground. He wore bits and pieces of homespun clothes and Confederate uniform parts. He appeared as if he hadn't seen a barber, a bath, or any other hygiene in some time. "You with the Missouri gang led by the fella they call the Shadow Commander? Is it Nate Morrow?"

Elijah reached down, tipped the man's hat off his head, and saw that he might barely be considered a man. He was perhaps twenty, but no boy if he fought in the war and rode with guerillas.

The prisoner looked up at all of them, then shot a look at Sheriff Carter when he slumped to the ground. "Are y'all gonna help him?" the young man's voice quivered.

Marshal Hawkins turned to Sheriff Carter, then back to the prisoner. "I'm afraid there isn't much we can do for him by the looks of it. You, however. We need information from."

The prisoner's eyes darted between the men, his face reflecting fear and uncertainty. Before he could respond, a sudden eruption of gunfire in the distance shattered the tense silence. The rapid, distinct pops echoed through the air, originating from the direction of downtown Omaha.

Marshal Hawkins' head snapped up, his expression grim as he assessed the situation. "That's gunfire in town," he said. "And there's only one deputy left around this morning."

Moses's eyes widened. "Time's not on our side," he said. We need to move now." He kicked the man over with his boot and drew his revolver to his side. "Anything we should know about?"

The sporadic crackle of gunshots grew louder, punctuated by the distant shouts and cries that drifted on the wind. Elijah gave the prisoner a kick in the side, not enough to hurt the man but sufficient to get his attention. "Things can only get worse for you, son."

The prisoner tried to shuffle back to a seated position, moving his eyes from his captors to the town and back.

"Out of time," Moses declared. He pointed his revolver at the young man.

"We was a diversion," he stammered. He looked back at his dead friends, then up at Moses with pleading eyes. "I didn't know this was gonna happen; they just told me there was money in it for me."

Elijah and Moses both cocked their heads. "How many others?" Moses demanded.

The young man began to stammer, looking toward town, perhaps wondering if he had held out long enough. "Half dozen."

Elijah positioned himself to climb back aboard Bear. "Where they hittin'?"

"I dunno," he muttered.

Elijah stepped away from Bear; his kick might have bruised a rib this time.

"The bank," the prisoner groaned.

Elijah swung into his saddle and looked down at the marshal. "You stay here and guard the prisoner. We'll send someone back for him and the sheriff, then rendezvous with you." The marshal gave him a puzzled look. Elijah realized he had no authority to make demands, but decisions had to be made swiftly.

Marshal Hawkins nodded. "I wanted your help; I guess I got it. Hargrove is the deputy marshal on duty. Lean man with a brown mustache and chin hair. Leathery face, you won't miss him."

Elijah glanced at Moses, who was already preparing to ride. "We'll find Hargrove and sort this out," he said. He gave Bear a kick, and they were off at a gallop.

THE CLATTER OF HOOVES echoed through the streets as Elijah and Moses neared downtown Omaha. The town, peaceful and productive earlier in the day, was now a scene of turmoil, with frightened townsfolk scurrying for cover. Windows slammed shut, and the clanging of closed shutters echoed through town.

As they approached, the brothers could see smoke curling into the sky from an unknown source. Shouts and screams punctuated the sharp reports of rifles and pistols.

Elijah scanned the scene for Deputy Marshal Hargrove. He spotted the man Marshal Hawkins had described ducking behind a water trough near the bank, firing his pistol at unseen assailants, a shotgun lying nearby. Elijah pointed, and without hesitation, Moses followed him toward the bank. They could see a pair of outlaws, their faces obscured by bandanas, exchanging gunfire with Hargrove.

The brothers dismounted, pulling their rifles from the scabbards, then pointed the horses down an alley and encouraged them to get out of harm's way. Their movements were fluid, a seamless transition from riders to foot soldiers. Each move was calculated, a dance they had performed countless times on distant battlefields, now replayed on the familiar streets of Omaha. Ducking behind the trough with the deputy marshal, Moses levered a round into his Spencer, popped up, and squeezed off a shot at one of the robbers. The rifle crack joined the cacophony of noise, and one of the thieves tumbled forward into the dusty street.

Elijah shouted to the deputy marshal over the din. "Hawkins sent us." The deputy nodded, both men flinching when a shot splintered the boardwalk near them. "Just the two?"

Hargrove looked at Moses. "Well, one now."

"Just you and two fellas doin' all this shooting?" Moses's voice carried over the noise as he risked looking toward the bank.

The deputy shook his head. "Two others got away already. Some shootin' somewhere else, too."

Elijah looked at Moses for a moment. The sight of the smoke rising toward the livery sparked concern inside him.

He leaned close to the deputy. "You any good with a rifle?" Elijah held up his Spencer, and the deputy nodded. "Awful fancy, but reckon it'll suit me better 'n that scattergun. Didn't reckon I'd need the Sharps rifle when I left the office this mornin'."

Elijah handed him the rifle and grabbed the shotgun. "Count of three, we're all jumping up. You've got four shots left. Run that lever and fire toward the bank until we're well clear. Meet us near the livery if you can."

"Won't need but one shot for the remainin' man."

Elijah could not get over the deputy's calm demeanor. "Then the others are to keep any attention off us while we move."

The deputy nodded again, unfazed. Moses worked the lever on his rifle as Elijah cocked both hammers on the shotgun. They all leaned back against the trough and took a breath.

"Ain't the worst plan you've ever had, I suppose," Moses said.

"Maybe the last, though," Elijah deadpanned. He looked at his partners. "Ready?" Elijah's count hit three, and he and Moses took off through the street toward the livery, seeking cover along buildings once they cleared a cross street.

Elijah heard one shot from the Spencer as he ran and then froze when an armed man emerged from a corner near the livery and raised his weapon in their direction. Before either brother could react, Elijah heard the crack of the Spencer, and the man in front of them fell. Turning toward Deputy Hargrove, he saw him levering the rifle, the remaining bandit from the bank lying dead in the street behind him.

Elijah and Moses dashed down the boardwalk, their boots thundering against the wooden planks. They rounded a corner, emerging into the intersection at the heart of downtown Omaha, where the livery and freight operation sat. Smoke billowed from the freight yard, and a smaller amount of smoke and flames licked the edges of the central office. The sight struck a chord of fear in Elijah's heart.

The street was in disarray, with horses and mules panicked and scattered; a couple of lifeless bodies that appeared to be innocent bystanders lay strewn on the ground. Brutus, the loyal and formidable dog, barked at the door to the office, his stance defensive and alert.

Elijah scanned the street desperately, searching for Big Sam. He soon spotted him taking cover behind his parked freight wagon. Sam was working to unhitch the team of horses, alternating between that task and taking shots across the street and into the livery. The wagon offered him minimal cover as he fought to protect what was left of the business.

Moses and Elijah moved toward Big Sam, taking advantage of the cover provided by the buildings. As they approached, Elijah could see the determination and fear on his face. Usually calm and collected, Sam was now a picture of focused desperation, sweat dripping down his face.

"Sam!" Elijah called out as they neared the wagon and slid underneath. "What's happening?"

Big Sam ducked as another shot rang out, then popped up to return fire. "They came outta nowhere, Elijah!" he shouted, his voice strained. "Handful of 'em took the bank, set the office on fire, and started driving off the horses and mules!" He looked toward Brutus and the livery. His voice cracked with emotion, a rare glimpse of vulnerability from the giant of a man. "I tried to stop 'em, but there were too many. I ain't lettin' 'em destroy everything we've worked for, though." He took a breath. "I think Billy is in there, still."

Elijah's gaze swept across the street to the livery. Through the smoke, he saw figures moving in the freight yard and the stables, trying to herd the remaining animals away. His jaw tightened. This was more than a bank robbery; it was a coordinated assault.

Moses rolled to his stomach under the wagon, raised his rifle, and took aim at one of the figures trying to drive the animals away. His shot rang true, and the figure collapsed.

Elijah's mind raced with tactical options. He assessed their position, the enemies' movements, and the street layout, devising a plan on the fly.

With a shotgun in hand, Elijah focused on the office. Brutus's relentless barking indicated someone or something significant was still inside. "We need to get into that office!" he yelled over the noise. Big Sam finished unhitching the last horse, slapping its rump to send it galloping away from the danger.

Elijah looked down at Moses, who was in a good shooting position, scanning for targets. "Mo, give Sam and me some time to get to the door."

"Yeah," Moses yelled. He then squeezed off another shot and rolled to his side to lever the rifle before returning to his position. "I see one shadow in the office, maybe near the safe, and another is skedaddling that way from the yard."

Elijah looked at Big Sam, who nodded his readiness, and the two ran for the office door. Brutus stopped his barking only long enough to look at each of them, then resumed pawing at the door. Big Sam kicked with his massive boot, and Brutus rushed ahead of them, latching onto the arm of a man working on the safe. The thief screamed in pain, threw the dog off, and had just drawn a revolver to shoot the attacking hound when Elijah sprayed him with the shotgun, and Brutus finished his attack.

Elijah turned at the sound of a scuffle and saw Big Sam dragging a man across the floor, his flailing feet skimming along the ground. Sam launched the man through the glass front window, then climbed through himself, putting a boot on his neck as Moses climbed from beneath the wagon and joined them.

Elijah surveyed the burning office, searching for other intruders or trapped individuals. The heat was intense, and timbers began to groan and shift, threatening to collapse. He coughed as smoke filled his lungs, his eyes stinging from the heat and ash. "Billy, are you in here?" He called out. "Mr. Hennessey?" Brutus's ears perked up, and he stopped thrashing his victim and bolted around the corner to the back office. Elijah held an arm before his face, struggling through the smoke and flames.

"Mr. Barber. . ." came a raspy voice.

Elijah looked down and dropped to his knees when he saw Billy sprawled on the floor. "Billy, what happened?" He crawled to him, grabbed the young man's shirt collar, and dragged him toward the door.

"She didn't wanna leave, but I made her," Billy managed. He groaned, and before Elijah could even process what he meant, he saw the crimson stain on the front of his shirt.

Elijah looked the young man in the eyes. "We'll get you some help, Billy."

"I tried to get her out and keep them fellas away from the safe." Billy coughed, and a sick gurgling noise came from his throat before he managed to speak again. "They were askin' for you by name, boss, and seemed to have figured she was your gal."

Elijah emerged into the street, gasping for air, and dropped beside Billy. He removed his hat, tossed it on the ground, and wiped his brow. "You done good, Billy. Braver than anything I saw in the war." Elijah began to look around in a daze, but then his head snapped back to Billy. "You said you *tried* to get her out?" he asked suddenly.

Billy's head rolled from side to side, and he began to cry. "They took her, boss. I'm sorry."

Elijah stood quickly and scanned the area.

The boy stared up at the sky. "I'm dyin', ain't I, boss?"

Elijah looked at the burns on the young man's body, then ripped open his shirt to see what he knew was a fatal wound. He wouldn't lie to the boy. "We appreciate everything you've done for us, Billy. We'll make sure your ma is taken care of." He grabbed the young man's hand. "And it ain't your fault they took her. You're a hero, son."

A flurry of hoofbeats and shouts got Elijah's attention, and he looked up to see three riders emerge down the street. One of them tipped his hat to Elijah, just like he had seen earlier in the day, with a sickening grin. Two others looked on, one holding a rope tied to Abigail, struggling and screaming in the street. Time seemed to freeze for a moment, and Elijah's mind raced back to Iron County, Missouri, and the moment he stared at the man who killed William Jones.

The crack of a rifle shattered Elijah's thoughts. He saw the man holding onto Abigail bolt upright and then fall from his saddle. Elijah looked behind him and saw Deputy Hargrove lowering the Sharps rifle he had retrieved.

"Elijah!" Abigail yelled, beginning to run for him.

"Abigail, don't!" Elijah stepped forward as time slowed. He watched the same sickening grin appear on the face of the man who killed William as he shot Abigail in the back, almost without taking his eyes off Elijah.

"No!" Elijah yelled as Abigail tumbled forward. Moses, Sam, and Clay fired every round they had left at the remaining two men, who hollered and whipped their horses into retreat, staying low in the saddle to avoid the distant bullets.

Moses came up beside him, a look of frustration turning to sadness as he looked from Abigail to Billy. Then, anger. "We just gonna let 'em ride off?"

Elijah looked at his brother, his expression grave. "I think that might be what they want, and I ain't gonna fall for it." His face was white, and he stared at Abigail with vacant eyes.

Moses ran a hand through his hair, then stepped away.

Elijah's world narrowed to the grim tableau before him as he staggered forward. He knelt beside Abigail, his hand trembling as it brushed a stray lock of hair from her face, her features still echoing the terror of her final moments. He removed his coat and laid it over her face and torso.

As he stood, a sudden crash echoed through the burning office—the sound of a heavy beam collapsing under the relentless assault of the flames. The sound jarred him back to the brutal reality, pulling his gaze away from Abigail's still form and toward the livery.

His eyes caught something, and he stepped forward, bending down to retrieve his cavalry hat buffeted by the wind against a piece of debris.

He picked up the hat, brushing off the dust and ash that marred its surface. He looked at Abigail's lifeless form once more, then beat the hat against his leg before planting it on his head and staring at the retreating dust cloud to the west.

AN OLD FRIEND

— • —

E lijah closed a gate on the far side of the freight yard untouched by the fire, where they had been able to corral a handful of the spooked horses and mules. Hopefully, good-natured citizens would bring more in later.

Moses approached him and leaned against the gate. He blew a long, low whistle, then smashed his fist against the wood as he looked at the livery. "Gone. All of it." Perhaps realizing this was not the worst loss of the day, he looked at his brother. "How are you, Eli?" Elijah watched the bucket brigade and volunteer fire team pour water on the last flickers of the fire. "Sam enlisted a mule to pull the safe into the street," he managed.

Moses's voice became commanding. "Eli. . . That ain't what I'm talkin' about."

There was a long silence before Elijah spoke up without looking away from the smoke and ruin. "They're dead because of us, because of me," he managed. I knew she was looking for any reason not to be with me. . ."

Moses grabbed him by the arm. "Not your fault, Eli. You hear me?"

Elijah slowly turned his head toward Moses, then looked down at the arm grabbing him. He shook it off. "Her people already came and got her, and they wouldn't say one word to me."

Moses rubbed his beard. "It's hard for people to grasp these kinds of things. They ain't used to it like we are."

Elijah looked at him with something akin to disgust. "Not a point of pride, Mo."

Moses cleared his throat. "Listen, Eli, if you need to go do whatever you need to do, I can manage it here."

"I'm where I need to be," he said. They were quiet for a long time before Moses kicked at the dirt, then looked up and pointed at Deputy Hargrove, who milled near those working on the fire. "Bad as it was, he kept this day from getting worse."

Elijah replied, continuing to stare at the blackened building. "Acted like he didn't have a care in the world and was more than comfortable with that rifle." Elijah reflected on the deputy's unflappable demeanor amidst the gunfire. There was a story behind those calm, calculating eyes.

"Exactly," Moses said. "That feller has seen some fightin'." He turned toward Elijah. "On which side, I'm not sure."

"Ours today."

Big Sam approached, trudging through the freight yard. "Got a couple more critters tied up out front and a few lingering close by that we'll get back." He looked at the stable of animals near Elijah and Moses, then back to the buildings. "Plenty are gone, though. . ." He hesitated before continuing. "And more 'n a few burned up." He then removed his hat and looked at Elijah. "Boss, I am awful sorry for your loss."

"Thanks for what you did today, Sam," Elijah said.

Sam leaned against the gate. There was a heaviness in his voice, the usually stoic giant visibly shaken by the day's events. The loss, not just of life and property but of security and the familiar, seemed to weigh on him, who had already seen too much loss in his lifetime. "My job," he said. "You both been good and fair bosses and helped me make a livin'." He nodded to emphasize his point but said no more for a moment before adding, "Those are some bad men who done this."

Elijah checked his pocket watch, its case warm from being held tightly in his hand. The time showed well past noon. The watch, a relic from a past life, had belonged to Talbot Jones, their old mentor. Elijah kept it after the old sheriff was killed as a token of remembrance. Sometimes, he opened the watch, expecting to hear Talbot's voice offering guidance or a stern rebuke. Elijah doubted even Talbot could find words for a day like this. "We missed the meeting with Hawkins and Carter," he said.

Moses shrugged, his eyes locked on the smoldering remains of their livery, the fire now mostly out. "Reckon we had more pressing matters."

"We should go see Hawkins anyway and check on Carter." Elijah paused, glancing at Big Sam. "You wanna come with?"

Big Sam's face showed his weariness. "May as well. Ain't got nothin' left to guard or haul now, anyhow."

Elijah saw Deputy Hargrove approaching. "Deputy, we're headed to see your boss," Elijah called out. Hargrove's expression was unreadable, and he merely nodded his assent.

The group made their way through Omaha's devastated streets, the rhythmic clack of their boots echoing on the wooden boardwalk. The typical buzz of activity had been replaced by a somber quiet, intermittently pierced by distant shouts and the sounds of townsfolk and stable hands corralling horses.

Approaching the City Marshal's office, Elijah felt the day's turmoil weigh upon him. The town's once palpable sense of safety and progress—usually only shaken by bar fights, the bad manners of some rail workers, and the overcrowding of a growing frontier town—

seemed ripped away. He tallied a list in his mind, a scroll of those dead because of him.

A sharp voice halted their solemn procession. "Elijah Barber! How could you?!"

They turned to see a woman in her mid-twenties marching toward them, holding her skirt up. Her long brown hair was pulled back in a practical bun, her dark eyes ablaze with anger and concern.

Her hands were planted on her hips as she confronted Elijah. "You were right there at the livery! Did you even bother to look for my father?"

Moses looked at the woman with heavy eyes. "Ma'am, please, he—"

"I did look. . . Miss Hennessey?" Elijah managed. He had only met her once, some time ago.

She huffed as if he should know without asking. "Yes. Margaret Hennessey. My father owns that livery." Her voice quivered, betraying her inner turmoil.

"Ma'am, if you know our name, then you know that—"

Elijah cut Moses off with a stare, then whispered. "Not the time, Mo. She don't know, and she's just worried."

Big Sam, recognizing the surname, interjected with a gentle tone. "Miss Hennessey, we tried our best. Your father wasn't there."

A flicker of relief passed through Margaret's eyes, replaced by resolve. "I need to see the marshal," she declared. She marched past them toward the office.

They found Patrick Hennessey attempting to console his daughter inside the marshal's office. Margaret was animated, expressing her frustrations over her father's dismissal of her worries.

As Elijah observed the father-daughter dynamics, Marshal Hawkins, standing near his desk, caught his attention. "Elijah, Moses,

I'm glad you're alright. We've got some information from the prisoners," Hawkins began, motioning them over along with Clay.

Elijah's focus shifted. "What did they say?"

The marshal leaned in, his voice low but urgent. "The young one you talked to earlier has been chatting. It was Nate Morrow's gang, alright. But the twist is it was two members of the group who orchestrated this attack. Seems they did it without Morrow's knowledge. A couple of brothers by the name of Jack and Miles Crenshaw."

Elijah's mind drifted back to that fateful encounter during the war and the two men holding onto William Jones—two men who looked as if they could have been brothers. Shaking off the memory, he refocused on the marshal.

"And the other one?" Elijah asked.

Hawkins shook his head. "The one from the livery isn't saying much, too scared or loyal. But the young one seems to think the Crenshaws have their own agenda. Something about settling old scores."

Old scores. The phrase resonated with Elijah. The image of the man in the street earlier, tipping his hat with that evil grin, flashed in his mind.

Moses, who had been listening intently, broke in. "So, this was more than just a simple raid for cash?"

"It appears so," the marshal confirmed. "The Crenshaws might be using Morrow's gang for their own purposes." Marshal Hawkins shrugged, then pulled Elijah aside. "I'm sorry about the schoolteacher," he said in a low voice.

"Thank you," Elijah said. His mind swirled with the realization that the attackers had likely spotted them riding together, and he beat himself up even more. He grimaced, and Hawkins looked like he wanted to speak but was hesitating. "What is it, Elijah asked?"

"Her father came by. Said it was best you do not try to see them."

Elijah began to object to the marshal but realized he was only a messenger. "Alright."

The Marshal patted Elijah on the shoulder, then turned to his deputy. "Are you alright, Clay?"

Hargrove nodded and set the shotgun he'd brought back into its spot in the office.

"If you can't tell from his demeanor," Elijah began with a perplexed look, "he was in the thick of the fighting today."

Marshal Hawkins patted Clay on the shoulder. "Doesn't surprise me."

Elijah eyed the marshal. "Sheriff Carter?"

Marshal Hawkins looked at the ground and shook his head. "Doc said the *best* scenario right now is losing the leg." He looked up and rubbed his neck. Found out Bradley took a bullet inside the bank."

"Oh no," Moses said.

"And?" Elijah managed. The marshal just shook his head.

Hawkins turned toward Big Sam and approached him. "Don't believe I've met this fellow. I'm Marshal Hawkins." He stuck out his hand, and Elijah saw him grimace when Big Sam took it.

"One of ours," Elijah said, gazing out the window without saying anything further.

Moses looked at Elijah, and when his brother didn't continue, he took up the introduction. "Marshal, this is Sam Donovan. Missouri fella who wandered up after the war. He runs our freight wagon operation and spent his morning defendin' the livery and half 'a downtown, it seems." The two men shook hands, and the room fell silent momentarily.

Patrick Hennessey turned to his daughter. "Margaret, you should go home and wait for me. It's no place for you here."

Margaret's response was immediate and defiant; her eyes opened wide. "I am not a fragile flower, Father. I have every right to be here. This involves me just as much as anyone else."

Elijah observed the exchange and saw the pain in the livery owner's eyes. He had lost his wife, sons, and perhaps now a business. He likely could muster no other mindset toward his daughter than being protective.

Marshal Hawkins cleared his throat, breaking the uncomfortable silence in the room. "We should be heading to that meeting now," he said. He glanced at his pocket watch. "Though we're considerably late, given today's events, our presence is more important than ever." He looked at Deputy Hargrove. Can you hold things down here, perhaps check on the Sheriff after a spell?"

"Never was one for a cotillion anyhow," Clay said.

Sam spoke up as he took stock of himself in sweat-soaked shirt sleeves. "Reckon I'm not fit for such an event anyhow. I'll find some grub and check back in soon."

"Alright, then," the marshal began, gathering his things, "we'll see you after—"

"And you won't even humor me with a reason my father and I should not attend?"

Patrick Hennessey sighed. "Dear, it was not our meeting to be invited to."

She turned to him, seemingly perplexed by his attitude. "They burnt your livery. Our livery. How doesn't this involve us?"

"If I may," Elijah said carefully. He stepped toward the Hennesseys. "I have a terrible feeling the livery was targeted on account of my brother and me." He gestured to Moses but saw that his comment confused him. "I think there's more to this than just our burnt livery.

I fear this is personal." She wrinkled her nose when Elijah said 'our' but said nothing else.

Elijah prepared to explain further, but his thoughts were interrupted by a shadow falling across the doorway and a voice calling down the street. "I found them!"

A man stepped inside, his presence commanding the room's attention. His eyes scanned the room, then settled on Elijah and Moses as his associate joined him. "Been looking all over town for you two."

Moses stepped forward. "Wish I could say I was happy to see you right now." He shook the man's hand.

The man gave a small smile, then turned. "Elijah."

"Matt? My God. How are you?" The two shook hands, and Matt Hobbs shrugged, then gestured into the street. "Better than you, it seems."

"What are you doing here?" Elijah asked. He then saw the rest of the group eyeing them. "Everyone, this is Matt Hobbs. He's the Pinkerton detective we helped catch Frank Tucker with last summer."

"Other way around, I think," Hobbs said. He removed his hat when he saw Margaret Hennessey, then turned back to Elijah. "Union Pacific wired us in Chicago last week, wanting to talk about some work here in Omaha and down the track. Figured I'd surprise you, and when I heard you'd be at the meeting. . . well, I thought it might be a fun reunion."

Elijah looked past Hobbs to the young man in the doorway and realized it was Thomas, the bank teller.

"Oh." Hobbs guided the young man forward. "Went looking for any of you and ended up at the bank, and. . . Well, Thomas, you tell them."

"They took all your money, Mr. Barber," Thomas managed. He was clearly in distress.

Moses beat his hat on his leg, walked to a corner of the office, and folded his arms. Elijah looked at his brother, his world collapsing even more around him, then turned back to Thomas. "Thank you for telling me, but I reckoned that was the case."

Elijah saw Hobbs grimace and kept his eyes on him as he asked, "What am I missing, Thomas?"

Thomas looked around the whole room before returning to Elijah. "It was only *your* personal safe and deposit box they asked us to open, Mr. Barber."

SEND US

— · —

Matt Hobbs held back as the group left the marshal's office, gesturing for Elijah to join him. Sensing the deliberate nature of the request, Elijah fell into step beside the tall, dapper man with his well-groomed facial hair and fancy East Coast suit.

Hobbs's tone was serious, quite different from the interaction either would have wished for after not seeing each other for so long. "First off, I'm genuinely sorry about your livery. . . and the money."

Elijah gave a curt reply. "Appreciated, Matt."

Hobbs hesitated, gauging Elijah's mood. "Have you thought about why it happened? Have you crossed paths with anyone lately who might want to do this?" He appeared in thought for a moment. "Does it tie back to Tucker somehow?"

Elijah's steps slowed as he considered the question. "Maybe the latter." Elijah's mind wandered back to those harrowing days, the memories like faded photographs—blurred yet hauntingly vivid. He remembered the desperation in the eyes of those they pursued, the relentless chase through dense woodlands and treacherous terrain. His heart clenched at the thought that someone from that past might be behind this attack. "I'm not sure," Elijah said, his voice laced with uncertainty. "I might be imagining things."

"You know," Hobbs pressed, "sometimes a hunch is more than just that."

Elijah shot him a sidelong glance. "There was someone this morning on the street. I might recognize him from when we tried to re-capture Tucker during the war. But I can't be sure. . ."

The conversation lulled as they walked, the distance between them more than physical. Hobbs broke the silence, his tone softer. "Elijah, it *is* good to see you. Despite all this."

That stopped Elijah in his tracks. He turned to Hobbs, and a silence fell between them, filled with the unspoken language of old friends who had shared triumphs and tragedies. There had been a time when Elijah and Hobbs had stood shoulder to shoulder, two men bound by a common cause and the unyielding grip of war. They had saved each other's lives last summer in a noble cause but were quite different men.

"You know why I stopped writing back, Matt? Your letters stopped being about staying in touch. It felt more like you were trying to recruit us, luring us to a life I've been trying to leave behind." Elijah began to walk again. "You knew we didn't want any part of it, and once you believed me. . ." He stopped again and looked at his old friend. "We never heard from you anymore."

"I never meant to—"

Elijah cut him off, gesturing toward Moses, who was chatting with Marshal Hawkins ahead of them. "I've spent years trying to get us to a safe place, Matt. A stable life. And today. . ." His voice trailed off, the events of the day casting a long shadow over his words. "Well, don't take this the wrong way because I respect you. But it's quite appropriate we cross paths on the day things all blew up again."

Hobbs remained silent, allowing Elijah's words to settle. Then, as he often did, he returned to business. "You'll be meeting Pinkerton himself today," he said. "The railroad's taking security and protection seriously. I'm sure today will only further that."

Elijah furrowed his brow. "Seems like you'll get the chance to pull me back in after all," Elijah muttered. He looked at Hobbs, who seemed surprised. "You think I'm just going to sit back and take this?" Elijah's face hardened. "Matt, I've spent every day since the war ended protecting what's mine. The livery wasn't just a business; it symbolized the life Moses and I fought to build. A life that's now been threatened. I won't stand by while everything we've worked for is torn down. No, I'm not the same man I was during the war, but I'll do whatever it takes to protect what's ours."

They fell into silence again, watching citizens cautiously begin to refill the streets. As they neared the grandeur of the Herndon House, Hobbs ventured one last question. "Oh, you wrote about the schoolteacher? How are things with her?"

Elijah halted and looked at his old friend. "They murdered her, Matt." His gaze drifted to the horizon, where the setting sun cast a melancholic glow over the city. He glanced around the street, seeing the eyes on him. "Murdered her, and it's because of me."

* * *

STANDING TALL at the corner of Ninth and Farnam, the Herndon House was a proud symbol of Omaha's burgeoning status at the frontier's edge. Its grandeur, a striking contrast to the dusty streets outside, was unmistakable, a fact not lost on Elijah and Moses as they entered its opulent lobby, flanked by Marshal Hawkins and Matt Hobbs. The luxurious interior seemed worlds apart from their usual haunts.

Unable to hide his awe, Moses whispered to Elijah, "This place is something else, huh?"

Elijah agreed." The opulence around him was both intimidating and fascinating. Matt Hobbs, moving with the ease of someone accustomed to such surroundings, led them upstairs. They walked past the ornate decor, observing the curious glances and worried looks. Hobbs knocked on the grand suite's doors and then ushered them in.

The suite they entered was a picture of luxury. Plush armchairs, a lavish sofa, and a dining table set with fine china and silverware spoke of a world far removed from their own. Elijah felt Moses's nervousness as he whispered, "We're not dressed for this sort of thing."

Before Elijah could reply, a side door opened, revealing a group of well-dressed men. They all acknowledged Hobbs, who then spoke up. "You're well aware of the day's events, so I hope their delay is understandable." He forced an awkward smile. "Marshal, I'll let you make introductions."

"Gentlemen, allow me to introduce Elijah and Moses Barber," he said, gesturing toward the brothers. "I originally invited them to seek their assistance in any way that might be needed, given their backgrounds. . . And alas, they were needed before we could even discuss things." He glanced toward Elijah and Moses. "Their actions today were crucial in keeping things from worsening, though their livery was lost to the flames." Hawkins hesitated. "Elijah's, um. . . the woman he was courting, was among the dead."

"Among the murdered," Elijah said. The room shifted uncomfortably.

A robust, bearded man with a Scottish accent and a stern demeanor extended his hand. "Alan Pinkerton. Your help last summer was invaluable, gentlemen. I'm happy to meet you finally, and I want to thank you for your help." He cast a glance at Hobbs. "And for keeping my man safe. Sorry to hear about your livery." He turned to Elijah. "You have my condolences."

Elijah managed a thin smile. "Thank you, Mr. Pinkerton." Elijah and Moses both shook his hand. Elijah sensed the underlying tensions in the room, the mix of respect and resentment towards their unconventional involvement. He felt Hobbs's supportive presence beside him, a silent ally in a room filled with powerful men who viewed the world through the lens of law, order, and business.

There was a brief silence, and Hobbs stepped in to fill it, gesturing toward an impeccably dressed man, doing his best to radiate authority. "Gentlemen, this is Thomas Durant, vice president and general manager of the Union Pacific Railroad operations here in Omaha. He arranged for the meeting to be held here and has asked for Pinkerton's help to protect his interests."

Durant leaned forward to shake the brothers' hands. "A pleasure," he said, adding, "My condolences."

Marshal Hawkins then introduced Caspar Yost, the U.S. Marshal for the territory. Yost's attire was refined yet understated. The middle-aged man's expression was unreadable. Elijah felt his keen eyes assessing them, making him uneasy.

Hawkins then turned to an older gentleman with a distinguished air. "And this is Judge Leonard Whitmore, the territory's federal judge. He's here to discuss the legalities of our situation."

With his silver hair and sharp eyes, Judge Whitmore looked at the Barbers. "Gentlemen, your reputation precedes you." The man moved forward, shook their hands, and offered Elijah his condolences before moving toward the table.

As he did, Marshal Yost's deep voice cut through the room. "Time is of the essence, men. Far more than when we scheduled this. We should begin."

Moses whispered to Elijah as they walked to their seats. "I ain't sure if he meant our reputations were a good thing or a bad thing."

Elijah closed his eyes. "I think that was the point, Mo."

The group all sat down at the table. Elijah noticed that Durant sat at the head. Still, Judge Whitmore held up a hand, commanding the room's attention as he settled into his chair. The group fell into a respectful silence, waiting for him to begin.

"Gentlemen, we all know that this town has faced a direct attack, one that has not only impacted its citizens but also poses a threat to the progress of the Union Pacific Railroad. While the railroad's concerns are understandable, let's not forget the broader picture here." He paused, his gaze sweeping across the faces gathered around the table.

"This is, at its core, a federal matter. The gang we believe to be led by Nate Morrow has committed a series of crimes across state lines. These aren't local disturbances – they include assaults on travelers, freight holdups spanning multiple states, and now another bank robbery. Each of these actions has federal implications."

Judge Whitmore leaned forward, his hands clasped on the table. "It's crucial that we understand the situation. This is not just a threat to Omaha or even to Nebraska Territory. It's a challenge to federal authority and law, and it must be addressed as such. Our response needs to be coordinated, decisive, and within the bounds of federal jurisdiction."

Still absorbing Judge Whitmore's words, the room shifted its attention as Thomas Durant, a cigar in hand, turned in his chair and prepared to speak. The smoky scent wafted through the room, prompting Elijah to reach for his pipe, filling it with a sense of reluctant camaraderie. As he lit it, Durant began, his voice rich with the confidence of a man used to getting his way.

"While I have the utmost respect for Judge Whitmore's perspective," Durant started, his tone suggesting a veiled patronization, "we must also acknowledge the monumental significance of the Union

Pacific Railroad. It's a federal endeavor backed by the government and crucial to the nation. This project, which crosses state lines, symbolizes progress and unity for our country."

As Durant continued, emphasizing the railroad's importance, its role in national development, and Federal interest, Moses, leaning back in his chair, interjected. "Well, not yet, it ain't. It's barely a hundred miles out of Omaha as it stands."

The room fell into an awkward silence, broken only by the soft crackling of Elijah's pipe. Feeling amusement and exasperation, Elijah glanced at his brother, fighting the urge to reprimand him for the interruption.

Durant's face reddened, his demeanor shifting from composed to furious. "Who even invited these men, anyway?" Durant demanded, his voice rising in frustration, the cigar's smoke curling in front of his face.

Marshal Hawkins spoke up. "I did, sir. As I said before we began. When we first got word that Morrow's men might be lurking outside the city, I sought their experience and advice. I had hoped it would not be required, but. . . Well, when the meeting was planned, it was their role to offer their experience chasing such men." He looked at Moses a moment. "I'm quite sure that Moses regrets his comment."

Moses leaned forward, his elbows on the table. "I'm real sorry, sir. I say things that come into my mind. I ain't used to fancy affairs like this." At this, everyone in the group smiled but Marshal Yost, who shook his head, and Durant, who still appeared agitated.

As the room's atmosphere remained tense, U.S. Marshal Yost leaned back in his chair, regarding the group with a demeanor that suggested he was ready to steer the conversation back to more serious matters. His tone was measured, but his voice hinted at dismissal, especially when addressing the local concerns.

"I concur with Judge Whitmore," Yost began, "this situation has escalated into a federal matter. The Marshal Service will initiate a manhunt for Morrow and his gang, supported by a federal warrant and bounties, as authorized by the judge." He paused and looked at Pinkerton. "Naturally, we'll also coordinate with the Pinkerton Agency to safeguard the railroad's interests."

Turning towards Marshal Hawkins and the Barbers, Yost spoke. "Your willingness to assist is appreciated, and I extend my sympathies regarding the livery. However, the federal government is equipped to oversee this pursuit. We'll coordinate with the city marshal and county sheriff as necessary, and I trust you will ensure the safety of the city and county from now on."

Marshal Hawkins, visibly irritated by Yost's tone, retorted. "With all due respect, Marshal Yost, our sheriff is unlikely to survive the day, and if by some miracle he does, it'll be without a leg."

The room fell silent, Hawkins' words hanging in the air. After puffing on his pipe, Elijah eyed Moses, receiving a nod of approval. As Yost and Durant began conversing, Elijah's calm and steady voice carried across the room.

"Send us."

His statement shocked everyone. Durant let out a dismissive laugh, but Yost responded sternly: "The U.S. Marshals don't make a habit of sending civilians after dangerous fugitives, especially ones that might just be seeking revenge, warranted as it may be."

Elijah's retort was quick. "Last summer, the Marshals sent two poor farmers with only wartime guerrilla hunting experience after a wanted man, and we brought him in."

Yost interjected, his tone laced with skepticism. "I'm sure the famous Barber brothers love to brag about that, but as I recall, the U.S. marshal and an old sheriff accompanying you were killed, with an entire town shot up in the process." Yost eyed the other men in the room for a moment. "And now it is quite possible your past with these men has—"

"Don't you dare," Elijah interjected.

Moses, speaking with conviction, backed up his brother. "Those men died bravely last summer, helping us give a whole town their lives back and bringing the men responsible for the first-ever train robbery to justice." He then stared at Durant. "Got a whole mess 'a money back for the railroad and two banks." He turned back to Yost and pointed a finger. "And it ain't our fault evil men do evil things."

"They helped me more than I helped them," Hobbs added.

Observing the exchange, Pinkerton stated flatly, "It's true."

Durant glared at Pinkerton. "Whose side are you on, anyway?" He then turned to Moses. "And how dare you insinuate I only care about money?"

Moses leaned into Elijah as voices filled the room. "What does he mean, insinuate?" Elijah closed his eyes.

Before the argument could escalate, Judge Whitmore raised his hand, signaling for silence. "Enough," he said, his authoritative tone cutting through the rising tensions. "This is not the time for bickering or recounting past glories. We have a pressing matter at hand, and we need a practical solution." He looked at Elijah. "Marshal Hawkins has told me you had no desire to continue that life. Why the change of heart?"

"They burnt our livery, people in our new hometown were killed, and it was only our money they took from the bank." There was disbelief in the room as Elijah recounted the teller's story of two men entering, asking only for Elijah and Moses Barber's money. "I fear. . ." Elijah paused, unsure of himself. "I fear, perhaps, there is a connection to either Frank Tucker or our service in the war that has made this personal for Morrow and his gang." He puffed on his pipe. "For God's sake, they murdered my..." He cut himself off, emotion creeping into his voice.

Judge Whitmore nodded, but Marshal Yost spoke up. "You can't possibly think we will sanction some justice or revenge-seeking adventure with a badge, do you?"

"Are you of the mind that honest, hard-working men who are good with a gun and get results couldn't use such a motivation for the good of the law when properly authorized?" Elijah responded.

Yost offered no response, and Judge Whitmore took a moment to ponder, his eyes shifting between the Barbers, Marshal Yost, and the others in the room. The tension was palpable.

"Marshal Yost, I understand your concerns," the judge began, his voice authoritative. "However, given the urgency of this matter and the fact that your deputies are engaged in other parts of the territory, I believe we need to be pragmatic and get this search underway."

He turned his attention to Elijah and Moses. "I am willing to make you both special deputy marshals deputized only to find, apprehend, and deliver Nate Morrow to justice. This is not a blank check for vigilantism; you will be expected to uphold the law in your pursuit. You are acting for the U.S. Government, not yourselves."

Elijah and Moses exchanged a glance. "We understand," Elijah said.

Judge Whitmore continued, "If you require additional men for a posse, you will have to hire and pay for them yourselves, but this is an extraordinary situation, and we must act swiftly." Amid grumbles from Yost and Durant, Whitmore discussed the administrative details and ended any further discussion.

As the meeting adjourned, Judge Whitmore approached the brothers. "Good luck, gentlemen. I'll have all the necessary paperwork ready for you by the end of the day."

"Yes, sir," Elijah answered. "We'll aim to leave at first light."

As the group began to disperse, Marshal Yost passed by Elijah and Moses, his expression unreadable. "I'm not sure if I have any badges for you," he said.

Moses responded. "Oh don't worry. We've still got ours from last year."

The room slowly emptied, with Marshal Hawkins and Alan Pinkerton shaking the brothers' hands on the way out. As Elijah and Moses prepared to leave, Hobbs approached them with a determined look. "I was going to head west anyway to confer with the railroad foreman about their needs and investigate a few things. Pinkerton agreed to let me ride with you. . . If you'll have me again."

Elijah eyed Hobbs. "Whaddya think, Mo?"

Moses raised an eyebrow and then shook Hobbs's hand. "We ride again."

Elijah stuck his hand out. "Looks like we got our first posse man."

THE TRACKER

— · —

As Elijah and Moses hurried through the disrupted streets of Omaha, a list of tasks weighed on Elijah's mind. He was already calculating how many men he would need, what supplies they would require, and how they could best begin their pursuit.

A small, thin man with a rugged, sun-beaten face and a confident gait approached them, leading a string of horses. Elijah recognized the man with a thick mustache and gray hair pulled back under a sombrero. He also recognized most of the horses and saw some were branded with Patrick Hennessey's mark, indicating his stock.

The man tied the line of horses to a hitching post in front of the charred livery while watching the brothers approach. "I found them grazing near the river," he said, his voice carrying a Mexican accent. "Some have brands, some do not. But I believe they are all yours."

Moses climbed down from Copper and inspected the horses, while Elijah dismounted and inspected the man before him. He studied his sun-beaten face, the man's deep, soulful eyes revealing more sorrow than usual. Moses patted the final horse on the string on the neck. He nodded at Elijah, indicating they were indeed the livery's horses.

"Much obliged," Elijah said. He offered his hand. "We haven't seen you in a while. Nor have I ever gotten your full name."

The man shook his hand, then reached to shake Moses's. "Rivera. Augusto Rivera, and you are welcome." There was an awkward silence, and Augusto leaned back against the hitching post, his sombrero casting a shadow over his weathered face, a glint of cunning in his eyes. "These horses," he gestured towards the string with a sweep of his hand, "are of good value, especially now with your livery gone."

"It ain't wholly gone, friend," Moses said. Elijah could see his brother was unsure of the man's motivations, as was he. "Got a few buildings, some stock, and a safe of money yet."

Elijah furrowed his brow in thought. "My brother is right, but you make a fair point. You've done us a great service, Mr. Rivera." Elijah leaned a hip against the post. "What can you tell us about claiming to see Nate Morrow's outfit in these parts?"

Augusto raised an eyebrow, curious about how Elijah had this knowledge. "You believe they are the ones who did this?" Elijah nodded, and Augusto continued. "Two men came to me outside Council Bluffs and inquired about buying my horses for far too little. They felt like pure evil, and I refused. Then they called me all sorts of names. . . . I believe they would have killed me for them had we not been near a crowd."

Elijah and Moses exchanged a glance. "They look like brothers?" Elijah asked.

Augusto looked up, thinking. "*Si*," he replied. "*Es posible*."

"What happened next?" Moses asked.

Augusto sighed. "I returned to the corral later in the evening, and the horses I was keeping there to sell in the morning were gone." He lowered his eyes. "They even covered my gear in the stable with excrement."

Moses's eyes opened wide. "Horse or human—"

Elijah held up a hand, and Moses stopped his inquiry. "And you believe these fellas ride with Morrow?" Elijah asked.

"*Si*. A man like me makes it his business to keep track of such groups," August replied.

"And aside from regularly showing up with horses to sell us," Elijah asked, "what is it a man like you does?" Elijah did not hide his insinuation that he questioned how Augusto came about his stock, even if he felt bad for the man.

Augusto's expression softened. "I've been tracking and guiding for those heading west ever since the war."

Moses cocked his head. "Pardon my lack of manners, but you look a little seasoned to have fought in the war."

Augusto shook his head and squinted into the sun at the brothers. "The war before your Civil War. One day, I was living in and fighting for Mexico; the next, I was in an American territory." He paused and let the statement sink in. "I drifted from place to place, doing work with horses, guiding white men who came to the area. . . and tracking. I came here hoping the railroad could use any of those talents." He smiled and produced a half-smoked cigar, chewing on it. "But I know horses the best."

Elijah reached for his pipe, as he often did in conversational settings, but realized he didn't have time to discuss this much longer. "Tracking animals or men?"

Augusto did not hesitate. "Both."

The brothers looked at each other, and then Moses spoke up. "You as good with a gun as you are with horses?"

Augusto met his gaze. "I have had my share of needing to be."

Elijah was wary of hiring the near stranger with a questionable background. Still, he recognized their desperate need for skilled men, especially those with experience in the land west of Omaha. "You could earn a bit more beyond what I'll give you for the horses if you're willing to ride with us after the men who did this. I won't lie; I don't know what that looks like, but I'll compensate you as fairly as possible. The best I can give you is my word."

Augusto paused, considering the proposition. "I have heard only good things about the men you are, so I will accept your word."

Elijah shook his hand and jerked his head toward the horses. "Pick one you like, and gather what gear you need, but pack light." Elijah tilted his chin down the street toward the mercantile they frequented, then checked his pocket watch. "Meet us in two hours."

Augusto Rivera chose a large, dark black horse, its glossy coat and muscular build hinting at a spirited temperament that had deterred others. Augusto ran his hand through the horse's mane, whispering in Spanish, and calmed the animal. He then put it on a lead rope and walked away.

Big Sam arrived just as Augusto Rivera left, his towering figure casting a broad shadow in the late afternoon sun. He had just come from the doctor's office, where he and Deputy Marshal Hargrove had been keeping vigil. The look on his face spoke volumes before he uttered a word.

"Doc couldn't save the sheriff," Big Sam said, his voice heavy with sadness. "He passed not long ago."

Elijah and Moses both hung their heads, another layer of grief added to an already tragic day. Elijah's fists clenched at his sides, the anger inside him simmering.

Big Sam noticed the string of horses. "Where'd these come from?"

Elijah explained their encounter with Augusto, watching Sam's reaction. "He brought them in. He knew his way around horses. Said he's been tracking and guiding west of here."

Sam scratched his chin. "I heard of a fella like that. I can't say if it's the same man, but the word is he's a bit of a mercenary. Good with a horse, better with a gun."

"More or less what came out of our conversation," Elijah said. He noticed Sam looked deep in thought.

Moses grinned at Sam. "You just upset we haven't asked you to join us yet?"

Sam snorted as he started untying the rope from the hitching post. "Was coming either way."

Elijah looked at Sam. "How'd you know we'd go after them?" He turned to Moses. "Neither of you seems surprised I asked for this."

Sam sighed, his eyes drifting over the remnants of the livery. "Boss, no matter how often you say you've left that life behind, you ain't the kind to let something like this go. Not when it's personal and got people killed."

Moses walked alongside the string of horses, keeping them calm. "What he said."

The men began herding the horses into the stable's undamaged portion, putting out hay and fresh water. When the work was complete, they all stood quietly, taking in the day's events for a moment.

"Meet us at the mercantile in an hour," Elijah said, breaking the silence. "We'll need supplies, and we've got to figure out how to make this work. I reckon we're going to need every hand we can get." He removed his slouch hat, its reappearance in his life startling him, and ran a hand through his hair. "Would like to find a few more men, but regardless, we leave at first light."

Sam's eyes met Elijah's. "I'll be there. And Elijah," he added, "be careful who we trust on this."

Moses interjected, seemingly sensing Big Sam's apprehension and wanting to back his brother up. "The Pinkerton is comin' with us,

Sam." He made eye contact with Elijah and then looked back at Sam. "So is Deputy Hargrove, I reckon."

"If you trust 'em, I trust 'em," Sam said. "I'm gonna go take stock of my things."

Elijah's mind was racing with plans. He turned to Moses, their long shadows stretching toward the charred remains of their livery buildings. "Let's get moving. We've got a long night ahead of us."

Two More

— ◦ —

As the day waned, the warm glow of the setting sun bathed McAllister's Mercantile in a light that seemed to soften the day. The mercantile, a hub of local commerce and gossip, was abuzz with whispers and sideways glances as townspeople went about their business, all too aware of the undercurrent of tension gripping Omaha.

The wooden floorboards creaked under the weight of customers, and the air was thick with the mingled scents of leather, tobacco, and ground coffee. Elijah, Moses, and the growing posse navigated through the narrow aisles, setting aside crates of goods.

Elijah paused by a shelf, his mind half on the task and half lost in the day's events. He lingered in a row of farm tools, which reminded him of simpler times in Illinois that seemed a lifetime ago.

"Elijah Barber," came a familiar voice, deep and resonant. Elijah turned to see Isaiah "Ike" Taylor approaching. Known to many as a pillar of strength and resilience, he approached with the steady gait of a man who had weathered storms, both literal and figurative. His presence commanded attention, not just for his imposing stature but for the respect he had earned in the community. The years had started to sprinkle gray in his tightly coiled hair, and the lines on his face spoke of laughter, perseverance, and the deep sorrows of a hard, unfair life.

His attire was that of a working man - a sturdy shirt, durable pants, and well-worn boots.

Ike extended his hand, and Elijah shook it, feeling the firm grip of a man who had only ever known demanding work, not always by his own free choice. "Ike," Elijah greeted, a warm but tired smile on his face. "Good to see you."

Ike's eyes swept over the assortment of supplies Elijah and his companions were gathering—ammunition, dried food, medical supplies, and bivouac gear. "I'm awful sorry about. . . You have my condolences," Ike said. He eyed Elijah. "Goin' after 'em, ain't ya?"

Elijah met Ike's stare, seeing in his eyes a reflection of his determination. "Thank you, and we are," he replied. He hesitated as he considered his following words. "Can't let what happened today go unanswered."

Ike's expression turned serious. "No, I reckon not." Ike looked around the store, assessing the group with Elijah. You and your brother are leaders of men," he said. Folks want to follow someone unable to abide injustice, just like they followed you in the war."

Elijah wrinkled his nose, uncomfortable with such open praise. He felt a respect for the man before him, though. Ike Taylor was not only a veteran of a United States Colored Troops regiment during the war but had become a respected figure in the community, known for his skills as a carpenter, blacksmith, and with a plow. His presence in the mercantile, at this moment, seemed almost fortuitous.

"It true this was Morrow's outfit?" Fellas that rode with him in the war?"

Elijah looked around and then spoke in a low voice. "Appears so."

Ike rubbed a hand across his short beard. "You need another man in your posse?" he asked, his voice low enough to be heard only by Elijah.

"I seen and heard what men like him did during the war, and this. . ." He shook his head.

Elijah looked at Ike, seeing more than the seasoned warrior before him. He saw a man who had turned his trials into triumphs and whose moral compass pointed toward justice. Ike's offer was more than just assistance; it was a gesture of solidarity and shared purpose.

The idea of Ike Taylor joining them sparked a glimmer of hope in Elijah. His skills and experience would be invaluable, but Elijah knew Ike had much to lose. "We could use a man of your talents, Ike," Elijah admitted. "But I know you've got a life here, a new wife. You've saved enough for a home, and I know you're planning to buy land for your own farm and wagon shop."

Ike cut him off with a wave of his hand. "That's true, and you helped me get set up at the bank and introduced me to folks in town willin' to help a fella that looks like me. You been good to me, Elijah, and I owe you. And if you say I don't, I'll just say you have been a good enough man to me that I want to help you in your time of need." A forced grin came to his face. "Besides, I ain't gonna lie to you and say the thought of helpin' take down the likes of Nate Morrow wouldn't be good for my soul."

Elijah's eyes narrowed. Ike's willingness to join them, despite the risks, underscored the seriousness of their endeavor. This was about justice, about standing up for what was right, and it seemed Ike Taylor understood that as well as any of them.

"Alright, Ike," Elijah said. "I can't promise what I'll be able to pay you, but it'll be as much as I can."

"I'll take the goin' rate, Elijah. And be happy to do it."

Elijah gave the man a look of admiration and shook his hand. "Meet us at the Steamboat Saloon this evening. We'll talk it all over and leave at first light."

As Ike prepared to leave, Moses approached, greeting him. "Ike Taylor, good to see you. How are ya?" Moses asked.

"I'm good. Just signing up for a little adventure with you and your brother here." He glanced at Elijah. "I'd better head home and tell my wife about my plan."

"Good luck with that," Elijah said with a sympathetic grin.

After Ike departed, Moses turned to Elijah. "He's joining us?"

"Brings us up to seven. A suitable number, I think."

Moses's attention shifted to something else. "Oh, look at this." He gestured to his head, revealing a new hat, and held a rifle in each hand. "Got me a 'Boss of the Plains' hat," he said.

Elijah was more intrigued by the rifles than the hat. "New rifles? We don't need to fix what ain't broke, Mo."

Moses handed one of the rifles to Elijah. "It's a Winchester. Shorter, sturdier, and holds twice as many rounds as our Spencers."

Elijah inspected the rifle, noting the bronze receiver and the overall craftsmanship. The gun felt right in his hands, a perfect balance of form and function. "It's a fine piece, Mo," he admitted. "How much?"

"McCallister's giving us a deal," Moses explained. "He'll only charge us for one so long as we return and tell our story about how good they are. We can give our old Spencers to posse members."

Elijah, aware of their dwindling funds but recognizing the necessity of being well-armed, sighed. "Alright, let's hope we're successful enough to make good on that offer but not gone long enough for you to become boss of the plains."

THE STEAMBOAT SALOON, a usual hive of weekend activity, was subdued. Despite the diminished crowd, the murmurs were enough to echo the town's collective unease. In this subdued atmosphere, Elijah, Moses, Matt Hobbs, and Sam Donovan found a secluded spot away from the probing eyes and whispers of curiosity.

Moses glanced around the saloon, eyebrow raised. "I thought it'd be even quieter than it is tonight."

Elijah grunted an acknowledgment. He felt a twinge of irritation at the normality around them. It seemed to him that the nation, eager for progress since the war's end, was too quick to brush aside the horror and the pain. As if acknowledging the darkness would somehow halt their forward march. He mulled over these thoughts, his gaze drifting across the room. People laughed, talked, drank – life moving on as if the day's terror were just a minor interruption. *So long as someone else did the fighting*, he thought, *life could go on*.

His introspection was interrupted by the sound of Big Sam and Hobbs exchanging stories. Hobbs tried to engage Elijah in the conversation, but his mind was elsewhere, caught in his thoughts on justice, revenge, and Abigail.

Hobbs poured everyone a glass of whiskey, handing them around the table before he looked at Big Sam. "So, I hope that these Barber brothers have not been so humble that they didn't share what brought about the journey that landed them here in Omaha," Hobbs began.

Big Sam took a glass and cautiously looked at Elijah. "Well, let's just say I got the story overview," Sam replied.

Hobbs leaned in, ready to share their tale in full detail. He recounted how the Barber Brothers had crossed paths with a new U.S. Marshal in their hometown of Danville, Illinois, convincing Elijah and Moses to become deputy marshals. Their pursuit of a notorious killer, who had transformed from a bank thief to a train robber, had taken them from a small Indiana town to the decks of a Missouri River steamboat.

It was there that they had been forced to take the man's life just before reaching Omaha.

Elijah sensed Moses enjoyed the retelling, but his feelings were more complex. While he relished the excitement and meaningful work, the memories of death and destruction weighed on him—especially as he faced the task now in front of them. The marshal's death had saved Elijah's life, and another dear friend, an old sheriff who had joined their mission, had met a similar fate. Such experiences had left deep scars, and Elijah seldom spoke of the war or their previous days as marshals.

Big Sam bit his lip. Elijah could tell the big man sensed his unease but gave him a slight nod of approval. "That's more or less the story I got," Sam said.

"But they told you the best part, right?" Hobbs interjected with an infectious enthusiasm. "I mean, everyone learned who Frank Tucker was, but you know these two knew him first, right?"

Big Sam raised a curious eyebrow, prompting Hobbs to continue. Sam's eyes sparkled with excitement as Hobbs narrated how Frank Tucker, a bounty jumper during the war, had been captured by Captain Elijah Barber and then turned into a prisoner. However, Tucker's escape had set him on a collision course with Elijah Barber, who now had a reputation for never letting a fugitive elude him for long.

"So you can see why they'd be happy to have the Barbers on this case, no matter what that cranky old marshal thinks." Hobbs sat back in his chair, satisfied with his storytelling, and took a drink.

"He's right about the story," Elijah managed, confirming the tale to Big Sam. He turned to Hobbs. "We aren't some fame-seeking lawmen, however."

The lively piano music contrasted with the heavy atmosphere around the large table in the back corner. Elijah was about to speak when they were joined by Ike Taylor, Clay Hargrove, and Augusto Rivera, each taking a seat amidst a haze of tension and unspoken questions. Hobbs poured all the men a drink, Ike and Augusto accepting, but Clay held up a hand to decline.

Ike Taylor took a drink, then seemed to sense an awkwardness at the table. "What did we miss?"

Elijah rubbed his chin and made eye contact with all the men he had assembled to lead. "We were just piecing together the puzzle of today's events," he said. "The attack today wasn't just a random act. I recognized a man on the street beforehand and someone with him afterward. . . The ones we now know were the Crenshaw brothers." The men reacted in their own ways, each clearly surprised by the revelation.

Elijah took a deep breath. "They are responsible for freeing Frank Tucker after I had re-captured him. . . and then murdered our dear friend William." The men's looks let Elijah know he could leave unsaid what they did to Abigail.

Moses's jaw dropped. "The two that grinned at us before riding off? They're the ones that killed Will and set Tucker's exploits in motion?" Elijah nodded, and Moses finished the drink in his glass. "Which makes them responsible for Will's pa bein' killed and all the other horrors of last summer and now today."

Elijah sipped from his whiskey glass, then began stuffing his pipe with tobacco. "I fear they have some vendetta against us for taking Tucker down." He struck a match on the table and began puffing away on the pipe as the group absorbed this revelation in stunned silence.

"This has become more personal than you have said," Augusto said. Elijah could not read the man's opinion about his statement. Was he stating the obvious, or did it give him pause?

Clay Hargrove was fiddling with a toothpick in his mouth and then spoke up. "I'm joinin' this outfit to make right by the town after what happened today. . ." He trailed off, and Elijah realized it was the most he'd ever heard the man say. "Marshal Hawkins says you've got a limited mandate to find and bring in Nate Morrow and nothin' more." He paused, seeming to want to make sure everyone at the table knew that. "You got my full effort for that, but I won't join any pursuits of revenge."

"I understand your concerns, Clay. Let me be clear to everyone here," Elijah began. His eyes swept across the table. "Moses and I have been appointed as special deputy marshals to apprehend Nate Morrow. Our mandate is clear, and I won't ask any of *you* to do anything more."

Moses shot Elijah a knowing look that seemed to question the sincerity of his brother's promise. That or he recognized how carefully his brother had worded his statement. Elijah caught the glance but chose to remain silent on the matter.

"I assure you all, we will operate firmly but fairly," Elijah continued. "I led men in the war with the same principles. We will leave at first light, and I'll pay each of you the going rate for deputy marshal posse men, with a fair bonus upon completing our mission once our stolen money is recovered." He looked at Moses. "Mo and I can't take any bounty money, and we don't want to anyway, so you can split that as well."

The men eyed the Barbers, each seeming to sense there was more to say.

"Ain't gonna be easy, fellas," Moses said. He toyed with his drink glass. "Morrow was brutal during the war, and it appears these brothers with him are even more so." He glanced at Elijah as if unsure he should continue. "From what we saw from his type in the war, they either killed you in a fight or hung you from a tree."

The group shifted in their seats, fiddling with their glasses or rubbing their faces. "Now is the time to step away if you aren't with us," Elijah said, "I assure you, neither my brother nor I will think any less of you should you leave."

The men around the table exchanged glances, weighing Elijah's words. None stood to leave; their silent agreement to stay spoke volumes about their commitment to the cause.

As they discussed their plans for the morning, the saloon began to empty. Once the details were set, the men filtered out as well. As Clay Hargrove stood to leave, Elijah saw him nod toward the door before wishing the brothers a good evening. Elijah turned and saw Marshal Hawkins heading for their table.

Hawkins approached the table, pulled out a chair, and sat down with a sigh. He glanced around the empty chairs and glasses. "It appears you two put together a solid group," he commented.

"We appreciate you letting us bring Deputy Hargrove along," Elijah said.

Hawkins gave a wry smile, though his eyes betrayed a touch of sadness. "Didn't seem like I had much choice," he replied. "Sheriff's office can't spare a man right now, but folks in town want our own as part of this." The undertone of his words brought Sheriff Carter's death to the front of Elijah's mind. The table fell into a brief, contemplative silence; each man lost in their thoughts about the day's tragic events.

Breaking the silence, Hawkins produced two envelopes from his coat and placed them on the table. "Here's your warrant and the paperwork confirming your status as special deputies," he explained. Hawkins slid the first envelope toward Elijah. Then he tapped the second one. "And this is a letter from Marshal Yost. It spells out your limited mandate in detail. He wrote two, signed them both, and kept one." The marshal hesitated. "He's plenty serious about ensuring you stick to it."

Elijah picked up the envelope with Yost's letter but didn't open it. "Doubt there's any praise in here," he remarked, setting it aside.

"Or any words of encouragement," Moses added.

Hawkins laughed. "Marshal Yost believes you're up to the task," he said. "But he's also expressed concerns about your. . . let's say, limited experience in law enforcement, despite your recent successes."

The brothers exchanged a glance but shrugged off the comment. Elijah knew what they were capable of and knew Moses didn't need the praise of others either.

Hawkins hesitated as if contemplating whether to say more. Sensing his reluctance, Elijah asked, "Is there something else?"

Hawkins met Elijah's eyes. "It's not just Yost," he began. "There are others who worry that you won't stop until you've settled whatever vendetta these Crenshaw brothers have brought against you."

Moses looked at Elijah, his eyes seeming to search for a reaction. Elijah remained composed, his expression unreadable. "Are you one of those who are worried, Marshal?"

Hawkins sighed, his eyes never leaving Elijah's. "I don't know, Elijah," he admitted. "I wouldn't blame you if that's what you did, but remember, you're not sanctioned for a personal vendetta. You have a precise mandate." The marshal looked around the room and then back to Elijah. "They're embarrassed at their failures so far, embarrassed they had to resort to sending you. . . he won't abide you not adhering to this, Elijah." Hawkins pointed at the letter and sat back. "They'll come for you if you go outside it."

The table grew quiet again as Hawkins's words sank in. Eventually, he stood up, offering a sincere yet troubled look as he shook the brothers' hands. "Good luck to you both," he said.

When Marshal Hawkins had left, Moses leaned close to his brother. "You ain't gonna stop until the Crenshaws are dead, are you?" Elijah gave no response and Moses sighed. "Brothers versus brothers. The war remains. . ."

Elijah opened his mouth to respond, but before he could articulate his thoughts, Margaret Hennessey approached their table. Both brothers began to stand, but Margaret's gesture stopped them mid-rise. "Keep your seats," she said. "I doubt such courtesies will be extended on the trail."

The brothers shared a look of confusion, and Margaret's demeanor shifted. Her face took on a resolute cast that invited no argument.

"My father has bemoaned how I spent more time with my brothers in the fields than learning to curtsy," she began, indicating this was no mere social call. "Well, he's too old for what comes next, and my brothers. . . they're gone." Her voice carried an edge, reflecting a resolve born of loss and determination. "The Hennessey name has a stake in this, and I'm the only one left to uphold it. I'm coming with you."

THE OUTLAWS

— ◆ —

Platte River Valley, West of Omaha

The campfire's low, flickering flames cast a menacing shadow across Jack Crenshaw's sharp features, his green eyes flashing defiantly. The night air was cool in the cottonwood grove on sandy ground near the Platte River, where they had set up camp. A low bluff provided cover behind them, and a bend in the river covered the east and West.

Beside him, Miles was engrossed in softening some hard tack in his coffee. He appeared not to care about the intense argument Jack knew was coming. Morrow had been staring daggers at him all afternoon. Now that they were concealed in the cottonwood grove, he felt safe enough to start the argument.

At thirty-six, Morrow's lean, six-foot frame was a testament to years of rigorous living—the last few fighting alongside the likes of Bloody Bill Anderson and William Quantrill's Raiders. His face, marked by the trials of a harsh existence, held a permanent, grim countenance. The guerrilla tactics of The Shadow Commander, a moniker few dared to utter, were whispered about in awe and fear.

Morrow finally stopped and fixed Jack with a hard stare. "What the hell were you thinkin', Jack?"

Jack didn't look up right away, letting the silence stretch. When he met Morrow's eyes, his expression was unapologetic. "We did what we set out to do," he said, pointing towards the wagon load of stolen goods. "Got that freighter across, just like we planned."

Morrow's frustration was palpable. "And the bank? The livery? Don't recall plannin' that part."

Jack stood, meeting Morrow's height as he eyed him across the fire. "That money belonged to those Yank brothers who killed Frank Tucker. It was justice, not a robbery," he declared, his voice laced with a cold determination.

Jack saw some approving eyes turn toward him, and he raised his voice, stepping into the moment. "We're not just out here to settle old scores; we're taking back what was stolen from us. You always said that. They've torn through our lands and made fortunes on the backs of our suffering. It's not just a fight; it's reclaiming the life that was rightfully ours before them Yankees decided they could rewrite our futures." Jack pointed in the direction of the railroad. "Now they'll take it west and ensure that is theirs too."

The group fell silent, processing his words. Some nodded in agreement, their faces set in determined lines. In contrast, others exchanged uneasy glances, weighing this challenge to The Shadow Commander.

Morrow rubbed his forehead, struggling to maintain his composure. "That's a nice speech and all, Jack. But you've put a target on our backs. We needed supplies and to get that wagon across the river. You made it personal and put our feet to the fire even more." He looked at the two strangers Jack and Miles had vouched for in Council Bluffs who now joined the camp. "You bring folks we don't even know into our midst, then pull something like this?"

Jack ignored him, and Miles, leaning against the wagon, continued the argument for his brother. "We'd 'a had a target either way. But now, we've made our point." He took a bite of hardtack. "Now they know what they're dealin' with. Besides, the Barbers have given up that life. Papers made it seem like they wanted no more part of such things."

Morrow fixed a state of disbelief on the brothers. "Had we just made our way through town, they wouldn't know anything at all!"

Jack glanced at the other men, gauging their reactions. Some were loyal to Morrow, but some would come his way. In addition to the few he'd convinced to help him—although he regretted a few were now dead—Jack thought he could peel off more of the group. Regardless, he knew his path after meeting the two disgruntled Union Pacific workers in Council Bluffs.

Connor "Red" Sanders, so-called for the dirt he came from, his fiery red hair and matching temper that occasionally flared, was busy whittling while sitting against a wagon wheel but chimed in. "If it was them Barber boys we saw ride in toward the river and start shootin', I don't believe they've given it up." His deep voice sounded like rocks tumbling down a hillside.

A loyal member of Morrow's gang, fighting alongside Morrow since early in the war, Red was a man of few words but many deeds. His stocky build and weathered face spoke of years of living outside the law. He stood, blew the shavings off the wood he'd been carving, and looked at the Crenshaws. "If half 'a what the papers have said about them is true, and after today, I reckon it is, they'll be comin'."

Jack felt a twinge of apprehension but quickly masked it. They had planned for every possibility, or so he thought. The Crenshaws had counted on the Barbers chasing them and had the ambush ready to finish what they had started. Between the war and what they knew of the events in Rockville last summer, he thought the morally righteous

Elijah Barber would come for them without caution. But Red's words made him realize that the brothers might be more formidable than he had anticipated.

As if sensing Jack's doubts, Red threw a verbal jab as he resumed whittling. "If it goes bad for you again this summer, I don't reckon you'll be able to count on being in jail to avoid gettin' rolled up when the cavalry comes. How was it you two got so lucky again?" Red looked up from his whittling and stared at each of them. "Acting foolish worked out for you last year... doubt it will again."

Jack's lips curled in anger, and he stepped toward Red while Miles held him back. "Hey, Red, you ever wonder why folks call Nate the Shadow Commander?" Jack looked at Nate for a moment, then back to Red. "That's right, nobody ever sees him. It's almost like someone else did all his work for him."

"Watch it, Jack," Morrow interjected sharply.

Red gave Morrow a calming look, then pointed his knife at Jack. "That right there is what I'm talkin' 'bout, boy. Foolish, ungrateful, and hot-headed."

Jack lunged at Red, cursing, and Miles gripped him tightly.

"Enough," Morrow commanded. He stepped close to Jack. "Enough." He then turned to the group and announced their next move: to head west, paralleling the railroad. The plan was to offload their goods along the rail construction route and split the money; then, everyone would go their separate ways.

Jack scoffed at the man giving up on their mission to keep fighting the war but kept his thoughts to himself this time.

Morrow noticed, however. "You got a problem with that, Jack," Morrow stepped closer to Jack again, his face stern. "Red is right. You're damn lucky you made it out of Indiana, lucky we took you back, and even luckier that despite your decisions today, I keep you with us." He glared at Miles a moment, then back at Jack. "Understood?"

Jack bit his lip. "Yeah, understood." He eyed the men he would soon need on his side, attempting to assess how Morrow's browbeating affected his standing. However, he needed to play nice with Nate Morrow until they could get beyond the end of the track and close to Fort Kearny.

Jack pulled Miles and their new friends aside as the men settled for the night. "We need to watch our backs. Those Barbers, they won't let this slide." He turned and looked at Nate and Red, conferring off to the side. "And I reckon we really are on a short leash with those two." He turned to the former railroad workers from Council Bluffs. "You're sure about all this?"

"Oh, you bet," the taller one said. "We'll have the inside information."

Miles spoke up, his eyes hard. "And let the Barbers come. We'll be ready." He softened his gaze as he looked at Jack, however. "But maybe don't press on him so hard, Jack."

"Miles, I don't need you to—"

The conversation was cut short as Morrow approached them with Red. "Jack, Miles, I need your word—no more side schemes. You're good at what you do, and we've made ourselves a small fortune and struck victories for our ideals with your help. I'm sorry to cut your legs out in front of the group, but this is my crew. From now on, we stick to the plan." He looked over the newcomers. "And I guess I got no choice with you fellas now. But you best earn your keep. That gonna be a problem?"

Jack met Morrow's stare. "I guess not, Nate."

Morrow leaned in close, his voice low. "And watch it with your insinuations about the shadow business. This is still my outfit, last time I checked."

"Yes sir," Jack muttered, leaving *most* of the condescension out.

Morrow seemed satisfied, but Jack knew the man had his doubts. He watched Morrow walk away, his mind racing with possibilities. They needed to stay ahead of the law and Nate Morrow, biding their time until they could finish off the Barbers, get their take, and disappear.

Jack looked up at the dark sky, excitement settling over him. He had set this in motion, and now there was no turning back. They had learned much since the war and were ready to branch out with their own group. They would swindle the great Nate Morrow, dispatch the notorious Barber Brothers, and make a score that would have every outlaw in the West wanting to ride with them.

MOVE OUT

— ◆ —

The room above the bustling tavern was spartan. Sparse furnishings – a couple of simple wooden chairs, a worn table, and a narrow bed with a straw-stuffed mattress – defined their temporary dwelling, made necessary by the burning of their quarters at the livery. The walls, bare except for peeling paint, echoed the room's utilitarian purpose. This was no place of comfort or rest; it was a mere necessity, a rare available shelter in the growing, ever-busy town of Omaha.

In the pre-dawn darkness, Elijah sat upright in one of the chairs, his silhouette barely discernible in the dim light seeping through the small, grimy window. Moses lay asleep still, his breathing steady and deep, undisturbed by Elijah leaving for hot water and returning to shave. He envied his brother's ability to rest when required.

Elijah was lost in thought, replaying a dream that lingered with unsettling clarity. In his dream, their old mentor, Sheriff Talbot Jones, had come to him, his face as clear and stern as it had been in life. 'Beware the path of revenge, Elijah,' the Sheriff had warned, his voice echoing with a gravity that transcended the dream. 'It's a road that changes a man, often in ways unseen until it's too late.'

The warning hung in Elijah's mind, intertwining with his waking thoughts. Talbot had told stories of what he'd seen revenge-seeking do to a man. He knew the Sheriff's words were not just figments of his imagination; they embodied his deep-seated fears and doubts about the journey they were embarking upon. Could he lead this posse without letting his thirst for justice turn into a quest for vengeance? Would acting outside his legal mandate be immoral or just illegal? *Was there a difference?*

Outside, the first faint hints of dawn began to dispel the darkness, casting a soft, diffused light into the room. Elijah rose from the chair, his movements slow and deliberate. He glanced at Moses, still sleeping peacefully, then assessed the few possessions he had left to his name. The brown sack suit he wore, the dark gray one he'd been gifted last summer at the beginning of their marshal work, Talbot Jones's old pocket watch, his slouch hat from the war, and their weapons and ammunition.

He lifted one of his saddlebags from the ground, dragging it on the floor louder than need be, and plunked it on the chair beside him, hoping to rouse Moses. Inside, he studied the only money he had left from their day-to-day safe at the livery. After buying supplies and giving the remaining stable hands a week's pay, he had an amount he hoped was enough to pay the posse and cover any incidentals. This after stopping by to give Billy's mother the sad news and offering her far more of his future wages than he had intended before seeing her face to face. When he arrived at Abigail's parents' home to do the same, he was turned away.

Elijah's fingers traced the contours of the worn saddle bag. Just a year ago, poverty had been an all-too-familiar companion. They had clawed out, only to find themselves teetering on the brink once more. Then, they only had themselves to care for and were willing to do almost anything. Now, the lives of so many others were involved.

"Mornin,' Eli," Moses murmured, rubbing sleep from his eyes. He sat up, squinting in the dim light, his gaze settling on his brother. "You always were up early when we were gonna put men on the move."

Just thinking about what's to come," Elijah replied.

Moses swung his legs over the side of the bed. "We've been through worse, brother. We'll see this through, just like we always do."

Elijah managed a half-smile, appreciating Moses's attempt to lift his spirits, though his doubts lingered. He didn't think Moses was any less concerned than he was, but he always did a better job of hiding it. "I'll meet you downstairs," Elijah said. He turned for the door, paused, reached in his saddlebag, and turned back toward Moses before tossing his brother one of their deputy marshal badges from last summer.

Moses stopped buttoning his shirt and caught the badge, turning it over in his hands. "Never thought I'd put it on again," he said.

As Elijah glanced back at the room, he noted how their few belongings occupied only a tiny corner. Soon, even that modest space would be empty as if their brief stay had never happened. The room would hold no trace of them, just like the countless other places they had passed through in their tumultuous lives.

Elijah descended the narrow staircase, the creaking of the steps echoing in the stillness of the early morning. As he entered the dining room, he noticed Big Sam and Clay seated at a table, a sense of tension hanging between them. Elijah chose not to delve into whatever might have transpired, instead opting for a lighter approach.

"Surprised to see both of you up and about this early," Elijah commented.

Big Sam, with a plate piled high, grinned. "Well, never know if we're going to be gone a day, a week, or a month. Figured I might as well get some good grub in me while I can."

Elijah turned to the tavern owner, who was bustling about and preparing their early meal. "Thanks for this and the room," he said, acknowledging the owner's hospitality.

"No trouble at all, given the circumstances," the owner replied before retreating to the kitchen.

Elijah made himself a modest plate, selecting a couple of strips of bacon, a piece of cornbread, and a scoop of eggs with a cup of coffee. The food was simple but hearty – just what they needed for the journey ahead. As he sat down and began to eat, the room fell into a momentary silence.

Sam broke the quiet, his voice casual but carrying a certain weight. "Elijah, did you know Clay here is also from Missouri?"

Sensing the direction this could head, Elijah simply nodded, then took a sip of coffee.

"Yeah, 'course," Sam continued, "he fought on a different side than I did. Than we did."

Elijah glanced at Clay, who seemed more interested in his food than engaging in an early morning debate. He was relieved; the last thing they needed was an argument to start the day.

"No sign of the others?" Elijah glanced around the room.

"Not yet," Clay mumbled.

"Bet that Pinkerton fella is gettin' a fancy breakfast at his fancy hotel before we ride out."

Elijah bit his lip, refraining from getting after Sam before the trip started. He had never known anyone who worked harder than the mountain of a man, but he was an agitator who seemed to say everything that popped into his mind.

Boots echoed down the staircase, and the three men looked up and acknowledged Moses, who shrugged his saddlebags off into a corner and began scooping food onto a plate. Noticing the atmosphere, he couldn't resist a sardonic comment as he sat down. "Been fussin' at each other already, or just not morning people?" he asked, raising his eyebrows as he ate breakfast.

Before anyone could reply, Augusto Rivera and Ike Taylor walked in. Elijah motioned them over. "Grab a plate, gentlemen. There's plenty."

Augusto and Ike helped themselves to breakfast. As they settled in, Ike made light conversation about the weather. "Warm but not hot. Should be good for travel," he remarked, glancing out the window at the brightening sky.

Augusto, finishing a bite of cornbread, added, "Clear skies should make the tracking a bit easier. A group that big will be making some dust, especially if they have a wagon, as Elijah says."

The group ate silently until Matt Hobbs arrived, his usual polished demeanor on display. "Morning, gentlemen. I must confess, I took advantage of the Herndon's comforts until the last minute." He winked, eliciting a knowing look from Big Sam toward Elijah.

Big Sam spoke up. "Seven's a good number. Enough to do the work, small enough to stay nimble."

Moses looked knowingly at Elijah, who cleared his throat before speaking. "Actually, we're going to have eight."

The table fell silent, everyone turning to Elijah with curiosity. Ike leaned forward. "Found one more man, did you?" he asked.

Before Elijah could respond, the door swung open, and Margaret Hennessey stepped into the room. Her long, chestnut brown hair was pulled back in a practical yet elegant braid. Her modest attire hinted at her inherent beauty—a simple blouse and durable trousers tucked into shined boots. She held a clean, wide-brimmed hat in her hands.

The conversation halted as she approached their table. No more chairs were available, and she stood at the end of the table, a condescending smile aimed at Elijah. "I take it these gentlemen were not made aware of my intentions?"

Elijah set down his fork and stood before grabbing his plate and gesturing toward his empty chair. As she moved toward it, all the men but Moses began to rise awkwardly before Moses waved them off. "She already said she don't want any of that."

Big Sam looked wide-eyed at the Barber brothers, then jerked a thumb toward Margaret Hennessey. "She's comin'?" Elijah nodded as he poured another cup of coffee. Sam looked at Margaret. "Listen, ma'am, I don't mean to be disrespectful or anything—"

"And yet you are." She sat, took a biscuit from a platter, and spread preserves. "And please, call me Maggie." She took a bite of the biscuit. "I don't care what any of you think. Were my brothers still alive, there's no doubt in my mind they would be joining you. They aren't here, so you must settle for my unconventional ways." She eyed each man. "As I told the Barbers last evening, the Hennessey name has a stake in this, and I'm the only one left to uphold it. "Is that a problem?"

"No, ma'am," Ike answered.

"*Es bueno*," Augusto said.

"Can you shoot?" Clay asked quietly.

"I can hold my own."

"Mind sleepin' outside?"

"No."

"Adverse to violence should it come to it?"

"These men brought violence to us first," Maggie answered calmly.

Clay looked around the room. "Well, if she's Pat Hennessey's daughter, I know she can ride." He piled the remaining breakfast food on a plate and slid it to her. "Better eat up, ma'am. . . And I hope you got more than just those brand-new duds you're wearing with you." He grinned slightly.

She feigned umbrage at the remark, but Elijah sensed they were, in fact, brand-new clothes. "Thank you, gentlemen." She looked at Matt Hobbs. "And what says the Pinkerton man?"

Hobbs raised his coffee cup in the air as if to toast. "I like your confidence."

Big Sam looked at each man, stopping on the Barber brothers. "I follow them."

"Alright then," Elijah said. He walked over to the tavern owner, handed him a few coins, and shook his hand. He grabbed his bags and turned to the group. "Don't reckon there's much more to say. It's time to start moving west."

The clatter of chairs and boots shuffling filled the room as the men and Maggie prepared to depart. Elijah felt a familiar sensation stirring within him as he watched the group gather their gear—a feeling he hadn't realized he had missed until now. The clinking of spurs and the rustling of saddlebags being strapped on were sounds reminiscent of the days before when the clatter of preparation was a prelude to battle.

The sound of Brutus's paws hitting the wooden porch drew their attention. The large dog hopped to the ground and trotted over to Big Sam, who was adjusting the saddle on his horse. The bond between the man and his dog was evident.

Moses watched the dog for a moment. "Are you sure Brutus is up for a journey like this, Sam?" he asked, his tone playful.

Big Sam finished securing his saddle and looked down at Brutus, who sat at his feet. "Brutus here's kept up on plenty of long trips," he confidently replied. "And who knows, we might be glad to have him around."

The group began to mount up, their movements efficient and practiced. Two pack horses, laden with their supplies and gear, were tethered to lead ropes, ready to follow the posse into the unknown.

Maggie approached Elijah. "I know none of you like the idea of a woman being with," she said, "but I can see they all respect you too much to say otherwise."

Elijah looked at her a moment. He had been ready to critique her attire after seeing the dress of the day before but had to admit that she was dressed the part—and looked good doing so. He sidestepped her compliment with a pragmatic tone. "If you pull your weight, nobody here will care you're a woman." He was attempting to be reassuring but carrying an undertone of caution as he, too, was weighing her presence in the group.

With a final glance at the group, Elijah mounted Bear and took his position at the front. Moses and Copper fell in beside him, a look of admiration in the younger brother's eyes. "Just like old times, eh Captain?" he said.

Elijah shook his head slightly, unwilling to romanticize the moment. "Get them in order," he commanded, his eyes fixed westward.

Moses turned to address the group. "Two by two, fall in!" he shouted. The group organized themselves into a formation.

Moses returned to Elijah's side. "We're ready," he announced.

Elijah spurred Bear. "Let's move out," he said, leading the group westward into the vast expanse of the frontier before them.

HELL ON WHEELS

—·—

As dawn broke over the Nebraska prairie, the posse set out from Omaha, heading west into the vast expanse of the American frontier. The early morning sun painted the undulating grassland in hues of gold and amber. Leading the group, Elijah felt a familiar sense of purpose reminiscent of his days during the war – the rhythm of travel, the cadence of hooves against the earth, and the camaraderie of a shared mission.

They journeyed through the sprawling canvas of natural beauty, where rolling hills gave way to vast open plains. Wildflowers in myriad colors dotted the green expanse, swaying in the prairie breeze. The Platte River, a shallow ribbon of water to their north, served as both a guide and a crucial resource, offering water for themselves and their horses while providing potential shelter spots along its banks.

As the sun rose higher, its rays warmed the earth, awakening the scents of the prairie. Leading the pack, Elijah inhaled deeply, the new fragrance of wild sage mingling with the dusty aroma of the trail. It was the kind of smell—mixed with the leather and horses—that brought back a flood of memories.

As they crested a low rise, Elijah's horse shied away from a prairie rattlesnake sunning itself on the path. Bear danced sideways, snorting alarmingly, and Elijah guided him around the serpent. "Watch your step, everyone," he called back.

"The land *es bonita*, but not without its dangers," Augusto said. He had warned them earlier, and the encounter reminded them of their journey's unpredictability.

The terrain was changing, transforming from the familiar outskirts of Omaha into the more rugged, untamed land of the western frontier. The posse's conversation was light, filled with stories and observations, casting an optimistic mood over the group. Elijah noticed the men neither ignored nor patronized Maggie, maintaining a respectful balance that he assumed she preferred.

Around mid-day, having covered a good twenty miles, Elijah signaled for a stop, their first that would last longer than the few minutes of previous breaks. They found a suitable spot near the river, with enough cover and space to water and feed the horses and themselves. "I don't want to stop long," Elijah told the group. "But I have to believe we are covering ground faster than they are with the wagon, and I don't want to burn these horses out."

As they dismounted, bickering between Big Sam and Clay punctured the otherwise peaceful scene. "You know, Clay, I can't quite wrap my head around how you could've fought for the South," Sam said, his tone edged with curiosity and judgment. "Here I was all excited to have a fellow Missouri man on this expedition, and turns out you was a gray back."

Clay, busy with his horse, paused and looked up at Big Sam. "Whereabouts in Missouri are you from, Sam?" he asked. His otherwise mellow voice had a hint of defensiveness.

"Northwest," Sam replied, "Near St. Joseph. Me and mine stood with the Union."

Clay resumed his work. "I'm from Southeast, down by Cape Girardeau. It's a different world there."

Sam scoffed. "That's no excuse."

Moses and Hobbs walked up alongside Elijah, who stopped on his trip with Bear to the water so he could watch the debate. "Want us to have them knock it off?" Moses asked.

Elijah shook his head. "Only if it comes to fighting. Let them get this out of the way." He pointed to Brutus with his pipe, milling at Sam's feet. "Don't let the dog rip Clay to pieces, though."

Elijah watched the exchange, his fingers tightening on the reins. He remembered too well the burden of command during the war, the constant balance between letting men settle their differences and stepping in to maintain order. Now, as then, Elijah felt the burden of leadership – guiding not just a mission but the lives entrusted to his decisions. He exhaled slowly, understanding that this journey was more than just a pursuit; it tested his ability to lead again.

Clay leaned against his horse, looking towards Ike, who seemed to be focusing on his tasks, before returning to Sam. "We were the poorest farm family in the poorest part of our county," he explained. "I don't know if we would've owned slaves if we could've, but we could barely feed ourselves, let alone anyone else."

Sam frowned, not quite understanding. "Then why'd you fight for the South?"

Clay scratched his head. "It wasn't about all that for us, not directly anyhow. A lot of folks around us owned one or two. Friends of friends, you know? Neighbors. When Union soldiers came, telling us what to do, taking what little we had. . . I had to pick a side. I chose the one that promised to get soldiers off our land and make life easier for my family."

Sam and Clay's conversation grew more intense, and their voices rose as they repeated their arguments. Ike, working on his horse nearby, cast uneasy glances their way, and Elijah noticed his discomfort.

"We *all* had to make hard choices," Ike said, his voice steady. "Choices that haunt us." He paused as if to ensure he had their attention. "It's a horrible thing the life I was forced to live, but I also did things I never want to think about again to escape it. His words seemed to hang in the air. "What my kind went through was going on long before there was a war over it. "Ain't neither of you or your kind innocent in it."

Elijah looked at Moses and Hobbs and, assessing the worst was over, tipped his head toward the river.

Sam's expression softened, but he still seemed unconvinced. Sam turned back to Clay. "I suppose we all got our reasons for everything. I reckon war has a way of blurring lines of right and wrong."

Sam and Clay exchanged a look, the tension between them easing somewhat. Elijah sensed an unspoken agreement forming – a truce of sorts, born of shared hardship and the recognition of a common goal.

"Agreed," Clay said. He seemed to want the conversation to end but pointed toward the West after a moment. "Those fellas we're chasin', though. . . They came from places like you're from. Union occupied, so they had to adopt the tactics they did. So now you and me are on the same side, and we agree about that, I reckon."

Elijah had observed the conversation, noting the subtle shifts in expression and tone. It was more than a discussion about past allegiances; it was a testament to the scars that still lingered a year after the war's end. "We all carry burdens from those days," he interjected. He met each man's eyes. "What matters now is the path we choose going forward."

Augusto crossed between Sam and Clay, leading some horses to the water. He stopped and eyed both of them, then grinned. "Both of your sides had leaders who fought my people in Mexico." Augusto shrugged and began to walk again. "So if it makes you feel better about each other, I dislike you both for that."

Both men laughed, and Elijah gave Augusto a wink as he passed him. It wasn't much, but Elijah was glad to have his first potential leadership crisis of the trip behind him.

The group resumed setting up their mid-day camp. Elijah realized that the men's experiences had led them to take up tasks with little direction. Maggie, however, watched from a distance, looking for a way to insert herself.

Wishing to avoid embarrassment or having any men think she wasn't pulling her weight, Elijah approached her and spoke in a low voice. "Do you know how to hobble your horse?"

She looked around as if worried someone would overhear. "Of course I do."

Elijah pointed to where Augusto was bringing horses back from the water. "Why don't you go get your mount a few swallows, then find a good spot of grass? Then you can give us some help making camp."

As Maggie walked away, Elijah watched her. She moved with a purpose, her actions speaking of a determination to prove her worth. He spied Moses, pulling out a pan and a coffee pot, and called after her. "If you can find some wood that would work for a small cook fire, that would be helpful."

She looked about to offer a retort, but Elijah cut her off with a raised hand.

"I ain't gonna put you in charge of cooking just because you're a woman." Her expression softened, and she headed for the water again before Elijah added, "Mo does the cooking, and I wager is way better than you anyhow."

She turned and glared at him, and Elijah laughed for the first time since the attack in town.

AUGUSTO'S DISCOVERY just before evening had set the tone for a restless night. After covering another fifteen miles after their mid-day break, the posse made camp under the vast sky, the stars their only canopy. The sign that Augusto had found—a veering off of a wagon and numerous riders from the well-trodden trail—brought a renewed focus to what had been casual travel. The trail, marked by the passage of countless settlers following the Platte River towards distant dreams, now branched off toward a different story.

As dawn broke, they resumed their pursuit, the sign leading them southwest. By mid-afternoon, the sounds of civilization encroached upon the natural quiet of the plains. The Union Pacific Railroad's construction was in full swing, a testament to the unstoppable force of progress. Man and beast brought rails forward, placed them, drove spikes, and continued down the graded path with military precision. The construction work was both awe-inspiring and jarring.

The juxtaposition of the wild, untamed plains against the bustling railroad construction was striking. Where the prairie whispered of freedom and a life beholden to no one, the railroad sang a different tune – one of order, structure, and collective purpose. It was a symphony of human endeavor, each hammer strike and shout a note in a grander scheme that sought to redefine the nation's landscape.

As they observed the railroad workers, Elijah couldn't help but reflect on the implications. The railroad, a symbol of a nation trying to stitch itself back together after the Civil War, was a marvel of engineering and human determination.

"This railroad's going to change everything," Hobbs remarked. "Linking East to West, it's like healing a wound of a divided nation, one rail at a time."

Elijah looked back at Sam, Clay, and Ike and thought of the men they pursued. "Gonna take more than a railroad, though, I believe." He pondered Morrow's intentions. Could the gang hide in plain sight among the workers and peddle their stolen goods? Choosing discretion over a direct approach, Elijah led the posse to a campsite. As the late afternoon shadows arrived, he decided on a smaller party to scout the railroad camp. The decision was met with some resistance.

"Shouldn't more of us go?" Big Sam questioned. His eyes reflected concern, but Elijah sensed the big man just wanted to find a scrape. "There could be trouble."

"We need eyes here, on our horses and supplies. Besides, we can't march in there with the whole group; it'll draw too much attention." Tending to her horse, Maggie looked up at the mention of potential danger. Her eyes met Elijah's.

"I'll go with Elijah and Moses," Hobbs insisted, his tone leaving no room for debate. "U.P. is paying me to assess the security of their operation and this sure intersects."

Elijah turned to Sam and Clay. "If we're not back in a few hours, come looking. But do what you need to do to take care of the group."

As Elijah issued his instructions, he caught the nuanced looks exchanged between Sam and Clay. Despite their differences, there was a silent acknowledgment and mutual understanding that they had a shared responsibility. Elijah's leadership wasn't just about giving orders; it was about fostering trust among men who, under any other circumstances, might have been at odds. It was about turning a group of individuals into a cohesive unit.

The makeshift town, a chaotic sprawl of tents and shanties, was alive with revelry, the workmen having just finished their daily labors. Mud and makeshift wooden planks lined what might have been called the main street in a civilized town. The air was heavy with the smell of cooking fires, blending with the acrid bite of tobacco smoke. Voices carried tales of fortune and misfortune alike, each a fragment of the larger narrative of the West.

Entering the tent that served as a saloon, the trio was met with a wall of noise. Laughter, music, and boisterous conversation filled the space. The conversation soon dwindled, however, as eyes turned toward the badged men. It was a palpable shift, a collective pause in the rhythm of the night, before the din resumed – a little louder, a little more forced, as if trying to cover the unease their presence had brought.

Moses leaned toward Elijah. "Don't reckon we achieved that low-profile visit you wanted."

As he spoke, two men looked up at the three of them, then exited the back of the tent. Hobbs noticed and followed, and without a word, Elijah and Moses went out the front.

FINDING HELP

—◆—

T he filthy space behind the saloon tent was a dark, twisting
labyrinth in the fading light. Hobbs emerged from behind the
tent just in time to see the two men who panicked and turned only to
run into Moses. Both men's eyes widened, and without a word, they
spun around, choosing a different route, only to find Elijah blocking
their path.

Elijah's stance was firm, his hand resting near his gun holster, his
eyes steady and assessing. The men, surrounded and shaking, looked
from Elijah to Hobbs and back, their options dwindling.

"Why the sudden exit, gentlemen?" Hobbs asked. His keen eyes
scanned them, searching for any telltale sign of guilt or deception.

One of the men, taller and leaner, swallowed hard, his eyes flickering toward Hobbs's detective badge. "Oh man, a Pinkerton. . ." he
muttered.

"You think that's something?" Moses chimed in, stepping closer,
his deputy marshal badge catching the dim light. His tone was casual,
but his posture was all business.

The revelation drained the remaining color from both men. They
exchanged a look, their shoulders slumping in resignation. The shorter
one, with a scruffy beard and nervous eyes, spoke up. "We ain't lookin'
for no trouble. Just tryin' to make a livin' here, that's all."

Elijah studied them for a moment longer, noticing they both looked more capable than they were portraying themselves. "You're not rail workers?"

"No, sir," the taller one replied. "Just drifters, tryin' to catch a break. Heard there was work, but. . ." His voice trailed off, the unspoken hardships of the frontier life hanging in the air.

Hobbs stepped forward, his eyes sharp. "So why did you skedaddle so quick when we came in?"

The shorter man squinted into the setting sun. "You looked like fellas searchin' for folks."

"Something here we'd be searching for?" Elijah fixed the man with a stare.

"Not no more, I reckon." The shorter man had barely uttered the words when the taller one elbowed him.

"Shut your yap, Jed."

"Dangit, Wes, what am I gonna do? Lie to a couple of deputy marshals and a Pinkerton?" He hung his head. "I shoulda stayed home." Elijah chuckled, realizing he often shared the sentiment.

Hobbs looked at Elijah and Moses. "Now, gents, I know you aren't master detectives like me, but something tells me these two just might have interacted with some folks passing through. Some folks we might be looking for."

Elijah looked at the shorter one. "You two got a tent or somewhere we can talk in private, Jed?"

The evening shadows stretched long across the makeshift town as the group followed Jed and Wesley through the unsavory camp. The air grew thick with the musk of sweat and dirt, mingling with the smoky scent of campfires. As darkness fell, the camp's transient nature became more pronounced, with figures moving like ghosts between tents and shanties, their faces flickering in the firelight.

The night was alive with clinking bottles, raucous laughter, and drunken songs. Passing a tent adorned with a simple wooden cross on a table out front, Elijah noticed a middle-aged man in a reverend's collar, his weary eyes watching the camp's inhabitants with a mix of hope and resignation. His presence seemed almost incongruous amid the rough-and-tumble of the railroad camp.

Wes and Jed led the trio to a small decrepit tent patched together with various fabrics, starkly contrasting some of the more orderly set-ups. A flickering oil lamp lit the cramped canvas walls as they ducked inside. The interior was as sparse as the outside suggested, with a couple of cots with threadbare blankets and a small, battered chest serving as the tent's only furnishings. Elijah thought it looked abandoned more than occupied.

Elijah sat down on the small trunk and began lighting his pipe. "Get anyone through here recently trying to sell some goods or cause any trouble?"

Moses stepped forward as Hobbs brushed off a spot on one of the cots with a disgusted-looking face before sitting. "Perhaps a rough-looking group with an overburdened freight wagon?" Moses asked.

Wes shifted his weight, glancing at Jed before responding. "Yeah, a group like that came through first thing this morning before work began. They tried to offload a bunch of goods, but the foreman put a stop to it."

Jed chimed in, "Foreman said he didn't like the look of 'em. Said the railroad had its own contracts and wasn't interested in outside supplies."

Hobbs raised an eyebrow. "Surprised they didn't resort to threats or violence. Seems like their usual style. They just moved on without a second thought when the foreman said to leave?"

Wes scratched his head. "We thought the same, but they just packed up and moved on."

Elijah puffed on his pipe, his mind working through the information. "Did they leave anyone behind? Someone to keep an eye on things?"

Jed glanced at Wes and then back at Elijah. "Actually, yeah. They offered us money to tell them if anyone was on their tail. They said someone would be back after dark."

Elijah stood up, stretching his legs. "You boys got any place around here we can get some chow? And did that group with the wagon pay you yet?"

Wes perked up a bit. "There's a cook tent down the way. And, uh, they paid us half. Said we'd get the rest when their man come back."

Elijah grinned. "Well, it's your lucky day, gents. The U.S. Marshals won't find out you were helping Nate Morrow, I'll pay you the other half of your money, and I'll even buy you dinner before you take me to the meeting spot."

Wes and Jed nodded eagerly, leading the way toward the cook tent. As they walked through the camp, the two men glanced around nervously, seemingly to ensure they weren't drawing unwanted attention.

Elijah, however, trailed behind, his gaze fixed on the preacher and his modest tent. The man's presence seemed to emanate a quiet dignity in this place that lacked any.

Moses called back, "Eli, you comin'?"

"Just a minute, Mo," Elijah replied, his eyes still on the preacher.

After a moment, the preacher noticed Elijah's attention. "I've never been one to force folks to come over," he said, "but I must say, you're the first to stand and look this long."

Elijah offered a polite smile. "Sorry, you remind me of someone." The preacher was a tall, lanky man who looked like he could work all day without tiring. He evoked memories of Elijah's father, or at least what little he remembered of him before his sudden death when Elijah was young.

The preacher extended his hand. "I'm Reverend Thomas."

"Elijah," he replied, shaking the preacher's hand. "You just look like my father is all."

The preacher's eyes held a knowing look. "Is that the only reason you stopped by?"

Elijah hesitated, caught off guard. "I'm not sure," he admitted.

Reverend Thomas's eyes fell on Elijah's badge. "After that group that passed through earlier, I suppose?"

Elijah nodded, somewhat surprised by the preacher's awareness. His eyes drifted to the small cross, a Bible sitting beside it. "Is there anything in that book about revenge?"

"Have these men committed some sort of wrongdoing, or do you seek revenge for something behind the cover of a badge?" He looked at Elijah with a stern face for a moment before the slightest appearance of a grin emerged.

"The former," Elijah said. He then dropped his head. "But I worry the latter is also true."

The preacher considered the question. "Well, there's Romans 12:19 – 'Vengeance is mine; I will repay, saith the Lord.' It suggests leaving vengeance to God, as do a lot of other verses. And Mark wrote that when we pray, if we 'hold anything against anyone, forgive them, so that your Father in heaven may forgive you your sins.'"

"My father could recite scripture like that as well," Elijah said. "But I fear both myself and the men I pursue would require far too much prayer to have our sins forgiven."

"I sense you are a man who knows that isn't true, Elijah." Reverend Thomas looked up at Elijah's cavalry slouch hat, seeming to notice it for the first time. "I also sense you are a man on the righteous side of this pursuit but have done things that will forever make you unsure. It is a good thing you wonder about your motivations."

Memories of righteous and regrettable past deeds flickered in his mind like the dim campfires around him. He looked at the reverend, then glanced back toward the cook tent. "I should go find my men. I thank you, reverend."

"Take care of yourself, Elijah." Reverend Thomas watched Elijah prepare to leave, adding, "And remember, the path of righteousness is often the most difficult to walk, but it's the journey, not the destination, that shapes a man."

A New Path

—·—

The moon was a slender crescent in the ink-black sky, casting a feeble light over the Nebraska plains. In the cover of the scrubby underbrush, Elijah, Moses, and Hobbs lay in wait. The drifters were fidgeting in a clearing, their lanterns casting a glow that flickered with their every tremulous movement.

"Those two are gonna run away if they catch sight of their own shadow," Moses said with a chuckle.

Hobbs swatted at an insect swarming near his face and surveyed his dark surroundings. "I've gotta stop spending my summers with you two," he said. Elijah looked at him with irritation. "This seems like a stretch to bear fruit, Elijah." He looked out toward Jed and Wes. "Especially when it hinges on that fidgety pair," Hobbs added.

Elijah, his eyes not leaving the clearing, replied in a low voice, "It's a gamble we need to take."

"What if Jed and Wes are in cahoots with Morrow's group?" Hobbs asked.

"What if they aren't, and this rider can lead us to Morrow?" Elijah replied.

"What if he doesn't say a word, and we get one of us shot in the process?" Hobbs countered.

"C'mon, Matt," Moses whispered. "Give it a chance." They all fell silent, Elijah grateful for his brother's support.

Elijah considered his history of taking chances to meet his objectives. He recalled their pursuit of Frank Tucker and how Hobbs was willing to take risks. Instead of leaning forward now, the Hobbs he had met last summer was a more cautious man.

After a few moments, however, Hobbs broke the silence once again. "Isn't it odd that they each led a horse out here?" The three looked past Jed and Wes to two mounts tied to a tree branch nearby. "It sure looks like a couple of fellas looking to make some tracks before we realize what has happened."

Minutes turned into hours; the only sounds were the occasional rustle of the wind across the prairie or noise from the nearby camp. A gnawing sense of doubt gradually replaced the anticipation.

Hobbs broke the silence again. "We've been out here for hours, Elijah."

Elijah was irritated but couldn't deny the truth in Hobbs' words. "Maybe the rider got spooked," he suggested, trying to salvage the situation.

Moses squinted into the darkness. "Or maybe we were fed a tall tale. Matt could be right, Eli. These two might have been playing us from the start."

"See, Moses gets it," Hobbs quipped.

"I heard you both," Elijah replied.

"Fellas, don't argue over this," Moses said.

"I'm just saying that—"

Elijah cut Hobbs off. "I know what you're saying. We got duped, and Morrow's gang made that much more traveling while we sat here."

As the realization dawned, a heavy silence fell upon them. Each man lost in his thoughts the weight of wasted hours and lost opportunity pressing down upon them like the night sky above.

As their argument fizzled, the three men looked up to realize they could no longer see the lantern light coming from where they'd left Jed and Wes. Leading their horses over to where the pair had stood, they discovered the men and their horses were gone.

Elijah climbed atop Bear. "Let's get back to camp."

Back at the camp, the atmosphere was subdued. Sam and Clay had been preparing to depart in search of the trio, and the group was disheartened by the explanation of the fruitless night.

"Now they'll know there's a couple of deputy marshals and a Pinkerton after them and where we are." Hobbs gave the group a gloomy look.

"Sure enough," Elijah admitted. "But we accomplished one thing at least. . . They don't know there's five more with us." Elijah didn't need Hobbs to remind him of his failure and was glad to put a positive view on the situation.

"Fair enough," Hobbs conceded.

Augusto spoke up. "If they are not here, maybe they are heading toward Fort Kearny. Many people do trading there, and soldiers are always looking to get their hands on things. It is a place where a group like Morrow's could make money and try to blend in as settlers or miners heading west."

Elijah eyed Augusto, who had continued to work over a cooking fire while he talked. "How far to the fort?" Elijah asked.

Augusto stood, wiped his hands, and stared toward the west as if the dark view would give him the answer. "Two days if we ride hard. Close to three if careful."

Elijah turned his gaze westward, thinking of all the times he had stared at a dark sky during the war, and made plans for the next day. He looked back at the old tracker. "Figure they're a full day ahead of us now?"

"Perhaps more," Augusto replied.

Elijah looked down to see the pot of beans, some meat Augusto had prepared, and some biscuits. He eyed Moses, who nodded, and Hobbs, who gave a reluctant look of approval.

"I just need to check in with the foreman come morning and send word back to Omaha," Hobbs said. He stared into the fire a moment before looking back at Elijah. "Haven't left you yet. I'm still with you."

"Everyone eat up and get some rest," Elijah said. "Make sure your horses are cared for and ready. We will put in a full day starting at first light."

The group ate, mostly in silence, Moses taking out his harmonica and playing for a while as everyone relaxed. Elijah noticed some small talk among Sam, Clay, and Ike, but the three men still did not appear they would become friends anytime soon.

Sam returned from cleaning his mess kit and passed Elijah sitting on his blankets, smoking his pipe. The big man stopped, turned, and looked down at him. "I'd 'a done the same thing today, boss." He looked toward the west. "And I reckon checking out the fort is as good a plan as any now."

Elijah puffed on the pipe and then looked up. "Thanks, Sam."

Sam appeared uneasy and looked around the camp before squatting next to Elijah. "Listen, boss. I know I made some stink about the woman joinin' us, then what happened earlier with Clay and Ike—"

Elijah put a hand on Sam's shoulder. "We're good." Big Sam stood and began to walk off but then lingered.

"What is it, Sam?" Elijah asked. Moses's harmonica playing became quieter as he listened in.

Sam bit his lip as if unsure whether he should speak. "Well, it's just that. . . I feel like I was your right-hand man and that we've fought and worked for the same things, but now you're sometimes takin' sides with this Johnny Reb, and then that ni—"

Moses's harmonica playing abruptly stopped, his voice low. "Don't you say it, Sam." Moses stared at Sam, and Elijah saw that while not a look of anger, it was one of firm conviction. A staunch abolitionist of a father had raised them. While Elijah always tried to be pragmatic, he knew the reason for the war was always evident in his brother's mind.

"Moses is right, Sam. We aren't going to have that kind of talk in this posse. Nor are we going to worry who was on whose side because we're all on the same one now." He did his best to give a reassuring look. "I told you we were good, Sam, so let's keep it that way."

"Besides," Moses added, "Elijah is *my* right-hand man, and that's how this all works." He smiled and resumed playing his harmonica as Sam sauntered off, before giving Elijah a reassuring look.

As the evening wore on, sleep did not come to Elijah, and he sat up against his saddle in the stillness of the night, the ambient sounds of the prairie enveloping him. The persistent chirping of crickets blended with the occasional buzz of a lone mosquito hovering nearby. Far away, the haunting call of a coyote echoed, punctuating the night air. The gentle whoosh of the night breeze through the grasses added a soothing undertone to the symphony of nighttime sounds—including the snores and other bodily noises of the men around him. Occasionally, the distant hoot of an owl from the shadowed trees lining the nearby riverbank could be heard.

Elijah turned his head toward a sound nearer to hand, reaching toward his revolver. "You did what you thought was best today," Maggie whispered.

Elijah looked up, surprised by her presence. "I should have known it wouldn't be that simple," he said in a low voice. "We could have made another few hours of travel."

"They could have been here trying to blend in with the railroad camp." She sat beside him, shifting her petite frame on the ground until she could rest against the saddle, their sides touching.

Elijah was uneasy, not from her proximity but from the thought of what others might interpret from their closeness. Maggie seemed indifferent to such perceptions. She leaned back, her eyes fixed on the dying fire. "You've led enough to know it's not about always being right. It's about making the best decisions and looking out for your people." She looked at him. "Not just about riding and fighting. I saw you keep the emotions in check with Sam, Clay, and Ike."

Elijah listened to her words, reminding him of the fine line he walked between duty and his demons. He responded, his voice low. "That's true, but it doesn't make those decisions any easier." He shifted slightly, his discomfort apparent.

Maggie caught his unease and smiled. "Don't worry, Elijah. I'm not trying to ruffle feathers. I'm sure you've got a woman back in Omaha."

"I don't, or rather, not anymore." He flushed with anger or embarrassment; he wasn't sure.

"I'm sure she'll wait for you, Elij—"

"It was the schoolteacher," Elijah said flatly. He tossed a stick in the fire.

Maggie's mouth froze open, and she covered it with her hand. Her face was white when she spoke. "Elijah, I had no idea; I am so sorry."

"It's fine, you didn't know," he said softly.

She looked at him momentarily, then shook her head and turned away. "Oh, and I came after you the way I did in the street, and it had just happened. . ." She looked back at Elijah. "And yet you were so calm and respectful when the others tried to come to your defense."

He stared ahead at the fire. "I've become too good at processing the loss of folks in such awful ways." He shook away the thought and looked back at her. "It's fine, or rather, you're fine." He looked at the ground. "She's dead because of me. Like a lot of others."

Maggie shook her head and looked at Elijah. "From what my father has told me, an awful lot of bad people are gone, and even more good people are still on this Earth because of you and your brother."

"Hmm," was all he could manage as he picked at some grass.

They sat quietly for a few minutes, staring at the fire. Finally, she turned toward him. "Have you sought out this life do you suppose, or has it just followed you somehow?"

"I think I'm just cursed." He didn't believe in such things but had no other explanation.

"Maybe this is just your path," she said. My father said it sounds like you put everything you had into taking care of your mother and the farm until she passed. You couldn't have expected to go to war for three years and come back and succeed at it." She leaned her head back and gazed at the stars. "Your family is Moses, and you provide for him. . . you help provide for others."

He was glad it was dark and hoped she couldn't see him grimace at the thought of it all. "Well, until I can stay in one spot and not have that past keep finding me, I doubt that's the kind of providing women like Abigail were, or are, looking for." He touched the scar on his face.

"I've noticed you do that," Maggie said.

"Do what?" Elijah stopped touching the scar, knowing that's what she meant.

"You touch that scar when contemplating where your past has landed you." Elijah eyed her, then turned away after catching a grin that meant she knew she was right.

They sat in comfortable silence for a while, the proximity neither acknowledged nor dismissed. Eventually, Maggie stood, stretching. "We'd better get some rest," she said. "Thank you, Elijah, for everything. For my father, for this." She gestured around them. "For letting me be part of it."

Elijah surveyed the night around them, then looked back at her. "Goodnight, Maggie."

"Goodnight, Elijah." She walked back to her bedroll, leaving Elijah to his thoughts. With her departure, a sense of calm descended on him, and sleep seemed within reach for the first time that night.

THE COMING STORM

— ◦ —

As the day dawned, Elijah's decision to head toward the fort, spurred by Augusto's suggestion, gave the posse a sense of direction. They broke camp, eager to make up for lost time.

Leaving the bustle of the railroad behind, the group ventured into the open expanse of the Nebraska plains. The terrain unfurled before them, golden from the rising sun painting the endless grasslands and wildflowers swaying in the breeze. The Platte River meandered to the north, its course a shallow thread through the landscape. The land rolled here, with low rises and shallow valleys that stretched toward the horizon. The air was fresh, tinged with the earthy scent of wild sage, and the only sounds were the rhythmic thudding of the horses' hooves and the occasional distant cry of a hawk soaring overhead.

The posse's departure from their camp had been early, executed with a quiet efficiency that spoke to their growing sense of purpose. Before they left, Elijah had ridden into Hell on Wheels to confer with the foreman, updating him on their intentions and attempting to gather any last bits of information about the movement of goods and men through the area. Hobbs took advantage of the railroad's telegraph to send a brief update back to Omaha.

As they rode, Elijah was pensive, his mind turning over the previous night's failure and Hobbs's critical words. Despite Maggie's reassurances, doubt gnawed at him. He was used to making tough decisions, but the responsibility for his makeshift posse's lives and their mission was heavy.

He found himself mulling over his conversation with Reverend Thomas the previous night. The reverend's words had stirred something in him. Though his parents' deaths had left a void, they had maintained the simple habit of praying before meals, a ritual more out of remembrance and familiarity than conviction. Elijah pondered the reverend's insights on righteousness and vengeance, wondering if his pursuit of justice blurred into something darker.

Elijah's contemplations were interrupted as Brutus ran up alongside him, his tongue lolling. Seeing Big Sam approaching, Elijah seized the opportunity to clear the air and seek his advice. He respected Sam's judgment, especially when handling their mounts, but mostly wanted to ensure things were good between them.

"Sam," Elijah called out. "I wanted your thoughts on how hard we can push these horses today. It's warm but not terribly so. We need to make good time, but I don't want to run them into the ground."

Sam, riding up beside him, glanced over the horses, his eyes assessing. "Well, boss, these mounts are strong, but we gotta be mindful. We can push 'em hard for a spell, but let's give 'em regular breaks, plenty of water, and a good rest come nightfall. The good news is we got plenty of grass. They'll carry us far if we treat 'em right."

"Thanks, Sam. Keep an eye on them for me today, and let me know when we need to swap mounts or rest." He tipped his chin toward the front of their line of riders. "Why don't you ride point with Augusto for a spell and confer with him on the same." Big Sam tapped the brim of his hat and spurred his mount toward the front.

Elijah reined up on Bear and waited for Clay to ride alongside him. "You and Sam good?"

Elijah's question seemed to draw Clay out of his usual reserved demeanor. "Yeah, we're fine," Clay replied. He paused as if in thought. "I try not to fault a man for his convictions held in good faith. . . but Sam is a stubborn man." He looked straight ahead as he rode. "He's firm in his beliefs."

Elijah's voice was light. "He shares many of *my* beliefs about the war, you know."

Clay glanced over, a slight grin breaking his stoic expression. "I respect you and Moses for your convictions. Fighting for the Union, against slavery. . . That's something I can understand. But Sam just picked the side that made life easier where he was. In Missouri, folks coulda gone either way and given his family's farm. . ."

"I understand what you're saying," Elijah offered.

Clay's voice returned to its stoic nature as he looked toward Ike. "Ain't right what people like him had to go through, but I ain't sure it's right that it was ended through force and destruction, either. When Union soldiers came, dictating what we should do, taking what little we had. . ."

Elijah noticed Ike riding ahead. "It's true, the suffering caused by slavery was a wrong that needed righting. But you're also right that the war brought ruin to many lives, especially down south." Elijah looked over at the quiet Southerner. "I understand your perspective, Clay. But remember who started—"

Clay raised his hand in a conceding gesture. "I know where you're goin'. All I can say is we didn't join the early secession, and my kin was never for it. Folks like me just wanted to be let alone."

"I respect that," Elijah said after a pause. He wanted to demonstrate he understood without abandoning his own beliefs. "Having firmly held convictions, even if we don't agree on all points, is better than having none at all."

Clay seemed to appreciate Elijah's words, and mutual respect became evident. "Thanks, Elijah."

They rode silently for a few moments, and then Elijah spoke without turning his head from the horizon. "You were a sniper, weren't you?"

Clay dropped his head momentarily as if the vague mention of it distressed him. "I was." Elijah nodded, and they were quiet briefly. "You ever been real good at somethin' you wish you weren't?" Clay asked.

Elijah laughed without any emotion. "Story of the last four years of my life."

"Yeah," was all Clay could manage.

Elijah turned and looked at him. "Let's do our best not to need that sniper skill on this trip." He put a finger to the brim of his hat and trotted Bear toward Moses and Hobbs, who were discussing the day's journey.

"We should think about stopping soon for a mid-day rest," Elijah suggested, scanning the terrain for a suitable spot.

Moses squinted at the sky, a concerned look crossing his face. "I don't like the look of those clouds gathering up ahead." He pointed to a mass of dark clouds on the horizon. "Doesn't seem like there's much around here that could shield us from a bad storm."

Hobbs assessed the view to the west. "I don't know much about the weather out here, but I know that won't be good if it continues this way."

"We can't predict the weather, but we can prepare for it," Elijah said. "Let's find the best spot we can and hope it holds off." He looked unsure of himself but then doubled down on his decision. "The horses need to rest a spell, and I suppose we all do too."

The group agreed and dismounted in a relatively flat area with a few scattered trees offering the barest hint of cover. They set about their tasks, watering the horses and preparing a quick meal of hard tack and jerky. Sitting on a rock, Elijah watched the clouds inch closer, a sense of foreboding creeping over him. *I don't need any extra tests thrown at me,* he thought.

THE WAGON

— • —

No sooner had they packed up and resumed their journey than the early summer storm hit with a vengeance. The wind howled across the open plains, bending the tall grasses to its will and whipping dust and debris into the air. The sky turned a menacing shade of gray, then black as dark clouds rolled in.

The first raindrops fell heavy and hard, soon becoming a torrential downpour. Visibility dropped, the landscape blurring into a wet haze. The posse, drenched to the bone, struggled to keep their mounts under control as the animals balked at the wind, driving rain, lightning, and thunder that seemed to shake the ground.

His hat pulled low against the rain, Elijah rode from one posse member to another, offering encouragement. "Keep moving! We need to find some shelter!" he shouted over the howl of the wind. The group, hunched and miserable, could do little else but pull on their slickers and keep their heads low against the relentless assault.

The storm seemed to sap their energy, each mile feeling more prolonged than the last. The wind howled like a banshee, the rain stinging their faces like a thousand tiny needles as Elijah wondered how long it could last. The ground beneath their horses' feet turned into a slick, muddy mess, making each step precarious.

While the wind and lightning eventually ceased, the downpour continued unabated. As dusk approached, the posse, weary and drenched, stumbled upon a small stand of trees offering a semblance of shelter from the unyielding rain.

Exhausted, they dismounted, their movements sluggish, each step a struggle against the muck and the fatigue that weighed them down. The horses, equally spent, lowered their heads, their sides heaving. Elijah surveyed the dismal scene, his heart heavy with the responsibility for those who had believed in his cause and trusted him to lead.

They attempted to kindle a fire with great effort, but the rain had soaked everything through. They managed only to produce a small flame, enough to warm a pot of coffee. They huddled together, the cold seeping into their bones, as they shared a meager dinner of cold biscuits and jerky, their spirits as dampened as their clothes.

The rain ceased sometime during the night, but it brought little relief. The air, though mild, felt icy against their wet clothing. Shivering and miserable, they tried to rest, but sleep was elusive. At first light, what little there was, the group roused themselves to continue. The promise of a warm cup of coffee was their only solace, but even that was denied as the rain returned, drenching them again.

As they trudged through the sodden landscape throughout the day, morale sank. The on-and-off rain and the uncertainty of their pursuit weighed on every mind. Elijah felt the burden of his decisions. He couldn't help but question what they were doing, chasing ghosts in the rain. Elijah glanced back at the line of bedraggled riders. "What are we putting ourselves through?" he muttered, his gaze fixed on the horizon, searching for anything that might give this journey meaning.

They made a brief stop midday, and through sheer determination, Augusto constructed a fire that warmed some beans and coffee while the horses rested and fed. Back in the saddle, steady rain continued falling from a gray sky, enveloping the Nebraska plains in a curtain of water. The posse's journey felt endless, each mile an ordeal against the elements.

"I almost miss the wind," Moses mused. He could not muster his usual optimism, although his sarcasm remained evident. "At least it blew some of the water off you."

As late afternoon wore on, the group encountered a slight rise in the terrain, its gentle slopes hiding what lay beyond. Augusto, riding beside Elijah, suggested caution. "We should scout ahead," he said, his voice grave. "It does not look like much, but any change in the ground can give an attacker an advantage. I will look."

Despite the group's groans over anything that slowed their pace even further, Elijah agreed. Augusto knew the land better than any of them, and the old tracker's wariness was not lost on Elijah.

Clay, who had been near the front, dismounted and handed his reins to Moses. "I'll go with him," he said. There was mock applause and cheering from the posse, causing Clay to shake his head. The group watched Augusto and Clay move toward a dip in the rise, their movements deliberate and calm.

They crawled the last few feet, their bodies hugging the earth. Augusto used a field glass to survey and then passed it to Clay. Moments later, the two men returned, drenched and muddy. Clay, attempting to wipe off the muck, was met with chuckles. "As if you weren't wet enough already, Moses said."

Ignoring Moses's comment, Augusto announced, "There is a wagon over the rise, two men struggling near it. Looks like they are stuck or working on something."

"How far?" Elijah asked.

Clay looked at Augusto. "Three or four hundred yards, maybe?"

Augusto nodded. "*Si*." He looked to Elijah. "Overloaded wagon and this wet terrain do not get along." He made a gesture implying the wagon was partially tipped.

"Gotta be Morrow," Elijah said.

Moses maneuvered Copper alongside Bear and spoke in a low voice. "He could be settin' up an ambush." Elijah looked ahead to the west.

"I know you two have the federal badges on, but we don't need any secrets being told right now, boys." Hobbs's tone appeared to be joking, but Elijah thought he sensed some resentment in it.

"Mo is thinking, and I am inclined to agree, that Morrow could be setting up an ambush."

"Seems like what he woulda done in the war," Ike said. "Guerrilla fighters use whatever they can to their advantage. . . turn a weakness into a strength." Elijah, Moses, Clay, and Augusto all agreed.

Elijah looked to Maggie, not wanting to leave her out of the decision-making process if danger was afoot. She adjusted in her saddle and sat up straight. "They certainly seem capable of such a thing based on their past."

Hobbs, however, shook his head. "Or, more likely, they got stuck in the storm like us, but they've got a wagon and draft animals, so they were even slower. We caught a break." He looked around the group for support. "How could they know we were coming behind them?"

"You were the one that warned me those guys in the railroad camp could be working for them," Elijah responded.

Hobbs rubbed his beard. "Yeah, I suppose that is true." He laughed under his breath. "Damn it, you've got a reply for everything."

Clay, who had been silent, spoke up. "If I were settin' up an ambush in this weather, there's a spot over there," he pointed to a slight rise in the terrain, "that I would use." He looked up to some parting clouds where the faintest sunlight emerged. "Puts what little sun there is in the eyes of someone trying to find him."

Elijah frowned, the possibility troubling him. "Clay, take Augusto and scout that position." He looked around at the rest of the group as he thought things over. He wanted to approach the wagon himself, so he would trust Moses to handle overwatch and prepare to react. "Mo, find a good spot to observe with Hobbs and Sam and be ready to counter anything." He looked at Maggie as confidently as he could. "I'll take Ike and Maggie down to the wagon."

Big Sam grumbled. "Can't believe I'm sayin' this, but I'm with the Pinkerton." He looked at Hobbs. "Ain't nobody settin' up an ambush on the wide-open prairie, 'cept maybe hidin' in that wagon. Good luck takin' us on that way, though." He looked at Elijah with pleading eyes. "I follow orders, boss, but we're just prolongin' our misery here."

Elijah had grown a bit weary of Sam's attitude. The man was a hard worker, but his familiarity with Elijah caused him to sometimes act insubordinate, risking morale issues. Now was not the time for bickering, however. "I understand your thoughts, Sam," Elijah said. "But this is the plan."

Big Sam gave a mock salute and joined Hobbs and Moses as Augusto and Clay maneuvered into position. Elijah rode over to Ike and Maggie and looked them over. Ike had a Spencer in a scabbard and was wearing his revolver. He nodded his readiness.

Elijah looked at Maggie. "Any sign of trouble, or if Ike and I start shooting, you find the nearest man that ain't either of us and pull the trigger on that scattergun." Elijah gave her the most confident look he could muster, and she seemed to do likewise.

Everyone was now in position. Elijah moved forward, his hand resting on the handle of his Colt, his senses on high alert. He guided Bear straight towards the wagon while Ike and Maggie swung around in a wide arc. As he drew closer, Elijah's grip on his weapon relaxed slightly; the men at the wagon's base were unarmed, struggling against ropes that bound them.

Elijah was perplexed. "They're tied up!" he called out. Maggie and Ike cautiously approached. Recognizing the man tied to the wagon as Nate Morrow from descriptions they had read brought confusion. Beside Morrow was a grizzled, red-haired man, unknown to them but apparently not a stranger to Morrow.

Elijah dismounted and squatted to face Morrow, who was no longer attempting to untie himself. Water dripped off Elijah's slouch hat as he tipped it up to get a good look at the man. He spoke loud enough to be heard over the steady drizzle and the animals still attached to the wagon. "Well, Nate. It's been downright unpleasant coming after you. Did you do this to set a trap, or did something go wrong?" Elijah peered around the wagon, desperate to know the answer to his question.

Maggie and Ike began to search the wagon, calming the draft animals struggling against their harnesses. The wagon, laden and tipping precariously, added to the dangerous scene.

Elijah continued questioning Morrow, trying to glean information, but the pair were not talking, only huddling up small, attempting to warm their shivering bodies. He tried to recall the information from the legal papers he hoped weren't ruined in his saddlebags. "You Red Sanders?" He slapped the other man's boot and got a look of disgust.

Elijah scanned the surroundings for other gang members. His gut told him something was off—the absence of Morrow's men was unsettling. "Ike, I don't like this. Is everything clear inside that wagon?"

Ike stepped onto the wagon and peered inside with his gun drawn. "I don't like it either, boss." The wagon looks clear, though." He jumped down and, noticing the wagon's instability and Maggie's proximity to the struggling animals, urged caution. "Careful there, Maggie. A mule kick or being crushed by this wagon will make things even more miserable out here."

Maggie laughed, but her smile disappeared. Elijah and Ike had concerned looks on their face, and she seemed to sense the men were uncomfortable.

"I'm not going to pretend to know how he came to be tied up," Elijah said. "But he is." He looked around. "Nothing else about this is good, though. Let's get back to the group."

Ike suddenly crouched down low and pulled Maggie behind him as he stared toward the rise Clay had pointed out.

Elijah followed his eyes. "What is it, Ike?"

Ike wedged himself behind a wagon wheel and in front of Maggie, then spoke in a low voice. "Caught a glint of something on that rise." He squinted. "Could have been a rifle barrel, coulda been nothin'."

"It won't be nothin'," Morrow grumbled.

Elijah stared at him. "Somethin' I should know, Nate?"

"Just that we didn't tie ourselves up and that there's some fellas nastier than me out there somewhere."

Elijah furrowed his brow and studied the rise. As Ike and Maggie moved along the leaning side of the wagon toward Elijah and better cover, one of the draft animals was spooked by their presence and a stray crack of thunder, setting off a reaction among the other animals. The wagon lurched and began to tip. Reacting swiftly, Ike pulled Maggie out of harm's way, pushing her and then stepping away from the wagon that nearly crushed them.

Elijah stepped away from the wagon, which was now leaning dangerously away from him, with the two men pulled upward on their toes. "Are we alright, Ike?"

"Yeah, boss. Just need to—"

A rifle shot tore through the rain. Ike collapsed to the ground, and Maggie screamed.

"Sniper!" Elijah shouted. He ran for Maggie, pulling her behind the cover of the wagon. The shot had come from the rise, the same direction Clay and Augusto had gone to scout. Elijah looked down at Maggie, trembling and sprayed with Ike's blood.

The ambush he had feared was unfolding, and they had walked right into it.

WHERE DO WE STAND?

— · —

The sudden stillness that followed the gunshot was almost more jarring than the shot itself. Elijah crouched over Maggie and felt a surge of anger. He quickly glanced around the wagon's corner, scanning for the shooter. The rise Clay had pointed out earlier seemed the likely spot.

He looked down at Ike, who lay in a pool of rainwater and mud, struggling to breathe, his pale face staring at Elijah. Blood mingled with the muddy water, spreading in a dark stain around him, the rain pelting his face. Maggie stared at Ike, her face covered with rain and blood, her body trembling.

"I'm sorry, Elijah," Ike gasped. "I couldn't tell. . . I tried to save her. . ."

"None of that," Elijah said. He looked back at Maggie. "You saved her. She would have been crushed or been the one shot."

Ike stared up at the sky. "Tell my wife—"

"You'll tell her yourself. I need you to lay still, though, Ike. Don't give him a reason to pull the trigger on you again."

"Ike closed his eyes tight and grimaced.

Elijah turned to the men tied to the wagon. "You did this," he growled at Morrow.

Morrow, his hands tied over his head to the wagon and barely able to stand, shook his head. "I didn't, but it ain't over, deputy," he said.

Elijah's mind raced. "How many?" he demanded, his voice sharp.

"Four," Morrow replied. "They thought they were facing just three of you. . ." Morrow strained to look around. "Thinkin' you got more, though."

Elijah grabbed Maggie by the shoulders, shaking her and calling her name until she looked at him. "They're going to come at us soon." He looked behind him, where Bear had shied away but not run off like Maggie's horse. "I'm going to ride into them and pull them away from the wagon."

She shook her head, unable to speak.

"You better listen to him, little lady," Morrow said. "What in the hell do you even have a woman with—"

"Shut it!" Elijah said without looking at him. He reached down and placed Maggie's shotgun in her hands. "Same as before. Anyone who ain't me or one of the rest of us gets near this wagon—"

She snapped out of her shock. "Got it."

Elijah turned on his haunches, gave Bear a quick whistle, and called his name. The horse inched over, and in one swift move, Elijah grabbed his reins and swung aboard.

Elijah sat atop Bear, watching the rise where the sniper had to be, sheltering himself with the wagon. He looked down at Maggie, who was still trembling. "You'll be alright," he said.

She looked up at him. "You're going to ride into three of them plus a sniper?" Her mouth hung open.

"Mo will know what I want him to do," he said. *I hope he knows me well enough to know what they need to do*, Elijah thought.

A roar of whoops and hollers cut through the air, and a sniper's bullet cracked into the wagon. "Oh Lord, here they come," Maggie hollered. She looked up just in time to see Elijah give Bear a kick and take off in their direction.

The world around him seemed to slow down, the raindrops falling like suspended crystals in time. Despite the scene, a deafening silence filled his ears, punctuated only by the steady drumming of rain falling upon his head.

As he closed on the riders, he pulled the Winchester from its scabbard and levered in a round, praying his practice with the new weapon translated to battle. Hopefully, if Moses didn't come, they would at least ride to Maggie's rescue and give Ike whatever slight chance he may have to survive.

As Elijah drew close enough to make out their faces, he recognized the one on the far left as the man who had called himself Jed at the railroad camp. The man had a devilish grin, clearly feeling good about his deception. Elijah raised the Winchester and leveled it toward the man, then sensing movement from his left, moved his aim to the right.

Jed's look of confusion was brief before blood sprayed from his head, a direct hit from Moses, and Elijah pulled the trigger on the center rider, speeding past him as the man slumped in his saddle. Looking to the rise, Elijah saw the sniper's rifle pointed at him from above some tall grass on a slight rise. Elijah levered a round, his heart racing as he realized he didn't have a shot. A moment later, he heard the crack of Clay's Sharps rifle, and the sniper slumped to the ground.

Spinning Bear one hundred and eighty degrees, Elijah saw Big Sam, Hobbs, and a speeding Brutus chasing the remaining attacker from behind, converging on him, the two men each taking a shot that ended the pursuit. Moses rode up alongside Elijah, his rifle held low but ready, scanning the horizon.

"That all of 'em?" Moses said.

"That's what Morrow said," Elijah replied.

Moses raised an eyebrow.

"You'll see." Elijah looked toward Sam and Hobbs. Can you take them and swing around the area to ensure we're clear now?"

"You got it." Moses kicked Copper and took off, stopping abruptly and turning back. "Ike?" Elijah shook his head. Moses looked at him momentarily, searching for the best thing to say to his brother. "You played it right, Eli. What else could we have done?"

"I know, Mo. Make sure there aren't any more of them." Moses touched the brim of his hat, and he and Copper were off.

Turning to face them, Elijah gave a grateful wave to Clay and Augusto, positioned on a distant rise, acknowledging their crucial role in providing overwatch. He pointed to Moses, Big Sam, and Hobbs and made a broad circling gesture, then pointed to himself and the wagon. Augusto waved an acknowledgment.

With the immediate threat neutralized, Elijah turned Bear and walked him back toward the wagon to check on Maggie, saying a prayer that, by some chance, Ike was still with them. The steady rain continued on his face as he approached, a nuisance he no longer noticed amid his problems.

Dismounting and ground-tying Bear, Elijah's boots sank into the soft, muddy ground. He looked ahead to where Ike lay, his head turned toward where Elijah had ridden, but his eyes were now lifeless. Elijah's heart sank but then began to beat faster when he saw Ike's revolver no longer lying next to him. Peering under the tipped-over wagon, he realized he only saw one pair of legs tied to the wagon.

Elijah rounded the corner of the wagon, his hand hovering near his revolver. The scene that greeted him was a tense standoff. Red Sanders stood with a revolver pointed at Maggie. She, in turn, was aiming a shotgun at him, her hands trembling.

Sanders's other hand was frantically working at Morrow's bindings, trying to free him from the wagon. Maggie's eyes darted towards Elijah, her grip on the shotgun tightened, her knuckles white against the rain-soaked wood. Seeing her glance, Red turned and saw Elijah. He began to shift the gun back and forth, pointing at Maggie, then Elijah.

"Take a deep breath," Elijah said. He heard Moses, Sam, and Hobbs approach and saw Sanders's eyes widen. Elijah held a hand up behind him, then spoke slowly and clearly. "Maybe you shoot me or the woman, but that's about all you're going to get out of it."

"Listen to him, Red," Morrow said. He no longer even struggled against his restraint.

"Shut up, Nate." Sanders spat. He stared at Morrow a moment. "You let those damn Crenshaws into our fold and ruined a good thing; now it's all over. I'll be dammed if I just give myself up without a fight only to be hanged." Sanders shook his head and spat again. "The Shadow Commander," he said in a voice dripping with disdain.

Elijah had many questions about the Crenshaws, but first, he needed to defuse the situation. "Red, think about this," Elijah urged. His voice was firm yet non-threatening. "You don't have to die here. There's a chance for you yet. None of us here have seen you kill anyone. You were a tied-up prisoner. Just lower the gun."

Sanders's arm wavered, his resolve flickering in his eyes. For a brief moment, it seemed like he might relent. The rain drummed steadily around them, muffling the world to this standoff.

But then, something in Sanders snapped. His face contorted with desperation and rage. He swung the revolver up, aiming at Elijah. But before he could fire, a shotgun blast echoed, and Sanders howled in pain. Maggie held the smoking barrel of the shotgun in her trembling hands, a look of panic in her eyes as Sanders turned toward her.

Elijah didn't hesitate. He drew his revolver and fired twice in a swift, fluid motion. The bullets hit Sanders in the chest, sending him staggering backward before collapsing into the muddy earth.

Morrow, still tied to the wagon, watched in stunned silence before turning away as his partner's body hit the ground.

Elijah kept his revolver trained on Sanders's still form for a moment, ensuring he was no longer a threat. Then he holstered his weapon, waved his brother over, and rushed to Maggie, who was staring at Sanders's body, her face a mask of shock.

Elijah reached out and lowered the barrel of the shotgun, which she still aimed toward Sanders. "Are you alright?" Elijah asked. His voice was soft but urgent as he took the gun from her hands.

Maggie was unable to find her voice, her eyes frozen on the lifeless body of Sanders.

"You didn't kill him," Elijah said. He knew that was the horror running through her mind. She stared blankly at him. "Do you hear me, Maggie? You gave me a chance to do it. You saved my life and your own." She handed Elijah the shotgun before walking away from the wagon.

Moses approached and swung down from Copper, inspecting Sanders's body and then looking up at Morrow. "That's a dumb friend you got there." Morrow hung his head.

"Find anything?" Elijah asked.

Moses, Hobbs, and Sam exchanged glances, and Moses spoke up. "Couple 'a fellas in Union Army coats strung up in a stand of trees." The entire group scoffed and showed signs of disgust.

"That'd be the bullwhackers we had driving the wagons," Morrow said. Elijah shot him a look, and Morrow replied quickly. "That was them that did that, not me."

"All clear otherwise," Hobbs said. "Found the tracks of maybe four or five riders headed west, though. Augusto can confirm."

Elijah then remembered the pair who had been providing over-watch. He stepped from behind the wagon, gave a whistle and a wave, and soon saw the two men riding toward them.

Elijah looked at Moses then cocked his head toward Ike's body. "Mo, can you see if there's a blanket or something in that wagon?"

Clay and Augusto arrived, and Elijah offered Clay his hand. "Good shooting. You were the first person to save my life this afternoon." He said nothing and shook Elijah's hand.

Moses finished covering Ike and returned to the group as Elijah began to speak. "We're going to get the dead buried, then see if we can't round up the horses those attackers were riding." He turned to Augusto. "Think you can get those critters pulling the wagon on a line?"

"*Si*, is no problem."

Elijah looked at Moses, aware that his next set of directives and questions would lead the group to some thinking. "How far off course are we from the main trail that leads by the fort, Augusto?"

August removed his dripping wet sombrero and shook the water out. "We are close. Likely to find it in less than one hour."

"They found some riders' tracks heading west from here. I'd like to follow them and confirm they meet back up with the trail. How far to the fort do you reckon?" Elijah asked.

Augusto gazed to the west. "I had wagered two to three hours before all of this happened." Elijah looked at his pocket watch and saw it was nearing six, but he couldn't remember when he last wound it.

"Boss, we even buryin' the ones who tried to kill us?" Sam asked.

"There were still men, Sam. Let's at least get them where critters won't dig them up." He looked around the group. "We'll get the animals ready, take on whatever supplies are worthwhile, and I want to leave within the hour." Elijah suddenly looked toward the trees and then back at his men. "Let's get those fellas cut down and buried as well."

There was a brief hesitation, but the men soon dispersed to their work, removing digging tools from the wagon or their gear while Augusto rounded up animals. Elijah walked over to Ike's covered body and removed his hat, water running down his face.

"Ain't anything you coulda done different other than turn around, Eli." Moses said before removing his hat.

"I know," Elijah replied. His eyes stayed on Ike's form. He began to speak as if saying a prayer or giving a eulogy. "This was a good man right here. He was a man who had all the reason in the world to be bitter and hateful, but he just worked hard and got through it. And now he leaves a wife behind and will not get to enjoy the long-coming fruits of those labors." He paused, looked at Moses, and then back down at Ike. "May we all be more like him, and God rest his soul."

"Amen," Moses said.

They each put their hats back on, and Elijah looked at Moses. "Well done on charging them in the flank."

Moses smirked. "Yeah, well, next time, maybe give us a little notice."

"Didn't have that luxury, Mo," Elijah said. He looked over to the glum-faced Nate Morrow, standing in the steady drizzle. "Be sure he's secured and ready to move," Elijah said.

"Will do," Moses said. He then lingered a moment.

"Something else?" Elijah asked. Moses pursed his lips and shook his head, and Elijah marched off across the muddy ground toward Maggie's horse. "Gonna go make sure she's ready to ride."

Moses set off for the digging parties and then stopped. He hesitated momentarily before stomping toward Elijah, his boots squelching on the muddy ground.

"Eli," he began, his voice low and measured, "I'm not looking to cross swords or question your judgment. But I need to understand where we stand, where you stand." He paused, eyes searching Elijah's face for any hint of his thoughts.

Elijah remained silent, his expression unreadable. Rain dripped off the brim of his hat, masking any emotion that might have flickered across his face.

Moses continued, "We got Morrow. Are we just riding west to find shelter and dry ground for the night, or is this chase far from over in your eyes?"

Elijah turned slowly to face his brother, his eyes stern and resolute under the relentless downpour. Finally, he spoke, his voice that of the wartime captain who had hunted guerrillas before. "Have everyone ready to leave within the hour, Mo."

FORT KEARNY

— ◆ —

Fort Kearny was a solitary sentinel on the vast prairie, its rough-hewn log walls standing stark against the vast, open sky. Built in the mid-1840s near the confluence of the Platte River, it was a crucial outpost in the untamed heart of the Nebraska Territory. Intended as a beacon of safety on the expanding American frontier, the fort was strategically positioned along the Oregon Trail, serving as a vital rest stop for weary travelers, gold seekers, and settlers heading westward. It was a nexus of trade and resupply. In this place, travelers could trade stories, replenish their supplies, and seek temporary refuge from the hardships of the trail.

Surrounded by rolling grasslands, the fort's sturdy outer walls painted a picture of rugged functionality. The air was often filled with the clanging of blacksmiths, chatter of traders, and the shuffle of soldiers. Amidst all this, the fort's men strived to maintain order and discipline, their decisions shaping the fragile balance between the wildness of the frontier and the creeping tide of civilization.

The posse had barely said a word after they finished standing over Ike Taylor's stone-marked grave until they arrived at the fort as the last light of the day faded. Having unleashed two relentless days of rain, the vast Nebraska sky chose this moment to relent, its clouds parting just as the riders neared. The twist of nature seemed almost to taunt Elijah and the weary travelers.

As they passed the makeshift camps of traders, travelers, and some natives outside the fort and approached the main gate, the sentries straightened, eyeing the group with caution. Elijah, leading the procession, wore his cavalry hat, the badge of his federal marshal status visible even in the fading light. The soldiers' initial wariness melted into respect as they recognized the insignia.

Elijah spoke with an earnestness that was authoritative. He explained their situation, the encounter with Morrow's gang, and their urgent need for shelter and rest. His words, coupled with the authority of his badge, convinced the officers to grant them access.

On three sides of the parade ground were the soldiers, officers, and quartermasters' buildings and stables. A row of cottonwood trees extended around the ground and in front of the buildings. The group found a sutler's store with a large stock of goods and even a post office.

The fort's command offered Elijah accommodations befitting an officer, but he declined, requesting that the favor be extended to Maggie for private quarters instead. Two of the very few officers' wives in the camp saw to her needs for the evening.

In exchange for their lodgings, Elijah bartered the spare horses and draft animals they had brought in. The trade provided the fort with much-needed livestock while securing the comfort of his weary group. The supply clerk had told Elijah he thought the fort was getting the better end of the deal, which Elijah intended to use as a bargaining chip in the morning.

Soon, they found themselves in the barracks among the enlisted men. While Hobbs made a sarcastic comment about it not being the Herndon House, the men appreciated Elijah's willingness to stay with them. The dry bunks, though humble, were a welcome respite from the relentless rain and mud they had endured. Fort Kearny's laundry service attended to their drenched clothing, finding them all some dry spares in the meantime.

After a hearty meal that revived their spirits and filled their bellies, Elijah and Moses made their way to the stockade. Elijah's steps were heavy as the guard stepped aside. The enclosure's wooden door creaked as Elijah pushed it open, stepping into the dimly lit interior to confront Morrow again.

The stockade was a stark, unadorned place, built more for function than comfort. The walls were made of sturdy logs, and the air was cool inside the tightly packed wood. Dimly lit by flickering torches mounted on the walls, the stockade cast long, dancing shadows that played across the rough wooden surfaces. The torchlight barely reached the far corners of the room, creating a sense of isolation and confinement.

Nate Morrow's cell was unembellished, with a thick wooden bar securing the door. Inside, the cell contained only the bare necessities: a narrow cot with a thin mattress, a small wooden stool, and a bucket in the corner. Despite its spartan appearance, the cell was clean and dry, a small mercy in the otherwise harsh environment.

Morrow sat on the cot's edge, his posture relaxed yet alert. He understood his situation—a criminal caught in the act—yet he had a certain dignity. His eyes, sharp and calculating, followed Elijah's movements closely.

Elijah pulled up a stool before the cell as Moses leaned against the wall. "How goes it, Nate?" Elijah asked. He struck a match on the leg of the stool and lit his pipe, savoring it. Elijah Barber had few material needs, but fresh tobacco at the fort after his had been soaked was one of them.

Elijah's question was met with a slight nod from Morrow. "Could be worse, I suppose," he replied, his voice composed. Despite his predicament, there was a sense of respect in his demeanor, an acknowledgment of the fairness he'd been treated with so far.

Standing by the wall, Moses observed the interaction with a keen eye. "Better treatment than the Crenshaws gave you it seems?" Moses smirked. "Lose control of your gang did you?"

Morrow ignored Moses's quip, and Elijah tilted his head toward his brother and shook his head. They wouldn't get anything out of this man by embarrassing him.

Elijah took a slow puff from his pipe, exhaling a cloud of smoke that drifted in the torch-lit air. He leaned forward, fixing Morrow with a steady stare. "Nate, you and I both know why you're here," he began. His voice was calm but carried an undercurrent of authority. That part is easy." He looked at Moses. "Despite my brother's ill manner, however, he asks a fair question: What happened with the Crenshaws?"

"I don't have a lot of cards left to play, deputy, but that is most certainly one of them."

Aware of the delicate balance he needed to strike in this interrogation, Elijah leaned in closer, his eyes never leaving Morrow's. He knew he had to tread carefully, offering just enough to coax the information he needed from Morrow while maintaining the upper hand.

"Morrow," Elijah began in a low, measured tone, "I understand you're in a bind, and I'm not here to make things worse for you. You're going back to Omaha, that's non-negotiable. But how you go back – that's still up in the air."

Morrow's eyes narrowed slightly, a hint of interest creeping into his stoic demeanor.

Elijah continued, "You give me something on the Crenshaws, and I can make sure it's known you cooperated. That you didn't resist capture. Might make things easier for you down the line." Elijah leaned back and puffed on his pipe. "Hell, your gang is all either dead, or with the Crenshaws and nowhere near Omaha. Who's to even say you've done what they say?" He paused, allowing the words to sink in. "And I won't make it public that the Crenshaws took over your gang by force," he added, watching Morrow's reaction closely.

Morrow's facade cracked for a moment, his pride wounded by the implication. However, Elijah could see a grudging appreciation in his eyes. It was a small concession, but it was something. But Morrow's expression then turned more calculating. "Deputy," he said slowly, "word I hear from the guards is that you're Elijah Barber. That right?"

Elijah glanced at Moses before answering. "That's right."

"I heard them Crenshaws talk about you. I read the papers, and I know the way you fought back in Omaha." Morrow leaned back. "So the man who won't quit until he's hunted down every last man who has done him wrong is now offering me a deal?"

"I'm offering you a chance to make things right, or at least less wrong. The Crenshaws are a menace that needs to be stopped. You help me with that, and it'll be noted," Elijah stated.

Morrow considered this. He grinned, clearly enjoying holding this over Elijah. "You know as well as I do, however, that the legal system doesn't always care for nuances."

Elijah puffed on the pipe. In this case, he was staking the rest of his life that the system *would* care. "I'm aware. But it's the best I can do." He hoped Morrow wanted to see the Crenshaws stopped as much as he did.

Morrow looked up at the ceiling and began to recite his story. Elijah sped him along through the portions before Omaha, ultimately getting out of the man that the Crenshaws, Jack in particular, had always been the ones to carry out the dirty work that made Morrow notorious during the war.

"That Shadow Commander name was good for business," Morrow said. "I had the influence and connections to recruit and get information and influence, and the Crenshaws. . . well they were the teeth of it." He rubbed his beard. "Guess I created a monster."

He sat back and recounted the Crenshaws waking up him and Red with guns to their faces in the storm, shooting one man, hauling off the wagon drivers, and holding him and Red at gunpoint as they tied them up and departed. "They got all the money, and I suppose planned to come back for all the stolen goods in the wagon," Morrow concluded.

Moses spoke up. "Why didn't they just kill you if they'd been able to have everyone turn on you? If they could get you tied up, a bullet in the head would have been easy."

Morrow snorted and looked at each brother. "Said it'd be more embarrassing for me to get caught. . . and that it would slow you two down when you stopped to deal with me. Plus, I guess they wanted it to look like someone was working on the stuck wagon for that ambush."

Elijah shared a look with Moses, each knowing this was how it had all gone. "So what's their plan now, Nate?"

"I have no idea, deputy."

Elijah tapped out his pipe, then stood and turned to leave but paused at the door, glancing back at Morrow. "Not giving me much more than a story, Nate. Just remember: We both want the same thing here – to see the Crenshaws brought to justice. If you want to help that cause and your own, I'll need more before morning."

"Dobytown," Morrow called out.

Elijah looked at him. "What?"

"Two or three miles southwest of here. That's where they'll be waiting for their guys to come back. They'll get liquored up, find a woman, get information from other lowlifes like them, and resupply and move on."

Elijah returned to the cell and stared at Morrow.

"I'm told Dobytown is the kind of spot where the rules of polite society don't hold much sway. . . Even less than usual out here. It's a rough-and-tumble settlement, brimming with traders, prospectors, and all manner of folk looking to make their fortune or just escape their past." Morrow smirked. "Just ask the soldiers. Any that say they don't know it are either Puritans or liars."

As Elijah left the stockade, Moses fell in step beside him. There was a tension in Moses's posture, a sign of the conflict brewing within him.

"Eli, you know as well as I do that any favor you try to curry for Morrow won't mean a thing if they find out we've gone rogue from our orders," Moses said, his voice low.

Elijah halted, his jaw set in determination. "I know, Mo. But right now, stopping the Crenshaws is what matters. We'll deal with the consequences later."

"So that's it, then? Decision made?" Moses stared at his brother.

Elijah removed the pipe from his mouth and bit his lip, glaring at Moses. He began counting names on his fingers. "William Jones, Talbot Jones, Marshal Foster, Willy from the livery, the bank manager, Ike Taylor. . . Abigail." He paused there a moment. "Not to mention the handful of men lost chasing them in the war and all the damage Frank Tucker did. Our livery, our livelihood, the life's work of Patrick Hennessey. . . Dammit, Mo, they stole pert near our whole life's savings to boot and—"

"I hear you, Eli," Moses interrupted.

"Do you, Mo?" He looked around, mindful he didn't want to make a scene, but his eyes flashed with anger and pain. "After all the violence of the war, coming back to no parents, watching the farm fail, leaving home last summer. . . We finally found a life for ourselves. And the Crenshaws. . . *they're* the ones responsible for all of this, Mo. Not Frank Tucker, not anyone else. The Crenshaw brothers." He attempted to soften his tone. "I don't want to spend the rest of my life looking over my shoulder, Mo."

Moses's expression softened, but his voice carried a stubborn edge. "That's not what you're talkin' about, Eli. We could take Morrow back to Omaha, and turn away from them. . . You're talkin' about revenge."

Elijah bristled at his brother's words. "And what? Just wait for them to come after us again? We thought we'd left it behind twice before, Mo." He stepped closer, his voice rising. "I can't – I won't – live like that, always waiting for the next attack. We have to end it."

"Elijah, I'm with you. You know that. But forgetting the fact that we got five others to take care of, that Morrow needs to be taken back to Omaha, and that we'll likely become outlaws ourselves if we do this." He looked into the distance for a moment. "Where does it stop?"

Elijah's face hardened, and he took a step back. "It stops when the Crenshaws can't hurt anyone else. Because of us. Because we didn't turn our backs when we had the chance to stop them."

Not Going to Stop

— · —

E lijah awoke well before the sun and roused Moses from the bed beside him. Even after the conversation with his brother the evening before, a dry bed had won out, and he had slept well. However, he wanted to get his day moving without delay and was set on finding the Crenshaws in Dobytown.

He left a note near the other men's beds asking them to gather their laundry and supplies and prepare the horses, then set off with Moses for the headquarters building.

The early morning was already warm, but a breeze caused the flag in the center of the parade grounds to snap overhead. Elijah looked up at the red and white stripes and the thirty-six stars inside the blue union. He had read that Tennessee might soon be the first seceded state to be re-admitted but knew the stars had never changed. The very Nebraska territory he now stood in would be an added star in the next year.

The brothers climbed the steps to the modest, but grander than the rest, headquarters building and entered an outer office. A few lower-ranking officers were beginning to trickle in, but the building was otherwise quiet. A lieutenant finished lighting an oil lamp on the wall and crossed the room to the brothers, his thick military boots knocking against the wooden floor.

"Good morning, deputies. I was told you'd be in this morning, but didn't expect you this early."

"We just want to be on our way and out of your way as soon as possible, Elijah said."

The lieutenant smiled. "Yes captain... or deputy." He laughed and shook his head. "The hat, but then the badge..." He pointed to some chairs. "I can bring you each a cup of coffee and will let you know as soon as the colonel is here."

They thanked him and sat in the chairs. Soon, they accepted the coffee and urged the lieutenant to go about his work and not worry about them.

"Were we ever that jittery in front of our superiors? Or perceived superiors?" Moses quipped before taking a sip of the coffee.

"We weren't ever on staff duty for a colonel."

"Thank God for that," Moses said. He took another sip of coffee. "He makes better coffee than me though."

Shortly, the lieutenant re-emerged. "The colonel is ready for you." He led them past some cluttered desks down a hallway full of maps depicting the territory, arriving at an open door, where still, the lieutenant knocked.

"Enter," came a deep voice.

A stocky man of average height with dark hair and a well-groomed beard sat in a high-backed chair behind a desk that was the most lavish piece of furniture on the entire military reservation. Without looking up, he examined a sheet of paper and spoke to the lieutenant. "Smith, what is this nonsense about some federal marshals needing to speak with me very first thing?"

Lieutenant Smith cleared his throat. "Sir. Deputies Elijah and Moses Barber to see you, sir."

The colonel looked up at the lieutenant.

"We are the nonsense needing to speak with you, sir," Moses said. Elijah's head slowly turned to his brother, the colonel following suit. "Good morning, sir." Moses smiled.

The colonel shook his head, dismissed the lieutenant, and gestured to chairs before his desk. He saw they had carried coffee mugs in, grabbed a pot from a stove, and set it before them. "Colonel Henry Redford," the man said. He sat, eyed them, and saw Elijah's slouch hat on his knee. "A cavalry officer?"

"A captain, yes sir. No longer though."

The colonel turned to Moses. "And you're his brother."

"Yessir."

"And you were also a soldier."

"Yessir."

The colonel grinned. "You've been waiting a long time to say something smart like that to a high-ranking officer, haven't you?"

"Yessir, I have."

Elijah shifted in his chair and scratched at his chin. "Sir, no disrespect meant, but we—"

"Are in a hurry, I'm sure." He set his papers aside and folded his hands on the desk. "Tell me your story, gentlemen."

Elijah leaned forward, his eyes locking with Colonel Redford's as he detailed Morrow's past, his gang's activities since the war ended, and the events leading up to and including what happened in Omaha.

"I'm familiar with Morrow from the war," Redford said. He took a drink of coffee and eyed the brothers. "I'm also familiar with your names." I get papers late, but I thought they said you two had given up this life.

Elijah sat back, realizing the colonel hadn't been asking about them during his introduction but confirming. Moses spoke up. "And give up all this?"

"You sure you don't want to re-enlist, son?" The colonel asked.

Elijah ignored them and continued. "We had a good thing going in Omaha, but the city and county had asked for our help just in case. . . and the case came. Then it got personal."

Moses filled in the remaining blanks. "The Territorial marshal made us special deputies with the mandate of stopping Morrow and his gang." Moses handed him the water-damaged warrant, bounty information, and deputy paperwork.

Moses continued. "We've got a posse of six more. . . well five now." He paused. "We caught up with them near here, sir. There was a shootout, and we apprehended Morrow." His tone was matter-of-fact.

"We've brought Morrow here for temporary holding," Elijah said. "We believe his gang is now being led by the Crenshaw brothers, Jack and Miles, however. They're dangerous men, colonel." He hoped the colonel wouldn't ask how much they knew so much about the Crenshaws. "Morrow says they are likely in Dobytown, but we're unfamiliar with it."

"That name I do not know," the colonel said. He handed back the legal papers. The colonel's expression grew serious. "But if they are the type of men you say they are, being in Dobytown does not surprise me. But what brings you to my doorstep with this problem, gentlemen? I hope you know, given my mandate to keep settlers and supply routes safe from Indian attacks, I am stretched thin. Furthermore," he motioned to the papers Moses now held, "I don't see that you have the authority to pursue things further with Morrow in your custody."

"We've been given federal authority to pursue and capture Morrow *and* his gang, sir," Elijah stated.

It was now Moses's turn to shift uncomfortably as the colonel stared at his brother. "Mr. Barber, I am not sure the law will see it that way, especially with Morrow in shackles and only a few, fleeing, members of his gang remaining free." He scratched his beard. "But let's say I see it your way. What *can* I do for you?"

"We need to leave Morrow here, under your care, while we pursue the Crenshaws to Dobytown," Elijah said, his request direct. "We need to act fast before they slip away."

The colonel hesitated, weighing his words. "I'll agree to hold Morrow, but on one condition: You bring the Crenshaws to justice, and you do it without causing more trouble than it's worth. I don't need a war breaking out in my jurisdiction." He eyed them both. "You pay for his food, and you're back within a day or two to take him out of here. Frankly, gentlemen, my hands are full enough as it is."

Elijah nodded. "We appreciate your cooperation, Colonel."

The colonel leaned back in his chair. "You see, it's not just settlers and supply routes I have to worry about these days. Now I've got this railroad work and all the trouble it has the potential to cause. There's a significant gold shipment coming from the Denver Mint, bound eastward. It's crucial for Union Pacific's continued expansion, I'm told. I've got men that have gone west to meet it, and will swap out again here to get it to the end of track. We can't afford any distractions or unexpected complications."

"We won't be a bother to your work, colonel," Moses said.

Colonel Redford stood, signaling their time was up. "If I have to hang onto him longer than two days or get stuck dealing with him in some fashion, it won't go well for you. . . Not that I'm sure this will anyway."

"A fair bargain," Elijah said. "We'll be discreet and quick," he assured him. The brothers stood and shook the colonel's hand.

As they were about to leave, the colonel stopped them. "One more thing. Be careful in Dobytown. It's a lawless place, and these Crenshaws won't be easy to corner. General Sherman made a visit and called the whiskey he got served tanglefoot. . . and said that was the least objectionable part of the settlement. If the man who brought the South to its knees didn't want to be there, I should think you won't either."

ELIJAH STEPPED BACK OUTSIDE the headquarters building, the morning sun glinting off his badge. He pulled his slouch hat down as he marched toward the barracks. He didn't wait for Moses, who was a few steps behind.

Moses quickened his pace, catching up to Elijah. He reached out, grabbing his brother's shoulder and spinning him around. "This the part where you lecture your little brother for not taking things seriously?" he asked.

Elijah, taken aback, looked into Moses's eyes. He put his finger on the badge on Moses's chest. "You are a federally appointed agent of the law, and that man is an army colonel. At some point, you have to grow up."

Moses bristled, biting his tongue. When Elijah continued walking toward the barracks, Moses matched his stride and leaned close to his ear as he walked. "I'm gonna ignore that growing up part for the time being and ask if maybe you don't think I'm just tryin' to make sure we have people thinking as positive of us as possible." They reached the boardwalk in front of the barracks and paused. "We're gonna need all the allies we can get if we continue down this path."

"Are you not on board with my plan?" Elijah asked. He set his jaw and stared, unblinking, at Moses.

Moses threw his hands in the air and laughed. "Eli, I don't think there *is* a plan yet."

The debate escalated, their voices growing louder, while Moses's stance became more defensive, his eyes narrowing. Hobbs approached and coughed, drawing the brothers' attention. Nodding towards the barracks door, he pointed toward the other posse members standing outside, watching the argument unfold.

Elijah and Moses stopped their arguing, Moses stepping away from Elijah. Hobbs looked between them, Moses staring at Elijah and Elijah avoiding eye contact with both of them.

"What isn't there a plan for, Elijah?"

"I need to speak with both of you privately," Elijah said in a low voice.

"Tell him," Moses said. He then pointed to the remaining posse members. "Tell *them*."

"Mo, I'll have you show some respect to—"

"Dammit, Eli. This ain't the army no more. They ain't your soldiers." He pointed at the tin on his chest, then at Elijah's. "They gave us the same damn badge with the same damn mandate." He paused, gathered his composure, then spoke more measuredly. "Now we all follow you 'cause we respect you, and you're good at it, but by golly, Eli, earn it now."

Elijah stood before the group, his hat in hand, spinning it by the brim. The posse members looked on, concern on their faces.

"Morning, everyone," Elijah began, his voice steadier than he felt. "We've spoken with Colonel Redford. Nate Morrow will remain in their custody while we take a ride to Dobytown."

A murmur rippled through the group who thought that dried out and re-supplied, they would return to Omaha with Morrow. Elijah could feel their apprehension, their trust in him tested by the uncertainty of their mission.

"We have reason to believe the Crenshaw brothers, who've taken over Morrow's gang, are there," he continued. "That's what Morrow tells us at least."

"You believe him?" Clay asked without emotion. Big Sam nodded at Clay and then looked at Elijah with a raised eyebrow as if he wondered the same.

Elijah looked at them a moment. "I do, actually. I think he has been humbled by what happened to him but also realizes playing his cards right could keep him from the end of a rope. Maybe even allow him a second chance down the line."

Big Sam crossed his arms. Augusto leaned against a post, his expression unreadable but his eyes sharp. Clay nodded, accepting the plan with his usual quiet resolve. Maggie watched Elijah intently.

Moses spoke, bringing up something Elijah knew he had to but feared the response. "You all signed on to help us track down Morrow, and we did that," he said. "Elijah and I are going to do this, but anyone who doesn't want to can collect their pay and is assured their cut of the Morrow bounty."

Hobbs stepped forward. "Elijah, you do realize this is dangerous territory we're heading into, right? Morrow is already captured, and I don't know if the documents you carry authorize you to—"

Elijah met Hobbs's stare, understanding the unspoken implications. "I know what they say."

Hobbs scanned the group. "So, regardless of what happens in Dobytown, we're coming back here to escort Morrow to Omaha, right?"

Elijah hesitated, his eyes darting toward Moses. "Our focus now is on the Crenshaws," he said, avoiding a direct answer.

Hobbs bit his lip, looking from one brother to the other while shaking his head at the non-answer. "I'm going to see if I can get some decent breakfast in this damn place," he said and walked off.

"I will see to the horses," Augusto said.

Moses looked at Clay and Big Sam and spoke in a low voice. "You two hungry?"

"Starving," Sam said.

When Clay said nothing, Moses tipped his head toward Maggie, who had dropped down on a bench in front of the barracks and was staring blankly toward the parade ground.

"Yeah, I could eat too," Clay said. He joined the two men, Moses opening his eyes wide at Elijah and darting them toward Maggie as they walked away.

Elijah took a breath, gathering his thoughts, before he joined Maggie on the bench. He could sense her contemplation, her mind wrestling with the situation. She seemed to be in her own world, her gaze distant.

"Maggie," Elijah started, unsure how to broach the subject. "I just wanted to check in with you after everything that's happened."

She turned to him, a flicker of surprise crossing her face, replaced by a stoic mask. "I'm alright, Elijah," she replied. Her voice was steady, but her eyes betrayed a hint of vulnerability. "I knew what I was signing up for. . . more or less."

Elijah fiddled with the brim of his hat. "It's just that. . . shooting a man, it's not an easy thing. I didn't want you to think you're alone in this."

Maggie gave a small, humorless laugh. "Elijah, I may not have been in a shootout before, but I'm not some delicate flower. I can handle that." Her tone softened. "But thank you. . . for worrying about me."

They paused as they looked off into the distance, lost in their thoughts. Elijah sighed, and it drew a question from her.

"Do you ever think about the fact that you've killed people?" She continued to stare straight ahead.

Elijah dug a toe of his boot in the dirt and looked down at the ground. "Not all that often, honestly."

She continued to stare for a moment, then turned to him. "Does it bother you?"

He looked at her. "That I've done it, or that I don't think about it?"

"Either."

He touched the scar on his face, then pulled his hand away. "I think more about wanting to live a quiet life without always chasing someone, or looking over my shoulder, or wondering when Mo or I. . . or someone I care about gets killed." He picked a rock off the ground and tossed it, turning silent again.

"Elijah, what *have* I gotten myself into?" Maggie broke the silence, her voice steady. "I can't risk my father losing his last child, his last remaining family, yet here I am in the middle of this madness. But I can't turn my back now. Not on you, not on Moses, not on doing what's right." She looked at him. "It's what either of my brothers would have done and what my father would do were he a younger man."

Elijah's expression softened. "I know it's a lot. And I won't lie; it might worsen before it gets better."

Maggie's eyes searched his. She moved closer to him on the bench. "Maybe when this is over, I could take a more active role at the livery. Help grow my father's business. . . your business. Alongside you."

He knew the path he was on might not lead back to Omaha. "I'd like that," he said. As he had done countless times before, he allowed himself a moment to imagine a different, more peaceful life. He looked away. "I really would."

They sat in silence, each lost in their thoughts about the future and the risks ahead. Elijah knew he had given everyone the option not to go to Dobytown. Still, he hoped Maggie would continue to stand by their side. She had proven herself more than capable, and her presence was a steady comfort. He didn't want her to go, but he also would not change anything about his plans to keep her, or anyone else, by his side.

Eventually, Elijah stood up. "We should get ready." She smiled and looked into his eyes before standing as well. "You should get something to eat," he said. "And when you see Moses, tell him to make sure we are provisioned for any eventuality. He'll understand."

"Alright," she replied, pulling back from him a bit. She began to speak, then stopped, bit her lip, and looked away. She turned back and looked at him with wide eyes. "You aren't going to stop until you kill the Crenshaws, are you?"

She stepped to him, but he had already moved on from the conversation. "I'm going to check with the stockade once more, then meet you all at the stables."

Her smile faded as he walked away without another word.

CROSSING A LINE

— • —

E lijah stopped by the stockade, ensuring the guards were briefed on Nate Morrow's situation before departing. He wanted no misunderstandings or complications arising in his absence. After the brief but critical discussion, he managed to grab a quick bite, his thoughts on the journey ahead, but not knowing when he would eat a proper meal again.

Finishing his breakfast, Elijah sought out Augusto, who was busy preparing the horses. He needed the old tracker's expertise for their arrival in Dobytown.

"Ready to do some high-stakes horse trading, Augusto?"

"*Sí,*" he replied. "You would like to sell more?"

Elijah shook his head. "How about selling to men in rough places? Desperate men. Perhaps men who would listen to the advice of an old tracker who knows the West if he knew where they were heading."

Augusto grinned. "I can be this man for you, Elijah."

Elijah told him to select two of the sturdier horses they had acquired after the attack but hadn't traded to the fort. He then shook Augusto's hand and held his other hand on his shoulder. "I told everyone if they weren't in support of my plan, they did not have to come. You do not have to do this."

"I believe in you, Elijah. I have also not felt this alive and useful in years. . ." He trailed off, eyeing Elijah.

"But?" Elijah asked.

"But *I* have lived this life. . . I have only to gain, nothing to lose." He took his hand back from Elijah and headed for the stables.

As Elijah walked along the wooden planks in front of the fort's buildings, heading towards the barracks to grab his things, he thought deeply, planning their approach to Dobytown. Suddenly, he bumped into a man exiting the sutler's store. He began to apologize, then looked up to see who it was. To his surprise, it was Reverend Thomas from the railroad camp.

"Reverend Thomas," Elijah said, "I didn't expect to see you here."

The reverend's calm demeanor soothed Elijah's preoccupied state. "Elijah Barber. Our paths seem destined to cross in the most unexpected places."

Elijah was amazed that the man remembered his name and smiled.

"I'm just here picking up some supplies." Reverend Thomas explained, gesturing to some loaded crates. "The camp moved west, and there are some men with basic needs I hope to provide for them. But tell me, Elijah, how are you? You look like a man with the weight of the world on his shoulders. Or perhaps it is that badge weighing you down. Did you find the men you were searching for?"

"We did." Elijah rubbed his chin, deciding to spare the reverend most of the details. "Well, most of them at least." He gestured toward the stockade. "The ringleader, a wanted man, sits in a cell here."

Reverend Thomas looked toward the stockade. "Be sure of this: The wicked will not go unpunished, but those who are righteous will go free."

"Sounds like Proverbs," Elijah said.

"Very good." The reverend smiled briefly, but it faded as he studied Elijah. "You do not seem unburdened by your success."

Elijah hesitated, struggling to decide how much to share with the reverend. Though he respected the holy man and felt a sense of familiarity that reminded him of his father, he also wrestled with a reluctance to expose his deepest doubts and fears to the man.

"Reverend, I'm conflicted," Elijah admitted. "It's not just about capturing that man or finding the others who have continued on. It's. . . everything. Leading this group, my responsibility to my brother. . ." Elijah trailed off.

Reverend Thomas listened intently, his eyes reflecting a deep understanding. He waited a moment, then spoke. "Elijah, leadership isn't about having all the answers or making perfect decisions. It's about guiding others, helping them to be their best selves, even amidst uncertainty."

Elijah glanced toward Moses, who was talking with the rest of the posse. He pointed him out to the reverend. "Moses and I, we've been through a lot together. The war, becoming marshals to avoid poverty, and it turning into stopping a notorious outlaw. I always felt it was my job to look out for him, to lead the way." He touched the scar on his face. "I've only ever wanted to provide him a safe and normal life."

"And do you not think Moses is capable of being his own man?" the reverend probed. "Or that, perhaps for you two, this life *is* normal?"

Elijah considered this. "I know he is. But it's hard to let go and not feel responsible for every decision and outcome. And no, reverend, I don't find anything normal about this kind of life."

"Sometimes, Elijah, the best thing a leader can do is step back and allow others the space to grow, to make their own choices," Reverend Thomas advised. "Your brother may just want to be your partner and not feel like decisions aren't his own."

Elijah took in the reverend's words. As they prepared to part ways, he felt compelled to seek one final piece of guidance. "Reverend. . . We're about to step outside our mandate. Pursue justice in a way that might make us outlaws." He summarized the devastation caused by the Crenshaws and what the law had told him he could and could not do. What should I do?"

Reverend Thomas looked at Elijah, his expression thoughtful. "In the pursuit of justice, one must sometimes tread paths that are not clearly defined by the laws of man. Seek justice, Elijah, but let your conscience be your guide. Act in a way that, when you look back, you can say you did what was right, not just what was lawful."

The thinnest of smiles came to Elijah's face. "I'm not sure I expected that answer from a reverend."

The reverend gestured broadly toward the plains. "There aren't many of us living this life." He laughed as if suddenly struck by a joke. "Besides, who am I to tell Elijah and Moses what to do?"

Elijah chuckled. "Would you believe my parents were "Joseph and Mary?" They both laughed, and Elijah offered his hand, the reverend accepting it. "I thank you, Reverend Thomas. I am glad to have encountered you."

The reverend put a hand on Elijah's shoulder. "I wish you good health and safety, Elijah. I hope we have the opportunity to cross paths once again someday."

Elijah rejoined the posse, who were all set to depart. Moses approached him, his expression curious.

"Who was that you were talking with?" Moses asked.

"Oh, him? He's that reverend from the railroad camp," Elijah replied. He tried to sound casual despite the profound impact of their conversation.

Moses squinted slightly as if making a connection. "He looks just like Pa, don't he?"

Elijah paused, pretending to consider this for the first time. "Oh, I guess he does," he responded.

Moses informed Elijah that the group was all ready to go. Augusto had already set out, playing the role of the horse trader.

"Good," Elijah said. "You and I will ride in together and not hide who we are," he continued. "I'll have the rest of the group filter in as unnoticed as possible to check things out." Moses nodded. "What about *our* preparedness?"

"I got Maggie's message from you and think I deciphered it right. Packed some ammunition, new dry bedrolls, and a few days' worth of dried food and hardtack. Got a couple of new canteens too."

Elijah expressed his gratitude, appreciating his brother's efforts. Moses looked at him for confirmation. "I'm assuming that was just for you and me?" he asked.

"Hopefully it doesn't come to that." Elijah eyed Moses. "You are your own man, Mo. Decisions might need to get made, and I want you to make them *with* me."

Moses considered this, and Elijah thought he looked appreciative. "Alright, then."

Elijah surveyed the group, noting their readiness and determination. The moment was ripe with anticipation, tinged with the unknown dangers ahead. He stepped forward and addressed them.

"I appreciate everyone sticking with this," he said.

"I follow the boss," Sam said. Brutus barked, and Big Sam looked down at him. "And he follows his." The group shared a needed laugh.

"In too deep to quit now," Clay added quietly.

Elijah looked at Maggie, who offered him a brave face but said nothing else; he then looked at Hobbs.

"Dobytown, then Omaha?" Hobbs asked.

Elijah stared at him. "That's the desired plan, Matt."

Hobbs bit his lip and shook his head, clearly unhappy with the ambiguous answer. He swung aboard his horse. "Like our member from Dixie said, too deep to quit now."

Elijah climbed aboard Bear and gave the loyal mount a hearty pat on the neck. "Let's get to it, then."

With those words, Elijah led the group outside the fort's walls. Moses fell in beside Elijah and looked back toward the fort and then east for a long while.

"What are you lookin' at, Mo?"

He turned back to the front and then looked at Elijah. "Reckon I ought to say goodbye to civilization just in case. . . What little is out here."

Elijah said nothing, knowing they were crossing a line they might not return from. Dobytown was only two miles west, though and he had no intention of stopping now.

DOBYTOWN

——— ◆ ———

The mid-day sun beat down on Dobytown, its harsh rays hardening the mud-baked street. The buildings, an assemblage of the namesake adobe and mismatched wood, leaned like drunks in the heat. The air was rife with the pungent mix of unwashed bodies, horse manure, and cheap whiskey.

Having observed from a distance to give Augusto and the rest of their posse time to blend into the town's fabric, the brothers made their way through its heart. They passed gambling dens where hollow-eyed men threw their lives away on the turn of a card and a bordello where laughter rang hollow and sad. Every man Elijah saw carried a weapon, most rather openly.

They hitched Bear and Copper to a post outside a building that seemed to sum up the spirit of Dobytown, an unnamed saloon held together by faded wood planks and rusty nails.

The brothers stepped inside to near darkness. The air was smoky and stale, quiet, with the occasional laugh, loud voice, or scraping of wooden tables and chairs on the rough floor. The handful of patrons were a motley crew of the most hardened men Elijah had ever laid eyes on. Some paused to size up the newcomers and their badges.

They approached the weathered bar, where a haggard old man wiped a dirty cloth on an equally dirty glass. The bartender sized them up as they came closer.

"Lawmen, huh?" The bartender's voice was rough as gravel. He chuckled, setting the glass down. "Can't say we get your type 'round these parts often. 'Round here, folks prefer to forget there's such a thing as law."

Moses took another look around and leaned against the bar. "Decent crowd for mid-day, ain't it?"

The old man stroked the curly gray goat beard. "Reckon so. There ain't much honest daytime work in Dobytown if that's what you're gettin' at."

"Is there honest nighttime work?" Elijah asked.

The old man grinned, revealing multiple gaps where teeth should have been. "Ain't much of that either, marshal."

"Deputy marshal."

"Doubt it'll make a difference," he said. He leaned in, his voice dropping to a conspiratorial whisper. "You know, you two might just be the first law types to set foot in Dobytown. And I reckon that's 'cause nobody's ever wanted to be the last." Elijah and Moses shared a look.

"Whiskey," Moses said. "And any information you have on a horse trader who mighta came in today. Goes by the name Augusto."

The bartender poured two shots of something Elijah thought looked undrinkable. "Might be I've seen a feller like that. But info like that costs more than a couple of drinks."

Elijah slid a coin across the bar, his eyes never leaving the bartender's. "I'm not much of a drinker, but I'm willing to pay for what I need. Let's start with these and go from there."

Moses put his hand on the glass and then made eye contact with Elijah. When Elijah rolled his eyes, Moses hesitated. "Go on," Elijah said. He started to lift his own but set it down when he saw the grimace on Moses's face.

"That must be the tanglefoot General Sherman referred to," Moses said with a cough. "Lord almighty."

The old man cackled and then looked at Elijah, who was showing his impatience. The bartender's laughter trailed off into a wheezy cough, and he wiped his hands on a grimy apron. "Alright, marshal. What do you need to know?"

Elijah relaxed a bit. "Need to know if you've seen the horse trader."

The bartender scratched his unkempt beard, his eyes narrowing as he recalled. "The quiet Mexican fella with the weathered face and eyes like he's seen too much of this world?"

Moses, still coughing from the drink, cleared his throat. "Yeah, that's him."

"Yeah, he was here all right. Kept to himself mostly, asked a few questions, and listened more than he spoke. Had a way about him, like he knew more than he let on." He eyed them both. "He some kinda bandit? Horse thief?"

"He's got a way with horses you can say," Elijah answered. "Is he still around?" He sensed movement by the swinging door and caught Big Sam walking in out of the corner of his eye.

The bartender shrugged. "Might be. He didn't seem the type to linger, but then again, Dobytown has a way of keeping folks longer than they plan." He looked at Sam. "Be right with ya, friend."

"Don't let me interfere with the law," Sam said playfully. "Dumb as they are for being here," he mumbled. Elijah made a mental note to tell Sam not to lay it on so heavily.

The bartender turned back to them. "Last I saw, he was headed towards the tables back there, talking to some rough-looking characters. Chatted one of 'em up quite a bit then left with him."

They thanked the man, and Elijah tossed another coin on the bar. When the bartender turned his back to get a whiskey for Sam, the brothers passed by the big man. "Got all our eyes on the place," he whispered.

As the Barbers walked to the back, the bartender leaned close to Big Sam. "Them rough fellers in the back might not 'a noticed, but it's clear as day to me that you're working with them marshals."

Big Sam downed the whiskey without flinching and slammed the upended glass on the bar. "Well old man, you on our side if it gets ugly?"

The bartender squinted toward Elijah and Moses, who were approaching a table in the back corner. "They the good kinda law or the ugly kind?"

"They're the best kind."

The bartender downed a glass of whiskey himself and then reached under the bar. He smiled as the click of multiple cocking hammers floated up. "It's been a spell since we had some excitement 'round here."

Elijah and Moses approached the back corner, where two men sat at a table, their conversation low and guarded. The remnants of a card game were spread across the table, along with numerous empty glasses. As they got closer, one of the men—a burly figure with a scarred face—looked up, his eyes narrowing.

"You lost?" he growled. A hand inched toward the gun holstered at his side.

Elijah held his hands up slightly, showing he meant no harm. "Just looking for some information."

"Don't reckon you'll find it here," the other man said.

Moses stepped forward. "Heard a man named Augusto was here. Mighta sold some horses. We need to talk to him."

A tense silence fell over the table. The scarred man snorted, "Augusto, huh? Skedaddled a while ago. He had some nice horse flesh but was too rich for our blood—not for others, though." He grinned. Why are you interested in a horse trader? He steals 'em?"

"We just need to speak with him," Elijah said. He didn't like the tension in the room.

The men exchanged glances, and the scarred man spat on the floor. "Maybe he found better company," he sneered.

A back door opened, and all eyes moved toward it. Elijah squinted and thought he recognized the short, haggard-looking man pulling his braces back over his shoulders. "Woo-eee, fellas. You been next door to see them ladies? Anyhow, has that Mexican already left? My bosses want me to bring them a couple more—" He froze and stared at Elijah.

"Hey there, Wes." Elijah realized it was the short man who had duped them at the railroad camp. Wes's eyes widened as he recognized Elijah, and his hand moved slowly toward his revolver. "Easy now, Wes. We don't need any bad decisions made."

Moses's voice cut through the tension. "Nobody needs to get hurt here. I promise you we just need to talk."

Outside, Hobbs's voice echoed in through the open door. "Elijah, if you can hear me, I don't like how quiet it just got in there."

Elijah called back, not taking his eyes off Wes. "We're alright."

"Four more men outside, Wes," Moses added. He then jerked his head toward Sam. "The fella at the bar too." Big Sam smiled and touched the brim of his hat.

Wes's eyes darted around the room. "Liars."

Elijah's tone was firm. "No, it's the truth. It's over now, Wes. Your deception at the camp, all of it. You caused us one heck of a mess, but you're out of room to maneuver now." He took a step and saw Wes's hand move closer to his weapon. Elijah held his hand out. "I can promise you though, that we are far more interested in what you can tell us than taking you in."

Wes turned to the men at the table. "C'mon fellas. You gonna believe these corrupt lawmen, or you on my side? I'll make it worth your while."

The men at the table looked confused, their eyes moving from Wes to Elijah and Moses. Wes's desperation grew. "They're lying! Don't listen to them! They'll stretch my neck sure as the sun comes up tomorrow."

One of the men at the table moved his hand toward his belt, and Moses did the same with a raised eyebrow. "You sure you wanna find out if I'm quicker?"

Suddenly, Wes spun and headed for the back door. Elijah couldn't see who or what was outside, but he saw Wes freeze, then pull his revolver before hearing a shotgun blast and seeing Wes fall to the ground.

The men at the table stood and pulled their weapons, but Elijah and Moses pointed their guns at them first.

"Look at that; I *am* quicker," Moses said.

Elijah looked towards the back door, where Maggie now stood in view, her shotgun still smoking. Wes lay motionless on the floor, his body peppered with shot.

Elijah approached the table, his gun pointed toward the men. "Guns on the table." They complied, and Big Sam hurried from the bar and took them.

"What did that man tell you?" He gestured at Wes. "What do you know?"

Hobbs and Clay rushed in, guns drawn, and Moses held up a calming hand. They each scanned the scene, both giving shocked reactions when they saw Maggie standing over the dead man in the back.

"Is that the fella from the—"

Elijah cut Hobbs off. "Yes," he said, turning back to the table. "One of you better start talking, and maybe losing your weapons will be the worst thing that happens to you today."

The scarred man scoffed in defiance, but the other began to ramble. "I ain't a bad man, marshal. . . just a failure and a lousy gambler. That lieutenant from the fort. . . He was a lousy gambler, too, but a good man, I 'spose. I think he was just tryin' to get out from under it. . . I think he told that gang that rolled in here somethin' that bought off his debts." He looked at Elijah as if wondering whether he'd given enough information. He pointed a shaky finger at Wes. "That one was with them, real eager to buy fresh horses."

"What lieutenant?" Moses asked, stepping forward.

The man's eyes were closed, but he took a deep breath. "I think. . . Smith?"

Moses looked at Elijah. "Redford's twitchy aide?"

Elijah stood up and removed his hat, taking in the scene. He rubbed his forehead and pinched his thumbs between his eyes, then suddenly planted his hat back on his head before storming toward the door.

"What are you thinkin,' Eli?" Moses called after him.

"They're gonna hit that gold shipment."

ERUPTION

— ◆ —

The pounding hooves of Bear and Copper were the only sound as Elijah and Moses rode away from Dobytown, the two-mile journey back to Fort Kearny feeling longer than ever. Elijah's mind raced as he urged his horse on, torn between pushing the animal faster and fearing for its well-being under such a pace.

"I hope these horses can handle this," Elijah said loud enough to be heard.

Moses looked over. "We don't know this is imminent."

"We don't know that it isn't," Elijah responded.

Rapid hoofbeats approached from behind, and Hobbs caught up with them. "Elijah, what in blazes is your plan?" he shouted over the noise of their horses.

Elijah's eyes were fixed ahead, but his voice was clear and firm. "We're warning the fort, Matt. We can't let that gold shipment fall into the Crenshaws' hands."

Hobbs looked ahead, urging his horse to keep pace but giving no reply.

"Did you tell Maggie to cover that back door alone?" Elijah yelled.

Hobbs's eyes flashed with anger. "She did that on her own, Elijah!"

"And you just let her?" Elijah realized his shouting was a mixture of concern for Maggie and frustration with Hobbs.

The heated exchange was cut short as they reached the gates of Fort Kearny. Elijah was relieved to see Augusto waiting outside.

The guards quickly opened the gates, allowing them entry. They trotted towards the headquarters building, urgency driving their every move. As they dismounted, Elijah looked at Augusto, who seemed eager to speak. "The gold shipment?"

"*Sí*, I fear so," August replied.

Elijah beat his hat against his leg and headed up the steps of the headquarters building, Moses alongside him and Hobbs, trying to keep up. Elijah turned and saw Big Sam coming across the parade ground. "Need you for a moment, Sam."

Elijah stormed into the headquarters building, his boots thudding against the wooden floor with each purposeful stride. Moses and Hobbs followed, and Elijah turned to see Big Sam moving quickly to catch up.

With a nervous demeanor, Lieutenant Smith jumped up from his desk. "Can I help you with something?" he stammered.

"As a matter of fact, yes," Elijah replied. He didn't miss the hint of worry in Smith's eyes, which only fueled his burning suspicion. "Sam, can you bring the lieutenant along with us?"

Without waiting for a response, Elijah marched the group straight into Colonel Redford's office. The colonel looked up from his desk, his face hardening at the sight of Big Sam hauling his lieutenant by the collar.

"What on Earth happened?" Colonel Redford shouted.

Elijah stepped forward, his expression grim. "Colonel, we need to talk. Now." He glanced at Big Sam, who tightened his grip on Lieutenant Smith and pushed him forward.

Redford's eyes narrowed. "Explain yourselves. This is highly irregular."

"We've just come from Dobytown, sir," Elijah began. "We've un-covered something you need to know about the gold shipment." Red-ford stared at Elijah a moment, then looked at Moses.

Moses turned toward Elijah as if he hoped his brother was right. "Sir, we think the Crenshaws are planning to hit the shipment." Elijah was glad at Moses's use of the word *we*.

Redford's expression shifted from anger to disbelief. "The Cren-shaws? The ones who had been with Morrow? Do you have proof?"

Elijah pointed at Lieutenant Smith. "We believe your lieutenant here might shed some light on this situation."

Smith's face paled as all eyes in the room turned to him. He tried to speak, but his voice came out a whisper. "I. . . I don't know what they're talking about, colonel."

Redford gave a look of annoyance. "Deputies," he began. He ad-dressed both of them but was looking squarely at Elijah. "I will not pretend to understand the full depth of what you are trying to do here, but I have seen the paperwork that you were tasked only with capturing Nate Morrow. He sits in my stockade, and I gave you a day before I wanted no more part of it." He sighed and inspected them once more. "I have had enough of all this."

Elijah's stare was unyielding. "Sir, you must listen. We have reason to believe that Lieutenant Smith has been providing information to the Crenshaws or their associates about the shipment. He's been com-promised."

The room fell silent as Redford stared at his aide. "Is this true, Lieutenant?"

Smith's eyes darted around the room, and his voice trembled when he spoke. "I was in debt. . . some folks offered me a way out if I had information about the escort. I didn't think they would actually. . ."

Redford's fist slammed onto the desk, his face turning a shade of crimson. "Dammit, Lieutenant. You jeopardized a crucial military operation for your debts?!" He turned to Elijah and Moses. "I'll deal with him. What do you need from me?"

"We need to warn and plus up the escort before anything happens," Elijah said.

Redford's expression was now one of determination. "I'll send word immediately. We'll fortify the escort. You did well to bring this to my attention, but you must understand our resources are stretched thin. A team just rode out to meet the shipment for an escort swap. Only a handful of soldiers are accompanying it to the fort for rest and re-supply before continuing to the railroad with more men."

Elijah grimaced. "That means for a few miles, the shipment is lightly defended."

"Exactly," Redford confirmed. "It has to be the Crenshaws' plan." He looked at Lieutenant Smith with disdain. "Being that they have such information."

Elijah looked at Moses, who shook his head. "Don't have time for you to muster troops," Elijah said to Redford. "We'll go now; you prepare men in case—"

"I understand, Captain." Elijah flinched at the mention of his old rank but knew the colonel was acknowledging his experience.

At that moment, Hobbs appeared in the office, his badge visible. Redford's eyes lit up. "Finally, the Pinkerton. I was told you'd be part of the escort from the fort to the railroad, but we're in a bit of a mess here."

Redford introduced Elijah and Moses to Hobbs, unaware of their prior acquaintance. The tension in the room grew as Hobbs and the Barbers exchanged knowing glances.

Disregarding the introduction, Elijah asked, "When did the escort leave?"

"Not long ago at all," Redford replied.

Without another word, Elijah stormed out of the office, followed by Moses, Big Sam, and Augusto. Hobbs trailed behind. Outside, they began mounting up.

Elijah, his voice laced with disdain, turned to Hobbs. "Can you handle organizing a response force with the soldiers here? You came to protect gold apparently, so protect it."

"Listen, Elijah, I—"

"Save it, Matt. You knew this shipment was happening and what Morrow's group or the Crenshaws were capable of. You didn't think that might be something Mo and I should've known?"

Hobbs opened his mouth to explain, but Elijah cut him off. "Just do your job, Matt."

Elijah rounded up the rest of the posse—Moses, Sam, Clay, Augusto, and Maggie. He paused, looking at Maggie. "Are you up for this?" The memory of the incident in Dobytown was still fresh. As a leader, he needed every gun, but he also felt a need to protect her and was unsure how she would react after killing a man.

"I'm ready," Maggie said. "I'm fine."

She conveyed a look to Elijah that led him to believe her. "Good," was all he could muster. He wondered if leaving Hobbs here but bringing her was more of an effort to put Hobbs in his place, but he put it out of his mind. She'd shown she could use her weapon, and he would keep her close at hand. With a yell to Bear, Elijah rode out hard, the posse following closely.

Moses rode up alongside Elijah, with Bear and Copper practically touching yet never interfering with each other. "They'll have a distraction; then the shooting will start."

Elijah reached up to secure his hat from their quickening pace. "It'll come from multiple directions and center on the wagon." He was silent momentarily, then turned and looked at the group behind him. "Need you to lead them if anything happens, and I'll work with the soldiers. Ain't any of them ever been in a fight like what this will look like, I fear."

"Let's pray it don't come to that," Moses said.

"Amen," Elijah muttered.

The tension was palpable as they neared the escort, the four soldiers looking wary as the posse approached. In the distance, the wagon could be seen coming, escorted by just two outriders.

Confused but defiant, the major leading the escort listened to Elijah's urgent explanation with skepticism. "I don't take orders from marshals," he finally retorted. He looked up at Elijah's slouch hat. "Or captains."

"I'm not trying to order you around, Major..."

"Harlan," the major replied dismissively.

"Major Harlan," Elijah continued. He did his best to sound deferential. "I'm trying to prevent a blood bath."

The major shook his head and removed a spyglass from his saddlebag. Looking toward the wagon, his tone was exasperated as he spoke to Elijah. "Let's not make something out of nothing, deputy." The group all fell silent, the only sound that of the labored breathing of the posse's horses and the faintest creaking of the approaching wagon. "We can handle the two miles back to the fort."

Elijah's jaw tightened as he watched the major's dismissive gaze return to the spyglass. The wagon, framed by the vast open prairie, inching closer. The sun, hanging high and harsh in the sky, cast a relentless glare over the scene. A knot formed in Elijah's stomach, the sense of impending doom growing stronger with each passing second.

Suddenly, the ground beneath them seemed to shudder, a violent eruption shattering the stillness of the landscape.

COLLISION

— • —

The explosion tore through the serene prairie landscape with great force. A deafening roar engulfed Elijah's senses, the blast reverberating through the ground and air. The previously clear sky was now a swirl of smoke, dirt, and fire, leaving a crater on the trail and obstructing the wagon from view.

Elijah struggled to maintain control of Bear, the ordinarily stoic horse rearing in panic at the sudden and violent noise. Around him, the rest of the posse grappled with their mounts, the animals spooked and skittish. Major Harlan, caught off guard, spurred his horse forward in a desperate bid to reach the wagon, its fate unknown behind the cloud of smoke.

"Major, wait!" Elijah's voice was lost in the din. He knew the major's reaction was what the attackers would want—a hasty charge into an ambush.

Elijah turned and eyed his posse. Moses had controlled Copper and moved among the group, helping them calm their animals. Maggie, who had been around horses since childhood, had fared better in the task than the rest of the men.

Moses turned to Elijah. "Boy, they don't train them West Point fellers up very well, do they?"

Elijah marveled at his brother's ability to always have a smart comment. He spun Bear in a circle, eyeing the terrain. "That stand of trees, to the north, and the dip in the terrain to the south. . ." Elijah pointed to each location and then locked eyes with Moses. "I want to ride like hell to that wagon and have a line of fire in both directions. Maggie and Clay with me, Sam, and Augusto, you're with Mo."

Elijah spurred Bear into a gallop, closing the gap as the major and his men raced towards the inferno. His eyes scanned the horizon, searching for any sign of the Crenshaws or their men. The landscape was a blur of movement, and he soon realized that the wagon, while not burning, had tipped over either from the blast or the frantic struggle of the frightened animals.

As Elijah rode around the crater and through the wall of black smoke, he saw the wagon. A driver lay crushed underneath, his screams for help piercing the air, while one of the outriders attempted to free him, his efforts frantic and futile. The other outrider was struggling to free trapped and wounded animals, their whinnies of pain and fear adding to the noise.

Major Harlan began to direct his men to dismount and help, but Elijah shouted over the din, "We can't help them yet! Perimeter first!" His voice was urgent, his eyes scanning the surroundings for any sign of the attackers.

The major, taken aback by Elijah's command, started to retort when the sharp crack of a rifle split the air a fraction of a second before the impact. The major jerked violently, a shocking spray of blood erupting from his head as he was thrown from his horse.

The posse froze for a split second, horror and realization dawning in their eyes. Elijah's heart pounded in his chest, adrenaline coursing through him as he shouted, "Where is he, Clay?" He knew they had to move quickly to avoid being sitting ducks.

"We need to be in front of or to the south of the wagon," Clay shouted.

As they dismounted and scrambled for cover, a second shot rang out, and one of the soldiers fell. "Damn it, everyone get down," Elijah yelled.

A great shout came from the stand of trees near the dip in terrain Elijah had identified. "Here they come," Moses shouted. He levered a round into his Winchester as Elijah did the same. Sam and Augusto chambered rounds into the old Spencers. Clay bolted for the crater in the trail, sliding in, then raising his Sharps rifle over the edge.

The two remaining men from the army escort gave Elijah a frightened look, and he realized he was now in command.

Moses shouted. "I see 'em coming from the trees."

"Same over here," Elijah yelled."

"Too late to go meet 'em, Eli."

Elijah agreed. "Everyone hand your reins to Maggie." He gave her a stern but caring look. "You're the best one to keep these critters calm, and that scattergun won't cut it." Everyone handed off their reins, and she stood inside the circle of horses, doing her best to keep them close.

Seven riders attacked with a fierce intensity, three from the south and four from the north, emerging from the cover of the terrain like specters of death. Elijah kept his eyes on the riders from the south, his hands steady on his rifle.

Two bullets slammed into the wagon with a thud, followed by a third that took out one of the outriders. A draft horse attached to the front of the wagon let out a sickening cry as it was hit, its enormous body thudding to the ground.

"Hold a moment longer," Elijah called out to his posse, his voice calm amidst the maelstrom. "Pick a rider and fire on my mark."

The posse waited, tensed for action. Elijah, Moses, Augusto, and Big Sam steadied their repeating rifles while the soldiers aimed their Springfields, ready to follow Elijah's lead. Clay, lying prone with his Sharps rifle, scanned the landscape, his eyes narrowed.

"Now!" Elijah shouted, and a volley of gunfire erupted from their position. Elijah saw one of the riders go down, hit by a well-aimed shot. Moses called out, "Got one here!" signaling another attacker had fallen on his side. Then, the distinct crack of Clay's Sharps rifle rang out, and yet another man fell from his horse.

Realizing their charge had faltered, the attackers rallied and retreated a distance, regrouping outside rifle range. Elijah quickly surveyed the situation, his heart pounding in his chest. The scene near the wagon was gruesome - the crushed man and the rider who had tried to help him both lay dead. One of the animals pulling the wagon lay motionless.

Augusto grimaced and attempted to slide closer to the wagon, a great deal of blood soaking through his trousers. His face contorted in pain, but his eyes were alert, watching for any further movement from the attackers.

Elijah looked at the man grimly. "Bad?"

Augusto gritted his teeth. "I will not walk on it again, but I can still shoot."

Elijah's mind raced as he assessed their position. They were exposed and vulnerable. The attackers could regroup and strike again at any moment. "How many came on your side, Mo?"

"Four," came his quick reply. "One down, another hit."

"We had three. . ." Elijah trailed off. "One down."

A heavy silence followed, broken only by the labored breathing of men and horses and the cries of the injured. Big Sam glanced at the brothers, crouched low, weapon at the ready. "They're not done yet," he said, a note of certainty in his voice. "They'd want more men for such a job, even without counting on us being here."

Elijah and Moses looked at each other, both scanning the surroundings. Moses's voice was low, almost a whisper. "Did you see them, Eli?"

"No. Not yet."

Another yell shattered the tense quiet. From his vantage point, Clay called out, "Two coming hard from the west!"

Without a word, Elijah climbed aboard Bear, pulling the reins from Maggie as Moses also made the connection and struggled to climb aboard Copper quickly. Elijah's face was set in a hard, unyielding mask, eyes burning with a deep, visceral hatred for the Crenshaws. He had not just the desire to stop the attack but an intense personal vendetta against the men he believed responsible for so much loss. He spurred Bear into a gallop, heading westward, his entire demeanor broadcasting a silent, fierce resolve.

As they rode out, everyone realized that the Crenshaws were likely the two riders leading this final charge. Maggie stood with one hand on the jittery horse's reins and took Augusto's rifle, trading him the shotgun as the posse tightened their formation, readying themselves for the confrontation.

Elijah and Moses charged across the open prairie, their horses' hooves drumming a furious rhythm on the hard-packed earth. Now a glaring orb in the sky, the sun cast long shadows of the four riders as they hurtled towards each other.

Elijah's eyes locked onto the older Crenshaw, a man whose face was etched in his memory. He saw an evil grin spread across the outlaw's face, the same twisted smile he had seen years ago when William Jones fell and when Abigail was gunned down. Elijah's grip on his rifle tightened, a comforting weight in his hands.

Moses glanced at Elijah. Was there a plan, or were they hurtling headlong into the attack? Elijah offered no sign, his focus laser-sharp on the brothers ahead.

The distance between them closed rapidly, the thunderous sound of the horses echoing across the open field, now joined by gunfire near the wagon. Bear and Copper, loyal and fierce, pushed forward, their breaths coming in labored heaves. Elijah felt a pang of concern for Bear, pushing the loyal animal to his limits.

Elijah's world seemed to narrow to this moment as they neared—two sets of brothers, driven by hate and revenge, hurtling toward each other at breakneck speed.

Just when it seemed they would collide, Elijah raised his rifle, and the Crenshaws veered sharply, splitting wide to either side. Acting on instinct, he fired, but his shot went wide. Beside him, Moses fired a split-second later, and Miles flinched. Elijah spun his head in time to see Moses had been hit in the shoulder but stayed upright in his saddle.

Elijah yanked hard on the reins to swing Bear around, and as he did, a loud thud echoed through the air. Bear let out a distressing cry, and Elijah felt the world lurch as his faithful horse crumpled beneath him, a horrifying whinny of pain filling the air.

Elijah's world spun as he lay on the ground, the skirmish swirling around him. His ears rang, muffling the sounds of gunfire and horses. Through blurred vision, he saw Moses clutching his left arm, pain on his face, but still upright and fighting. Around the wagon, a deadly dance unfolded as Sam, Maggie, and Clay returned fire, repelling the attackers who charged and retreated like waves against a stubborn shore.

The pained cries from Bear brought Elijah back to a clarity of thought, the realization that Bear was suffering, hitting him like a physical blow. His loyal companion, who had been with him through thick and thin, was now in agony. Bear was the one constant in a life that had often teetered on the brink of poverty and despair, the one nice thing he had held onto when everything else seemed bleak.

For a moment, time seemed to stand still. Elijah crawled to Bear, his movements sluggish with shock and grief. He placed a trembling hand on the horse's neck, feeling the labored breaths and the warm blood that coated his fingers. "Thank you, Bear," he whispered, his voice cracking with emotion.

With a heavy heart, Elijah drew his revolver. His hand was steady despite the turmoil within. He owed Bear this final mercy. Closing his eyes, he placed the muzzle against the faithful horse's head and pulled the trigger.

Elijah's heart ached as he rose, picking up his rifle with a solemn determination. The battlefield around him was a blur of motion and violence, yet his mind focused on survival and the task at hand.

Moses's voice pierced through the air just as Elijah stood. "Eli! The sniper!"

Elijah's instincts kicked in. His mind raced, trying to recall the direction of the initial sniper shot. He lunged behind Bear's lifeless body, seeking whatever cover his fallen companion could provide. A shot rang out, the bullet slapping into Bear's body. He was in the sniper's sights.

Peering cautiously from his makeshift cover, Elijah scanned the horizon. Then he saw them – the Crenshaw brothers, charging towards him. Whether they got the gold was still in flux, but they appeared to want to finish off the Barbers regardless.

As Elijah crouched behind Bear's body, he weighed his dire options. Rising to face the Crenshaws meant exposing himself to the sniper's deadly aim, yet staying down would leave him defenseless against their imminent charge. His mind raced, calculating every possible move.

That's when Moses, grim-faced and resolute, spurred Copper into a daring charge. His left arm hung low, a weak grip on his reins, his revolver clenched in his right hand, as he made himself a smaller target in the saddle. Elijah watched, heart in his throat, as Moses fired at the Crenshaws, his shot hitting the younger Miles again, who reeled but remained in his saddle.

Suddenly, Big Sam thundered past Moses and the Crenshaws, heading straight for the sniper's position with a barking Brutus at his heels. Riding like a man possessed, Sam raised his Spencer rifle and fired. He worked the lever with practiced ease, firing a second and then a third time, his eyes locked on the sniper's hidden location.

Elijah's attention was torn between the converging threats. He saw the sniper shift from behind a tree, lining up a shot at the oncoming Sam. Both men fired almost simultaneously. The sniper's body jerked and fell from behind the tree, but at the exact moment, Sam jolted upright in his saddle. It looked like he had triumphed for a fleeting second, but then he slumped, falling to the ground as his horse continued its wild run. Brutus was instantly at Sam's side, barking a loud, frantic alarm.

The Crenshaws spurred their horses into a hasty retreat, their last two men attempting to follow. Pushing through his pain, Elijah stood up and limped toward the wagon. His eyes caught Moses rushing to Big Sam's side, dismounting with urgency to kneel beside the fallen man. He scanned for any further threats even as he checked on Sam.

Elijah's eyes shifted to the remaining attackers, watching as Clay, with precise aim, took down one of the riders. Desperate to escape, the other turned his horse to join the fleeing Crenshaws. As the rider raised his gun to take a parting shot at Elijah, a sharp crack pierced the air. The man jerked and tumbled from his saddle, a lifeless heap on the ground.

Turning towards the source of the shot, Elijah saw Maggie near the wagon, her rifle barrel smoking. She ejected the spent cartridge with a calm efficiency, her hands steady and eyes full of intensity.

Stillness fell over the battlefield, the Crenshaws disappearing to the west, out of rifle range. Moses looked toward Elijah, a silent question in his eyes as he began to mount Copper, ready to give chase. Elijah raised a hand, signaling him to wait. The only sound was the grass swaying in the breeze and the horses nickering nervously, wandering without their riders or minders.

Elijah's gaze lingered on Sam's motionless form, Brutus still at his side, before looking back at Moses, who only shook his head. Their pursuit of the Crenshaws would have to wait. Now was a time for reflection and to tend to their wounded and fallen. The cost of their quest for justice was becoming painfully clear.

***

THE BELEAGUERED POSSE made their way back to Fort Kearny in silence. As they approached, a response force assembled, soldiers moving with urgency.

Upon seeing them, Colonel Redford paused mid-command, his eyes widening. The sight of Big Sam's lifeless body draped across a horse alongside the major and another of his soldiers brought shock to his face. "My God," he murmured under his breath.

Clay helped a grimacing Augusto down from his horse. Augusto, despite his pain, managed a brave face. "Just a shot of whiskey before the cutting starts," he joked weakly to a nearby soldier.

Another soldier noticed Moses's arm and approached to help. Moses, ever the stoic, allowed himself to be led away, though not without a loud declaration. "This arm ain't comin' off."

Elijah dismounted from the horse he had used for the return journey, his heart aching as much as his body. He stared westward, his face blank.

Colonel Redford approached him. "What now?" he asked.

Elijah turned, his face set in determination. "You'll need some men and animals to get that wagon upright, but the gold's all there, Colonel." He shifted his weight, grimacing. "I'm fine," he said in response to Redford's look of concern. There are more bodies out there."

"The Crenshaws?"

Elijah's response was cold, with a hard edge to his voice that matched the steely look in his eyes. "No, Colonel, unfortunately, theirs are the only ones *not* out there."

There was no need for further explanation; his tone and the grim set of his jaw said everything. The look he gave Colonel Redford was resolute, a silent vow that this wasn't the end.

LIFE LEFT BEHIND

— ∘ —

E lijah stood motionless in the dimly lit room of Fort Kearny's medical building; his eyes fixed on Big Sam's sheet-covered form. Brutus sat nearby, his head bowed as if understanding the finality of the scene before him.

In the background, the sounds of the fort ebbed and flowed—a distant reminder of life continuing outside these walls. But within, time seemed to stand still, punctuated only by the occasional muffled groan from other rooms. Moses's wound, a too-close call at his upper arm and shoulder, had just been dressed, and the frightening proximity to his chest left Elijah grappling with a silent terror. Just moments ago, the harrowing screams from Augusto's amputation had ceased, the man likely succumbing to unconsciousness under the surgeon's saw.

Elijah's thoughts were a whirlwind of self-reproach and grim determination. The cost of their pursuit laid bare before him: Ike, Big Sam, Augusto, all casualties of a path he had chosen. And Moses, his brother, his constant, now lying wounded. No amount of gold recovered, no bounty on Nate Morrow, could ease the weight on his conscience. The Crenshaws, the very source of this escalating spiral of violence, still loomed large in his mind.

Lost in his solitude, the soft sound of movement behind him barely registered until Maggie approached. Her presence was like a sudden ray of light in the oppressive gloom of the room. Her eyes met his, and Elijah searched for words but found none that could bridge the chasm of emotion that lay between them.

Maggie studied Big Sam Donovan's lifeless form and then turned to Elijah. "Are you alright?"

"He's dead because of me," Elijah muttered.

She shook her head. "That's not true, Elijah."

"No. He thought he had something to prove to me, and sacrificing himself to end this pursuit was his way of doing that."

"And so you'll blame yourself for Ike, too?" She said.

"And Augusto. That damn major and one of his men." He turned away. "Even Moses is now wounded."

"Perhaps they all just saw the goodness in your quest and chose to follow you."

He gave a sad-sounding laugh. "There's no goodness left in this."

Maggie's eyes softened with empathy. "But there's a reason you can't let it go, Elijah. And I think it's because you believe there's still a chance to do what's right, even when the path is dark."

Elijah looked at her. "Sometimes I'm not sure who I've become." He stared at Sam's body a moment, then back at Maggie.

She began to reply, but they were interrupted when two men entered the room with a wooden box to attend to Big Sam's body. Stepping outside, they continued their discussion under the vast, open skies. Elijah patted his leg, and Brutus reluctantly followed.

Maggie reached out, taking Elijah's hand in hers. Her words were heavy with unspoken emotion. "I have to go back. Someone must be there to rebuild the livery, to be there for my father."

Elijah opened his mouth to speak, but she stopped him with a gentle gesture. "Don't make promises you can't keep," she said softly, the implication clear in her eyes. She knew the choice he would make.

She leaned forward and embraced him. For a fleeting moment, his worries seemed to vanish, swallowed by the warmth of her embrace. She was the first woman who had ever entirely accepted him for who he was. Then, the moment was broken by Moses, clearing his throat as he approached them, his arm in a sling.

"Sorry to interrupt," Moses said. "I'm still among the living. They want me to keep the arm in a sling to keep the wound from opening up." He gave Maggie a polite smile and then turned to Elijah. "Otherwise, I'm ready for my captain's orders."

Elijah gave a nod, acknowledging his brother's resilience. "We need to check on Augusto."

Moses shook his head. "Resting now. Doc had to take the leg awful high up but said he's got a good chance."

Elijah stuck his slouch hat back on his head. "We better go talk to Redford, then." He looked to Maggie, ready to excuse himself, and she waved him on.

As the brothers walked toward the headquarters building, Moses turned back to Maggie for a moment and then looked at Elijah. "I'd say what I just saw portended us returning to Omaha, but I know that ain't gonna be it."

"I can either let her, or the Crenshaws, get away, Mo."

Moses whistled. "Maybe don't say it to her that way."

"She knows."

They walked in silence, the dirt and gravel crunching beneath them. "Sam say anything before he died?" Elijah asked.

Moses shook his head. "Dead when he hit the ground." He stared at his brother for a moment. "I know you, Eli, and I know you're going to punish yourself for this, but Sam Donovan was just a good soldier putting the mission before his personal safety."

"Maybe so," Elijah said. They arrived outside Colonel Redford's office, and he hurried up the stairs. Redford looked up as they entered, his face a mask of exhaustion and concern.

"Elijah, Moses," Redford greeted, his voice tired. "I just got the report on the wagon. The gold is secured now, thanks to you. I'm very sorry about your men, but you have our thanks."

Elijah sat and produced his pipe, relishing the long overdue moment to enjoy the comforting habit. He spoke as he began to pack and light it. "You're welcome, colonel, but I assume you know that other than stopping the men who attempted to take it, I care very little about that gold."

Colonel Redford leaned back in his chair, studying them. "I've been thinking about your situation. You've done more than anyone could have expected. Nate Morrow is in custody; the gold is safe. Those Crenshaw boys are alone and headed for the middle of nowhere. . . You said one of them is wounded too. Might be that it's time to consider this mission completed."

Elijah's jaw tightened. "The Crenshaws are still out there, Colonel."

"Don't count a pair of determined brothers out just because they're alone and injured," Moses added.

Redford said, "I know you feel you need to see this through. But you're treading a fine line, Elijah. If you leave Nebraska territory in pursuit, I can't promise the law will see it your way. . . if they ever could have to begin with." He rubbed his beard. "Right now, however, I believe you'd still be in the right."

Moses turned, his eyes meeting his brother's. "We understand," Elijah said. He puffed on his pipe for a moment. "Our man Augusto?"

Redford's eyes softened. "Augusto will get the care he needs here, a small gesture for his sacrifice. As for the rest of your outfit. . ."

Elijah spoke up. "Moses and I will head west. Augusto told us about Julesburg before his operation. Just inside Colorado territory. Says it's even more violent and lawless than Dobytown, and there's potential money to be made with the railroad coming. It's likely where the Crenshaws are headed."

"I'll arrange for Detective Hobbs to escort the gold and Morrow to the railroad with your remaining group. But as for you two and the dog," Redford added, looking at Brutus, who had entered the room, "you're on your own." He stared intently at each of them.

Elijah looked down at the tin on his chest and plucked it off his coat. "I reckon we are." Moses hesitated and then did the same before they each laid their badges on the desk as they stood. "You'll see that our group's efforts in capturing Morrow are recognized and that anything else is put on us?"

Colonel Redford narrowed his eyes and then gave a slight grin. "If a little extra paperwork keeps me out of trouble and gets your people taken care of, I'd be happy to." He shook each of their hands. "Good luck, gentlemen."

———

THE EARLY EVENING SUN cast long shadows across Fort Kearny as Elijah and Moses prepared to leave. Their mission didn't allow for delay, even after the day's harrowing events. They checked the supplies, ensuring they had enough provisions, ammunition, and food. Copper and three horses obtained during the fight were saddled and ready, their packs secured. The mood was somber as Maggie and Clay gathered to wish them goodbye.

"Can't thank you enough for everything you've done," Elijah said. He and Moses stepped forward and shook the southerner's hand.

"Was a pleasure to serve with you," Clay replied. Pausing momentarily, Elijah thought the man appeared as if the moment called for him to say more than usual. "Omaha thanks you, and I'll be sure to let people know the lengths you went to for justice."

Elijah bit his lip, uncomfortable with the praise in light of what he said next. "Will you be sure Ike's wife gets his cut of the bounty?"

"I'll see to it myself," Clay responded.

Hobbs approached just as Elijah was about to speak to Maggie, and she gave him a knowing look. Elijah pulled him aside. "Thanks for agreeing to oversee Morrow's transport and help ensure Clay and Maggie make it back to Omaha safely," Elijah said, extending his hand.

Hobbs accepted the handshake, a solemn look on his face. "About before, Elijah, I—"

Elijah cut him off. "You were doing your job as the Pinkertons and the railroad saw fit. I don't know that anything different would have happened if we had known. . . but I just thought we could trust each other more than that."

Hobbs's eyes reflected a deep regret. "I'll make sure they get back."

Elijah turned to see Maggie standing a short distance away. He walked over to her, his heart heavy. She reached out, taking his hand in hers. "I'll say it again Elijah Barber: Don't make any promises you can't keep," she said, her eyes glistening.

Elijah looked at her for a long moment, gathering the courage to speak. He looked down at the ground, then back up at her. "I have to do this," he managed.

She shook her head rapidly and wiped away tears. "Go find your peace, Elijah."

Elijah and Moses mounted their horses, Brutus at their side, the pack horses trailing close behind. As they rode through the fort's gates, the last rays of sun cast a golden hue over the landscape, the vast unknown prairie stretching out before them. Elijah glanced back one last time, seeing the sun dipping below the horizon behind them, its light fading like the life they were leaving behind.

In that fading light, a solemn truth settled over Elijah. With the shedding of their badges and embracing this pursuit, they had stepped beyond the bounds of the law they once upheld, venturing into a gray expanse where justice would come only by their own hands. This path marked a point of no return, a journey into a realm where right and wrong blurred and where each step forward bound them ever more tightly to a future they could no longer escape. The brothers rode on, silhouettes against the dying light, crossing the threshold.

A Visitor

— ◆ —

The early evening air was brisk, a coolness that surprised Elijah as he and Moses rode away from Dobytown, having briefly stopped to ensure the Crenshaws weren't there. The sun, a fiery orb sinking into the horizon, cast an eerie glow over the vast prairie landscape stretching out before them. The silence between the brothers was profound; each lost in their thoughts, haunted by the day's events and the journey ahead.

As the last light of the day faded, Moses broke the silence. "Eli," he began, his voice tinged with exhaustion, "I know Augusto said it'd be a three or four-day ride to Julesburg if we didn't find them first. But soon, we won't see a thing in this darkness."

Elijah considered his brother's words, the memory of Augusto's warning echoing in his mind. If they didn't catch the Crenshaws beforehand, Julesburg was at least three days away, and that was if they ignored the health of their horses. After losing Bear, Elijah wasn't keen on risking another mount.

He pondered whether the Crenshaws had stopped in Dobytown for their spare horses or lit out straight from the skirmish at the gold wagon. Perhaps they weren't even moving west. The uncertainty gnawed at him; they could be just behind the Crenshaws or chasing shadows.

"Alright," Elijah conceded. "We'll stop at the next decent spot to camp." He looked down at Brutus, who had caught back up after one of his occasional forays after a rabbit or other small creature. "I can't believe he keeps up."

Moses looked at the dog with a mournful face. "He knows Sam would want him to be with us."

Their camp that night was a humble affair – a small fire, just enough to ward off the night's chill and heat their meager dinner. The brothers sat in silence in a stand of scrubby trees just north of the Platte, the crackling fire punctuating the vast emptiness around them. Elijah's eyes occasionally swept the dark horizon, a habit born of a lifetime spent in uncertain situations.

With the first light of dawn, they broke camp. Elijah observed Moses wince as he prepared the horses and climbed into his saddle. As they rode on, the tension between them was palpable. It wasn't a tension of disagreement over their course of action but rather a deep, unspoken acknowledgment of what this journey meant for their lives going forward.

Moses's riding posture was not that of his usual cavalry-trained demeanor. Elijah couldn't help but feel a twinge of guilt for dragging his brother into this, for the pain Moses was enduring, and for the uncertain future they were riding into.

Around mid-day, Elijah paused to wipe the sweat from his brow, taking in the desolate terrain surrounding them. The land was a vast expanse of prairie stretching under the relentless sun. The only feature breaking things up was the Platte River, a meandering ribbon of life in the otherwise empty landscape.

The terrain was rugged and unwelcoming. Sparse vegetation dotted the landscape, offering little shade or comfort. The occasional rustle of a small animal or the distant cry of a hawk were the only interruptions to the overwhelming silence. The sun beat down, casting a harsh light that created a shimmering haze in the distance.

"Maggie asked me if I ever thought about the people I've killed," Elijah said unprompted. He didn't know why he brought it up and wondered if Moses would even want to discuss such a thing.

Moses turned his head. "What'd you tell her?"

Elijah scratched at the stubble on his face, unable to remember the last time he shaved. "That I don't really ever think about the actual killing part." They rode in silence for a moment. "Then she asked if that bothered me."

"The killing or the not thinking about it?"

Elijah snorted. "That's what I asked."

"Sounds about right." Moses looked at Elijah. "Bothers me a lot," Moses said.

The conversation trailed off into silence, the brothers content to let the vastness of the prairie swallow their thoughts. As the sun descended toward the horizon, casting long shadows across the landscape, Elijah spotted a suitable place to camp for the night. A small copse of trees offered some protection from the wind, and a creek coming off the Platte provided a much-needed water source.

The brothers set up a modest camp. They tethered the horses near the stream, allowing them to drink and graze on the sparse grass. Elijah gathered some dry branches and twigs, starting a small fire that flickered against the encroaching darkness. The simple act of setting up camp, something he had done countless times before, felt daunting now in this journey.

Dinner was a quiet affair, consisting of beans and hardtack, their flavor as bland as the conversation. Elijah felt exhaustion settling over him, the past days' events catching up. He leaned back against his saddle, using it as a pillow, and stared into the flames.

The crackling of the fire and the gentle rustling of the leaves in the breeze created a soothing backdrop. Elijah's eyelids grew heavy, the warmth of the fire lulling him into a drowsy state. He fought to keep his eyes open, but the exhaustion was too much. Within minutes, he succumbed to sleep.

At some point, he didn't know how long it had been; Elijah was jolted awake by a hand clamped over his mouth. His eyes snapped open, and he couldn't make out the figure crouched over him in the darkness. His heart pounded in his chest, adrenaline surging through his body. The figure leaned in close and pressed a knee against Elijah's arm when he went for his gun.

CUTTHROAT TROUT

— • —

The shadowy figure leaned in close, and a familiar whisper broke the silence. "Eli, it's me. Don't make a sound."

Elijah, staring at the stars above, nodded, and Moses removed his hand and knee, turning on his haunches toward the east. As Elijah's eyes adjusted to the dark, he saw Moses pointing.

"A fire?" Elijah asked. He sat up and threw off his bedroll, squinting into the night.

"Yeah," Moses whispered. "I couldn't sleep and was staring off that way. Watched it come to life. Tried to kick ours out, but didn't want to throw water on it and create a bunch of smoke with how concealed we are."

Elijah ran a hand over his face, trying to wake up, angry at himself for falling so deep into sleep. "And that's how you decided to wake me?"

Moses hesitated a moment. "You were mumblin' about something, and I've learned my lesson about waking you from one of your dreams. Didn't want you hollerin'."

Elijah ignored the comment. Moses was right, and there was nothing more to be said. "We can check it out, stay put, or get on the move," he said. "Reckon the last idea is no good."

"We'll make too much noise getting packed and trying to find our way in the dark," Moses said, looking toward the fire again. "You don't think they got behind us somehow, do you?"

"Don't know, but if that were their game, they sure wouldn't announce it with a fire." Elijah suddenly regretted that they'd used one, small as it had been. He pulled his Winchester from his saddle. "Let's try and sneak in there and see what we're dealing with."

The moon hung low in the sky, casting a pale, silvery light over the prairie as Elijah and Moses moved cautiously through the terrain. The only sounds were the soft rustle of grass under their boots and the distant calls of nocturnal animals. The world around them was bathed in shades of blue and gray, the landscape eerily beautiful under the moonlight.

Elijah signaled to Moses, using hand gestures that had become second nature after years of working together. Silently, they split up, approaching the campfire from opposite sides. Moses, his left arm still in a sling, held his revolver in his right hand. Brutus followed, surprising Elijah as he moved quietly and gracefully as if he understood the need for stealth.

As they neared the camp, the quiet nickers of two horses near the fire became audible. Elijah crouched low, using the sparse cover to remain unseen. He could now see the outlines of a bedroll near the fire, but it was empty.

Suddenly, the unmistakable click of a revolver's hammer being cocked broke the silence. Elijah froze, his heart pounding in his chest. A familiar voice called out from the darkness, tinged with relief, "Hoped it was just you two."

Elijah slowly stood with his weapon ready. From the shadows, a figure emerged, hands raised in a non-threatening gesture, a revolver visible in one of them. It was Matt Hobbs, his face materializing in the flickering firelight.

Elijah's grip on his rifle relaxed slightly, but he remained alert. "What are you doing out here, Matt?"

Moses joined them, his expression wary as he held his revolver low but did not re-holster. "Seems like a long way from escorting gold and a prisoner to the railroad," he said.

"Not to mention Maggie and Clay," Elijah added warily.

Hobbs eyed both of their weapons, then kept one hand in the air while holstering his revolver. "Have I fallen so out of favor with both of you that you don't put away your weapons?"

As Elijah and Moses exchanged sheepish looks and Moses holstered his revolver, Brutus, prowling the camp's perimeter, bounded towards the new arrival. Just as Brutus neared Hobbs, he recognized the man and stopped short, his stance relaxing but alert.

Hobbs chuckled, eyeing the dog. "Good to see you too, Brutus." He then turned his attention back to Elijah and Moses. "I got your group to the railroad, Morrow included. I arranged for them to get a ride back on the next supply train. Then I got two fresh horses and hurried back after you two."

Elijah and Moses exchanged a look, confusion evident in their expressions. Elijah's brow furrowed. "Why come after us, Matt?"

Hobbs glanced down at his badge. "Suppose they'll make me take mine off, too, once they find out what I've done." He plucked the badge off his coat and then looked up. "I've come too far with you two to let you go off on this alone without trying to re-earn your trust."

Elijah studied Hobbs for a moment. "You didn't have to do this, Matt."

Hobbs shrugged. "Maybe not. But I did." He paused, his expression turning serious. "You should know, that in the process of trading telegraph messages with Omaha, I was asked when we would all return. I told them Maggie and Clay were returning with a shackled Nate Morrow, but you two were continuing on after remnants of Morrow's gang. The response. . . was not positive."

In light of the meeting in Omaha and the farewell discussion with Marshal Hawkins, Elijah had anticipated this. Hobbs offered his conjecture. "Between the political aspirations of those making the call and the embarrassment over not being the ones to stop Morrow in the first place, there's a firmness in their decision. Regardless of why it is, there won't be any going back for us if we continue."

Elijah glanced at Moses, then back at Hobbs. "We've already decided. We head to Julesburg. If the Crenshaws are there, we'll find them. If not, we keep going."

Moses chimed in. "That's the plan. Our lawman days are over."

Hobbs nodded. "I'm still in." He looked toward the west and then back at the brothers. "There's no law out here, anyhow."

"Only what we make," Elijah said. He began to walk back toward their camp, calling back. "We're just up ahead, Matt. We leave at first light."

<hr>

THE HUNT CONTINUED the next day under a relentless sun, the three men pushing themselves and their horses to the limit. They often switched between mounts and pack horses, doing just enough to keep the animals and themselves cared for. The terrain was unforgiving, an endless expanse of dry grasslands and occasional rocky outcrops. It was a grueling but necessary pace.

As the sun descended in the sky late in the afternoon, Moses spotted something significant. He called Elijah and Hobbs over and pointed to the ground near a water access point along the Platte River. "It looks like two riders and two horses," Moses observed, examining the foot and hoof prints.

The men agreed the tracks were fresh. This was the first sign they had found, and it breathed new life into their pursuit. They followed the trail as long as the fading light allowed, but as dusk settled in, visibility became increasingly difficult.

"We should continue on," Elijah insisted. He was eager to close the distance if the tracks were indeed the Crenshaws.

Moses and Hobbs exchanged glances before Hobbs spoke up. "It's not wise to risk losing the trail in the dark, Elijah. Or worse, riding into an ambush without even seeing it coming."

"He's right, Eli," Moses said. "We need to make camp. We can pick up the trail at first light."

Elijah conceded their point. He knew the dangers of night travel, especially in unfamiliar territory. He dismounted, and the men set up camp, eating jerky and hardtack with a fire small enough to warm some coffee and keep the chill off.

The temperature had dropped significantly since sunset, a stark reminder of how harsh the prairie could be after dark. Moses rubbed his hands together, trying to generate some warmth. "Never thought I'd miss the heat of the day," he grumbled.

"The nights out here can be unforgiving," Hobbs added, pulling his coat tighter around him.

Elijah, leaning against his saddle, stared into the flickering flames, his face illuminated by the firelight as he puffed on his pipe. He was silent, lost in his thoughts, his gaze distant. He did not realize the other two were watching him.

Hobbs cleared his throat, breaking the silence. He seemed hesitant but needed to understand the mission. "Elijah," he began, "I just. . . I must ensure I understand exactly what we intend to do."

Elijah turned his head slightly, his expression unchanging. "The Crenshaws," he said, his voice flat but persistent, "murdered William Jones during what should have been an honest prisoner swap. They enabled Frank Tucker's brutality, leading to more deaths. And now, everything they've done since. . . I can't let them continue to inflict such violence on the world."

"There won't be any capturing for a trial, will there, Elijah?" Hobbs asked, his words measured. Moses bit his lip and looked at the ground.

Elijah turned to Hobbs. "You said yourself, there's no law out here. So I intend to compensate for that. I won't spend the rest of my life checking my back."

Hobbs absorbed Elijah's words. "About that," he began. He reached into his coat pocket to retrieve something, then stopped, seeming unsure of himself. "The rest of your life I mean, how will you spend it?"

Before Elijah could respond, Moses cut in. "We gotta take care of this first," he said firmly, his tone brooking no argument. Elijah gave his brother a grateful look, glad for his support. Moses nodded an acknowledgment, then shifted uncomfortably with a grimace.

"You alright, Mo?"

"Yessir," he answered eagerly. "Goin' to get some shuteye and hope we find that damn town tomorrow."

Elijah hoped they would, too. He just wasn't sure what they'd find there.

* * *

WITH THE FIRST LIGHT OF DAWN, the trio resumed their pursuit, picking up the trail they had left the previous evening. The freshness of the tracks from the day before gave them hope, but as the morning wore on, the trail became increasingly difficult to follow.

The terrain around them began to change, the dry grasslands giving way to more rocky and uneven ground. The hoof prints they followed became scattered and less distinct among the stones and sparse vegetation. Elijah dismounted, crouching to inspect the ground. "Tracks are getting harder to see," he murmured.

Hobbs scanned the area. "This rocky terrain is masking their trail. They could have gone any direction from here."

Moses, still on horseback, squinted into the distance. "We're losing precious time trying to pick up their exact path. Maybe we ought to aim straight for Julesburg."

As they continued westward, the landscape became more rugged, the rolling plains now interspersed with hills and scattered rock formations. The sun climbed higher in the sky, its heat relentless. Elijah wiped his brow. They had crossed into an even more desolate part of the territory, the signs of human presence exceedingly rare. At one point, Moses pointed to a weathered, barely legible wooden signpost marking their crossing into Colorado Territory.

Late in the morning, as they crested a slight rise, Elijah spotted something. Through the heat haze, the faint outline of buildings could be seen, a small cluster that had to be Julesburg. "There it is," he said.

They found a secluded spot to tie up three horses, switching to fresh mounts for the final approach. Moses staked out Copper, casting a glance at the loyal horse. "Don't need you sharing Bear's fate," he murmured.

As the three men rode into the edge of Julesburg, the town materialized from the haze of legend into stark reality. Known as the wickedest town in the west, Julesburg sprawled before them in a chaotic mix of buildings and tents. It was a place born from the confluence of the Oregon and Mormon Trails and the Pony Express, having grown into a notorious haven for outlaws and adventurers.

The town's streets were dusty and uneven, with saloons, traders, and dilapidated buildings. Signs creaked on their hinges, advertising goods and services to the transient population that ebbed and flowed through Julesburg. The air was heavy with the smell of livestock, smoke, and unwashed bodies.

Julesburg was a trading post and a site of back-and-forth massacres between its residents and Native Americans in recent years. Its reputation for lawlessness was well-earned, with tales of violence and vice fueling its infamy.

As they rode in, Hobbs's attention was drawn to a young man who spotted them and hurried down the decrepit boardwalk, disappearing into a rough-looking saloon. "They're here," Hobbs said under his breath.

Elijah gave a subtle nod, his eyes scanning the town. He noticed Moses, with a determined expression, remove the sling from his left arm, revealing the bandaged wound before he pulled his coat sleeve back on with a pained look. The action was a silent testament to his readiness for what might come next.

Elijah had tried to get Brutus to stay with the horses, but he looked down and saw the dog trotting between him and Moses. "Hope you know what you're getting yourself into, ol' boy."

They dismounted near the saloon, tying their horses to a hitching post. A wooden sign creaked on a hinge above the door, letting them know the establishment was called The Cutthroat Trout. The weathered sign depicted a carved fish, with Xs where the eyes should be and a dagger through its neck.

"Friendly-looking place," Hobbs quipped. He looked up and down the street. "This is the one the boy ran into."

Elijah and Moses each dug a second Colt out of their saddle bags while Hobbs pulled out a ten-gauge double barrel to go with his own Colt. Elijah took a deep breath, his hand resting on the butt of a revolver as he led the way into the saloon, pushing open the creaking wooden doors.

Inside, the room was dimly lit and reeked of tobacco smoke and stale alcohol. The few patrons inside glanced their way, their eyes lingering. The bartender, a middle-aged man with a scruffy beard and sharp eyes, studied them briefly before placing three shots of whiskey on the bar when Moses held up as many fingers.

"You lookin' for someone?" the bartender asked. His voice was a whisper, and he never looked up while serving the drinks and wiping the bar. The same boy they'd seen run in minutes before shot out the door after hearing the question.

"The fellas that lad was likely paid to warn," Elijah said. He took the whiskey, turning toward Moses and Hobbs as he spoke to the bartender. "Was in the same kind of hurry when he saw us ride in." Elijah downed his shot smoothly and watched two rough-looking men eye them as they slipped out the door.

Hobbs walked to the bat wing doors and peered over the top, watching the men momentarily before returning to the bar.

The bartender continued to wipe down the bar with a dirty rag. "Self-preservation's the law here. When a fight's brewing, I keep my head down and try to land on the right side of things." He moved to the back of the bar and fiddled with some glasses.

"Who says a fight is brewing?" Moses asked before downing his drink.

The bartender turned and looked at them. "Three type 'a folks in Julesburg: Ones bein' chased, one's doin' the chasin', and ones keepin' their heads down."

Moses peered at the man as Elijah examined their surroundings. "Which one are we?"

"Well I know for damn sure you aren't the ones keepin' your heads down."

"How's that?" Hobbs asked. He drank his whiskey and placed the upturned glass on the bar.

"A fella knows," the bartender said. He shook his head. "The less I know, though, the better. Two fellas came into town yesterday, and they've already created a lot of chatter. They heard I was a doc, and availed themselves of my services while taking bottles of liquor they didn't pay for."

Elijah cocked his head. "You're the doctor and a saloon owner?"

The man laughed. "I'm a failed doctor who runs a saloon in a place men are constantly getting shot." Elijah and Moses both raised an eyebrow. "Fellas, I give 'em whiskey and dig bullets out."

Hobbs moved to the door again and peered outside. "Handful of guns milling down the street, Elijah."

"Tell us about the two men, doc," Elijah said, showing his impatience.

"They are the ones running; I can tell that much. And from the looks of it," he glanced at Elijah's coat, then pointed to where he could see a star had once been pinned, "you're the ones chasing. I'm sure they've got it comin'. But it ain't my business."

"One's injured?"

The bartender nodded. "Shot twice. Once in the leg. Still plenty feisty, though."

"I knew I got him," Moses muttered. "What else?" he asked the bartender.

The man sighed. "Said they were out of supplies and killed their horses getting here. Word got around, and when folks got interested, they said one thing they had plenty of was money. Told a story about men trying to take it from them and hired some help. Said they aimed to make themselves, and any man who helped, rich."

Elijah touched the scar on his face. "Well, it's *our* money they stole, and a whole mess of people they've killed and property they've stolen and destroyed." Elijah looked to the dirty window and saw people moving indoors. "No law here?"

The bartender scoffed. "Every once 'n a while, we get a committee that elects some fella to try and keep the peace, but it never sticks. This place runs on being on the right side of the current strongmen and paying for guns willing to help you."

He continued as he refilled their glasses. "Justice has always been a flexible concept here. Hell, the place is named after a fella who shot a vigilante like yourself full of holes, only for the son of a gun to live and come back and kill and mutilate ol' Jules." He finished pouring and looked at all of them in turn. "So I tell folks it's best to keep your head down, get what supplies you need, and keep movin'."

"Well, we won't be movin' on just yet," Elijah said. He dug in his coat and produced far more coins than the drinks cost.

"Didn't figure," the bartender said. He sighed deeply as he looked at the coins. "Best I can tell, they're down at the Dusty Sparrow. Part boarding house, part bordello."

"Likely restin' up a spell and re-supplying before they light out again. Hired guns likely meant to slow us down," Moses said.

Hobbs returned from the door. "Or make a stand. With the railroad coming through, toughs with money and the ability to enforce their will could stand to make a fortune as this place formalizes."

The bartender nodded and pointed at Hobbs. "You're a smart one."

"He knows," Elijah said. He forced a grin when Hobbs looked at him. Elijah turned to the bartender. "Appreciate your time. We'll keep clear of here when it starts."

The bartender shook his head, his look not conveying confidence in them. "I know some of the men they've hired. I've seen their chicanery, and I've seen 'em fight. If there's money involved and the potential for more, they'll fight like the devil, even for strangers."

Elijah tapped the brim of his hat and moved toward the door with Moses and Hobbs. "I'd ask what you think, but I've already made up my mind."

"Too late to turn back," Moses said. "We've been in worse jams."

Hobbs clapped a hand on Elijah's shoulder, his shotgun still in his other hand. "Didn't ride all this way to bow out before the last act. I'm in, till the guns go silent."

Elijah pulled his hat down tight. "Then let's go finish this."

They stepped out of the Cutthroat Trout, squinting against the harsh glare of the midday sun as their boots thumped ominously along the boardwalk. The street was unnervingly quiet, the dusty thoroughfare now a stage set for a deadly play. Elijah looked down at Brutus and held up a hand. "Stay with the horses, boy."

With a nod to each man, Elijah stepped into the street, his boots crunching in the dust as Moses and Hobbs joined him. Looking toward the Dusty Sparrow, he saw the movement of a door, and two figures emerged.

Elijah paused, staring down the street. "Mo, when it starts, you're on Miles. Matt, you've got the first gun that jumps in. Jack is mine."

Hobbs nodded, but Moses looked at Elijah and spoke up. "How will we know when it starts?"

Elijah continued staring straight ahead, then began to walk. "You'll know."

A confrontation two years in the making was about to come to its final, irrevocable conclusion, and only one side would walk away.

TWO FAVORS

— ◦ —

The midday sun bore down on the dusty streets of Julesburg, casting long shadows from the buildings onto the ground. The town was silent, and the street was empty except for a few hitched horses. The only noise was the crunching of their boots as Elijah, Moses, and Hobbs made their way to the Dusty Sparrow. The heat was more than it had been their entire journey, and eddies of dust swirled around their boots as they walked.

Elijah's sharp gaze swept across the street, spotting shadows that flickered and moved with a stealthy grace that spoke of danger. One figure appeared briefly on a rooftop, the sun glinting off something metallic in his hands—likely a rifle. He looked at Hobbs and nodded up to the roof.

The Crenshaw brothers' boots knocked across the boardwalk, and they stepped out into the dusty, sun-scorched street. Elijah spied a pair of revolvers on each man's hips as they sauntered away from the Dusty Sparrow and positioned themselves in the center of the street. Jack Crenshaw's sickening grin was unmistakable even from a distance, his eyes gleaming with defiance and derision. Beside him, Miles, limping slightly, mirrored Jack's menacing stance.

Elijah, Moses, and Hobbs stood three wide in the street, directly across from the Crenshaws, and for a moment, time hung suspended.

The short distance between them was charged with silent tension; every eye locked, every muscle tensed. Dust motes danced in the sunbeams between them, the only movement in the otherwise still tableau.

Jack's voice cut through the silence, dry as the dirt beneath their boots. "Long ride just to find your graves, Barbers." He looked directly at Elijah. "Seems like a waste of a good *horse*."

Elijah narrowed his eyes, not giving him the satisfaction of bringing up Bear's death. "Dreamed of this for two years. What's a few more miles?"

"Shoulder still holding up?" Miles glared at Moses. Or you need another bullet to balance it out?" Miles quipped.

"Better than your leg it seems," Moses answered. "That or the weight of your sins makes you walk that way."

"Badges off and a man advantage," Jack shot back as he looked at Hobbs. He then turned back to Elijah. "Don't seem fair, I reckon." He laughed, and Elijah caught Jack's eyes looking toward something behind him momentarily. "Can't take us on without help, Barber?"

Elijah snorted, then paused momentarily as he sensed movement behind his left shoulder. He spoke up loudly, letting Jack know he had a bigger audience than the Crenshaws.

"All this started nearly two years ago when you backshot a fairly swapped prisoner. Now we find ourselves here in part because you backshot an innocent, unarmed woman just trying to run to safety." He paused, steeling himself for what was next, and took a breath. "Ain't gonna *end* with someone being backshot, though."

Elijah turned as his left hand brought up and cocked his revolver before anyone else knew what was happening, shattering the silence with a chest shot to the backshooter.

As Elijah turned back, his right hand drew, and he fired a shot toward Jack, striking him just below the collarbone. Jack stumbled back, his shocked face contorting in pain as he struggled to keep his balance, grabbing at the injury.

Moses reacted quickly, drawing with his good right arm as the echoes of the first shots bounced off the wooden structures of Julesburg. He aimed at Miles, squeezing the trigger. The shot went wide, missing as Miles ducked behind a nearby cart, retreating with Jack. Without hesitation, however, Moses turned and fired at another figure rushing out from the boarding house, dropping him with a clean shot to the chest.

The street transformed into a battlefield, with the sharp cracks of gunfire echoing off the close-packed buildings. The hired guns began appearing from the shadows and firing in earnest. Bullets sliced through the air, hurling clouds of dust upward and splintering the sun-bleached wood of the storefronts.

Hobbs turned and blasted one barrel of his shotgun into the dark mouth of an alley where a shadow moved ominously. A cry and a thud signaled his hit. As he reloaded, a sharp crack from above drew his gaze upwards just in time to see a man aiming down from the roof of a two-story building. Hobbs didn't hesitate; he fired his second barrel, the shot catching the man full in the face. The shooter cried out a ghastly sound before tumbling down to the street below.

Hobbs sprinted for the cover of a nearby wagon. Mid-stride, a bullet ripped into his leg, and he collapsed to his knees. Pain flashing across his face, he yanked out his revolver and fired back, dropping his attacker with a clean shot.

Across the street, Elijah and Moses crept along the sun-baked side of a clapboard building, their shadows long and distorted on the peeling paint. They dove behind an old water trough as bullets thudded into the wooden barrier, sending splinters flying around them.

The brothers traded shots with two men crouched behind the remains of a dilapidated cart. One enemy fell to Elijah's careful aim, the other to Moses's steady hand.

Elijah spun towards a rustling sound. As he faced the new threat, a bullet grazed his left arm, searing his flesh with a white-hot pain. Gritting his teeth, he aimed and fired.

Elijah looked up to see Moses on the move, but a bandit flanked him from a corner. "Left side, Mo!" Elijah barked over the gunfire.

Moses turned toward the man and raised his right arm, but the hammer only clicked. The bandit grinned, firing at close range, but the bullet merely whisked the top of Moses's hat, missing its lethal intent. Shock painted the bandit's face, a look that turned to horror as Moses dropped his empty weapon, cross-drew the one on his left, and fired. The man dropped to a knee, and Moses stepped forward and finished his work.

A shotgun blast boomed, and then the street fell silent except for the nervous whinnies of tied-up horses. Moses met Elijah's eyes, holding up his hat with a bemused expression. Together, they sought out Hobbs, who was limping but alive, his gun still smoking as he met them in the street. Covering each other as they reloaded and disarmed the wounded men, the trio centered themselves in front of the dilapidated old boarding house.

Hobbs looked down at Moses's hat. "Jesus."

Moses put it back on his head. "Boss of the plains."

Elijah turned toward the saloon and whistled loudly. "Brutus!" he yelled. The dog ran toward them, spinning in circles at Elijah's feet until he held out a hand and told him to sit.

"Now you want him?" Moses asked.

"Might not be standing here had I gone into the livery in Omaha without him." Elijah forced a slight grin, then inspected his partners. "You both alright?"

"Shot me in the damn meaty part of the thigh," Hobbs replied. "A pain, but I'll be fine."

Moses bit his lip and looked at Elijah, who was eyeing his shoulder. "It's holding up." Elijah could see it was bleeding again but didn't say anything. "How about you?" Moses asked.

"Fine," Elijah said. He held up his arm, a hole in the sleeve just below the elbow. "Ready to finish this?"

They both nodded, and Elijah led them forward a few steps and pointed to a large front window. Hobbs stepped onto the rough boardwalk near the boarding house, his eyes scanning the dusty window for any sign of the Crenshaws. Elijah and Moses assumed positions out front, facing the building squarely.

Elijah called out, ringing clear and robust in the now quiet street. "Jack and Miles Crenshaw! Your time is up, and your game is over!" His words echoed off the buildings, hanging in the air.

The sun seemed to beat down even harder, adding to the anticipation as sweat ran down from under their hats. A tense silence enveloped the street, broken only by the groans of a couple of the hired guns. Brutus, however, did not even seem to notice. His eyes were locked straight ahead, just like those of the brothers he stood between.

After a moment, there was a response from inside the Dusty Sparrow. It was Jack, whose voice was cold and ruthless despite his situation. "I gotta hand it to you, Barber," he began, "you are a relentless man." Another period of silence. "But how many of your friends did we kill along the way? Those guns out there mean nothing to me. . . Your money is gone, your business is burnt. And oh, that sweet red head back in Omaha. . . I hope killin' Frank was worth it. Seems like life ain't gone the way you thought it would since then."

Elijah's eyes narrowed on the front door. He could see Moses holding a hand to his shoulder inside his coat from the corner of his eye. His eyes, however, scanned the boarding house, attempting to figure out where the voice was coming from in the building.

"I ain't the one who ran inside and hid," Elijah said suddenly. "But I 'spose you can chat with Frank soon enough. Ask him what *he* thinks."

"You still out there or that shoulder bleed out yet?" Miles called out. "Maybe I'll come out and finish you off."

Moses removed his hand from his shoulder, and Elijah saw blood on his hand. "Reckon you're the one who needs put out of his misery."

Jack Crenshaw laughed, a harsh, mocking sound. "You two have become quite the heroes, haven't you? But let's be clear: You're no better than us. You're here for blood, the same as we are." There was a brief pause. "Time to see who's best at it."

"All this talk's just wind," Hobbs called out from the corner of the building. "Let's see who's standing when it dies down."

Elijah's eyes scanned the front of the Dusty Sparrow, his hand resting on the revolver at his hip. Silence fell once again, and Elijah turned to Moses.

"You ready to—"

A gunshot from inside the building broke the silence. A window near where Hobbs was standing exploded in a shower of glass, followed by what sounded like the scream of women inside the building. Hobbs ducked and then, without hesitation, thrust his shotgun through the shattered window, firing a blast into the room beyond, a loud groan coming from Miles Crenshaw.

Elijah charged the building, with Moses and Brutus close behind. As he reached the doorway, Elijah saw a shot splinter the wood. They ducked, and then Moses turned inside, firing his revolver back toward the source of the shot. His bullet found its mark, and another pained shout came from Miles Crenshaw.

Before Moses could react further, Miles, wounded but driven by rage, charged at him. The two collided with a thud, Moses crying out as he was knocked to the ground, the assailant landing on his already injured shoulder.

Elijah was about to rush to his brother's aid when a shot rang out from the top of a short, narrow staircase. Jack Crenshaw stood there, gun in hand, aiming down at them, causing Elijah to duck for cover.

Inside, the struggle between Moses and Miles intensified. Miles Crenshaw put a knee into Moses's bloody shoulder, bringing a horrible shout of pain, and pulled a knife from his boot. Elijah was about to risk exposing himself when he saw Hobbs's shotgun barrel clear the remainder of the glass, and Hobbs fell through the window shortly after. He stood and fired, and Miles Crenshaw grabbed at his neck and fell backward.

Moses crawled toward the corner of the room, and Hobbs moved forward to grab his good arm and drag him when a shot came from the staircase. Hobbs's eyes shot wide open, and he stared at Elijah a moment before falling on top of Moses and waving Elijah toward the stairs.

Elijah emerged angrily from the doorway, cursing at Jack Crenshaw and firing two shots up the staircase. Seeing the man move for cover, Elijah charged upward, Brutus bounding past him.

Elijah glimpsed Jack grab a woman, using her as cover while dragging her into a room. But Brutus, with a mighty leap, latched onto Jack's arm. The outlaw yelled in pain, releasing the woman and dropping his gun as he kicked Brutus away. Crenshaw began to reach for the weapon as Brutus charged back at him, and they both froze when Elijah called out, "No, Brutus!"

Elijah entered the room, his revolver drawn, facing Jack Crenshaw. "Pick it up," he commanded. Jack Crenshaw reached for the revolver, and Elijah fired a shot that splintered the floorboard as Crenshaw drew away. The woman screamed and hurried under a bed.

As Crenshaw stood up straight, his eyes locked on Elijah. His shirt was stained red, and he held his head awkwardly. "I guess you win, Barber." He spit tobacco on the faded floorboards and winced. "But see. . . We ain't so different."

"Sure we are," Elijah said. He holstered his gun.

Elijah inclined his head toward the bed and called to the woman. "You can come out; it's safe now." The woman's head appeared from under the bed, and she trembled as she looked at Elijah. "It's alright, I'm the good guy." He wasn't sure if he was trying to convince *her* or *himself*, and he cringed when Jack grinned.

"Go on now," Elijah said to the woman. He pointed toward the door, urging Brutus in front of her. "He'll protect you." The woman finally left, and Elijah returned his gaze to Crenshaw.

"Pick it up."

Crenshaw tilted his head, and a twisted grin came to his face. He bent slightly, clearly in great pain, keeping his eyes on Elijah as he reached for the weapon. The two men stared at each other as Crenshaw straightened and holstered his gun.

"Cast in the same mold we are, Barber." Crenshaw tipped his chin toward the door. "She knows it. We're *both* killers."

"Maybe so. . ." Elijah said, his eyes never leaving Crenshaw's.

Jack Crenshaw stared back at Elijah momentarily, then licked his lips and smiled before going for his gun.

A shot rang out, and Elijah's bullet hit Crenshaw square in the chest, dropping him to the ground as women screamed from the adjacent room.

Elijah stepped over him, his revolver still aimed at the fallen man. Crenshaw began to speak with a disgusting grin, but Elijah cut him off.

". . . Cast for a different purpose, though." Elijah pulled the trigger again, ensuring Jack Crenshaw would never harm another soul.

Elijah momentarily looked at himself in the mirror, then straightened his jacket and hat. He entered the hallway and peeked inside the room where Brutus was guarding the women who cowered when they saw him. "Stay," he said to Brutus. Elijah then looked at the women. "It's over."

DESCENDING THE STAIRCASE, Elijah heard the weak sound of Moses trying to pull Hobbs closer with his good arm. As Elijah's footsteps approached, Moses raised his weapon, then lowered it, recognizing his brother. The scene before Elijah was grim. The arm of Moses's coat was soaked in blood, his face growing pale as he pressed a hand to his bleeding shoulder. Hobbs, slumped against the wall, was in worse shape, a pool of blood beneath him.

Elijah quickly stepped outside, scanning to ensure no further threats. He saw the bartender standing outside his building down the street and waved to him, shouting, "Bring any medical supplies you've got, doc!"

Returning inside, he knelt beside Hobbs, whose face was contorted with pain. "Gutshot," Hobbs managed to say before coughing blood.

His voice was full of resignation, yet with a hint of Matt Hobbs sarcasm. "I've seen how this ends."

Elijah turned to Moses, trying to assess his brother's injury. Moses's breathing was labored, and his eyes flickered with pain and fatigue. "Hang in there, Mo," Elijah urged. We'll get that bleeding stopped."

Moses looked at Hobbs, no doubt realizing their friend's fate. "Just worry about him first."

The bartender returned and stopped in the doorway, taking in the scene. He looked at Hobbs, and Elijah shook his head and pointed at Moses. A couple of the women from upstairs came down and began to help the bartender, who was doing nothing more than pouring alcohol on Moses's shoulder and attempting to pack the re-opened wound.

Lying against the wall, Hobbs looked up at Elijah with a wry smile. His voice was weak, but the humor was still there. "You remember, Elijah," he coughed slightly, "I told you I should've stopped spending my summers with the Barbers."

Elijah, kneeling beside him, felt a strong pang of guilt. "Matt, is there anything, anything at all, I can do for you?" He looked at his friend, trying to think of some explanation or apology. "It wasn't supposed to go this way."

Hobbs rolled his head from side to side and gave a slight grin. "I've been telling myself that since Antietam," he said.

"Yeah. . ." Elijah had no response to the simple yet profound statement.

Hobbs's eyes flickered with a tiny spark of life, and he reached into his coat pocket with a shaky hand. He pulled out a letter, the envelope stained. "There *is* something you can do, actually," he said, handing the letter to Elijah. "You can take this."

Elijah took the letter. "I'll make sure it gets to whoever it needs to go to," he promised.

Hobbs shook his head. "It's for you, Elijah. Told her I'd get it to you. So you'll take it, and I at least die knowing I did that."

Elijah looked down at the letter, recognizing Maggie's handwriting on the envelope. His heart skipped a beat as he stared at it before folding it and placing it in his coat pocket.

Elijah's eyes, usually a bastion of stoicism, now shimmered with emotion. He looked down at Hobbs, who lay with his eyes closed. Suddenly, Hobbs turned away, and a violent cough broke his peaceful demeanor. Elijah winced, running a hand over his face. Hobbs wiped his mouth and composed himself, turning back to meet Elijah's eyes.

Hobbs took a weak breath. "I've got two favors to ask of you," he said, his voice weak but determined.

"Of course," Elijah responded.

Hobbs's eyes held Elijah's. "Whatever the future holds for you, I hope you continue to stand up for what's right, no matter how boring and peaceful of a life you might try to forge."

Elijah chuckled softly, biting his lip to suppress his emotions. "I'll try, Matt." He grabbed Hobbs's hand.

"And the second," Hobbs continued, "I'll haunt you if you don't write Maggie back."

Elijah's grip on Hobbs's hand tightened. "I promise, Matt."

"Just thought of another." Hobbs's eyes were closed, and his speech labored and raspy. "Go find that life now for you and your brother. . . and live the hell out of it."

"I will." Elijah put his arm around his shoulder, and they shook hands, a firm grasp that lingered. "Thank you, Matt," Elijah whispered, sitting beside his friend. "You're a good man."

"I know," Hobbs replied.

As the minutes passed, Hobbs's breathing grew slower, and the room fell into a peaceful stillness. The women had left, and the bartender stepped outside. Moses, his face pale, sat in the corner of the room, an excessive amount of cloth wrapped around his shoulder. Elijah looked at him, and Moses shook his head.

"Don't you die on me, too," Elijah said.

NOWHERE TO GO

— ◦ —

A heavy silence enveloped the room as Hobbs's life ebbed away. Unfortunately, there would be no time to pause and reflect.

The bartender returned and saw Elijah removing Hobbs's coat and covering him. "I'm real sorry about your friend," the man said. He hung his head a moment, then looked up again. "I reckon even a real doctor couldn't have done anything. And best I can do for your brother is give you some bandages and whiskey."

Elijah stood and nodded, attempting to convey understanding in his eyes.

The bartender looked at Moses before continuing. "I know it ain't a good time, but whisper around town already is that the types that run this place with the threat of violence ain't happy about some vigilante types bein' around." He looked back at Elijah. "And them fellas that lived. . . Well, they've seen your faces."

Moses's head slumped as if to say he had no more fight in him. "About as I expected," Elijah said. "We can't stay put anyhow."

"Don't rightly know if you have somewhere to go. Fort Sedgwick is only a few miles distant. A proper doctor." He sighed. "I wish I could help, but—"

Elijah cut him off. "I know." He knelt and helped Moses to his feet, draping his good arm around his shoulder. "If you can help me load them up, we'll be gone. I'll be back shortly to trade you some horses for any supplies you can offer, and then you'll never see us again."

They slung Hobbs over his horse's body, Elijah cursing the undignified manner in which it had to be done. He tied a lead to his horse, then began to do the same to Moses's mount after the bartender helped him climb aboard.

"I can ride," Moses said. He grimaced as he swatted Elijah's hand away.

Elijah didn't want to waste time arguing and climbed aboard his mount. He then hopped down, hurried back into the Dusty Sparrow, and went up the stairs. He returned with two saddlebags that rattled with the sound of coins and had some paper currency sticking out.

After attaching them to saddles, he looked at the bartender. "That's *our* money," he said. At least what's left of it." The bartender held up his hands and gave no argument, and Elijah led the slow procession out of town.

Thankful the animals and their gear were undisturbed, Elijah climbed down and helped Moses do the same. He was about to ask his brother for help but stopped when he saw Moses slump against a tree. Elijah retrieved a shovel from the supplies and walked a short bit to the softer-looking ground underneath a stand of trees.

Burying Hobbs was a grim task. Elijah plunged the shovel into the earth; each thrust was a physical manifestation of his turmoil. Sweat beaded on his brow, and Elijah paused, considering whether the end of the Crenshaws brought any sense of closure. He realized that proper judgment of his actions could only come after ensuring Moses's survival and finding a new path forward. Regardless, the shadows of Hobbs, Big Sam, Ike, and the marshal and Talbot Jones from last summer loomed in his memory – good men who had fallen alongside countless innocents, casualties in a relentless cycle of violence and retribution since he went to and returned from war.

A profound thought struck Elijah, as raw and vivid as the harsh landscape around him: In pursuing justice, a man often walks a line as thin and sharp as a razor's edge, where each step can uphold righteousness or plunge into darkness. It's a path that leaves its mark, visible or not.

With this thought echoing in his mind, Elijah finished the grave, a simple resting place in this place so far from civilization. He returned to where Hobbs's body lay. Carefully, he lifted Hobbs under the arms and shoulders, his muscles straining as he dragged him toward the grave.

Moses attempted to stand but swayed and held a hand to steady himself. "Let me help—"

"No, Mo," Elijah interrupted, his tone gentle yet firm. You need to rest." He saw Moses's frustration but also his recognition of his current limitations.

It was a harsh, unceremonious task, but it was all he could manage as Elijah worked Hobbs's body into the earth and arranged him as best he could. He leaned on the shovel and caught his breath.

"He was a good man," Moses said in a weak voice. He struggled to where Elijah was and stood beside him. "It bothers me to think that were it not for the war and everything we've seen since, we would never have met him in this life."

Elijah bit his lip and looked at the ground. "And yet, it's why he's dead." They were silent for a while, and then Elijah scooped up some dirt. "A good man who served others and was loyal to the end. Give him some peace Lord." He threw the dirt on the body and scooped some more as Moses walked away.

Brutus turned toward Moses momentarily, then returned and sat at Elijah's feet. Elijah looked down. "I'll take some of that peace for us, too."

___ ⁄⁄⁄ ___

RETURNING FROM TOWN after trading two perfectly good horses for a moderate supply of foodstuffs, Elijah consolidated their supplies, loaded the pack horses, and saddled Copper. Thankful for the loyal horse's seeming understanding, he struggled to get Moses atop the mount, then climbed aboard his.

In the fading light of the early evening, Elijah guided his small convoy of weary horses through the rugged terrain northwest of Julesburg. Given his unknown situation in the eyes of the law, he had decided against the fort, a decision he was already questioning as he watched Moses's condition deteriorate. He stayed close to the Overland Trail, hoping to find a stagecoach station or small settlement, his eyes constantly darting to Moses and attempting to keep him alert as he swayed in the saddle.

As the sun dipped below the horizon, painting the sky in hues of orange and purple, Elijah stopped at the first suitable spot to make camp. A small copse of scrubby trees offered a semblance of shelter, and a trickle of a creek – a meandering offshoot of the North Platte – provided them with water.

With great effort, Elijah helped Moses down from Copper. Moses's movements were sluggish, his face showing pain and exhaustion. Elijah unsaddled the horses, staking them near the water and sparse grass.

When Elijah got Moses comfortable and arranged the spartan camp, the night settled in. The sky was a vast canvas of deepening blue as the first stars twinkled in the expanse. The air was cool, a gentle breeze whispering through the trees, carrying with it the faint sounds of the night—the distant howl of a coyote, the rustle of grass in the wind.

Elijah started a small fire, heated some beans, and found a few biscuits in the bag from the Julesburg bartender. He was concerned at how little Moses was talking but grateful that when he handed his brother a tin plate of food, he ate some with a trembling hand.

Elijah leaned back against his saddle, his tin of food untouched in his lap. His body ached with fatigue, but his mind truly felt the strain. He stared into the fire, lost in thought as he smoked his pipe. They were alone, miles from any help. He couldn't risk returning to Julesburg, nor could he risk being seen at Fort Sedgwick. He would press in the morning, hoping to find a stagecoach or its station and concoct a reason for their distress.

A sense of helplessness crept over him, a feeling foreign and unwelcome. He always had a plan, the one who knew what to do next. But now, as he looked at Moses, watching his brother's shallow and uneven breathing, doubt gnawed at him. He touched the scar on his face, now feeling unfamiliar with it covered by his growth of facial hair.

Elijah moved over to Moses, knelt, and held his hand to his forehead; he was burning up. He began to reach for his coat to inspect the wound when Moses spoke up.

"Please don't, Eli," he said softly. His eyes remained closed. "It hurts like the devil is prodding at it, and I don't have to see it to know it's infected."

Elijah sat back onto the bare ground and ran a hand through his hair. "Do you want me to turn us around and head back?"

Moses opened his eyes briefly, then closed them again. "No good options, Eli." He smacked his dry lips, and Elijah held a canteen to his mouth. Moses drank his fill before continuing. "Kearny or the railroad is too far, Julesburg is askin' for us to be killed, and the fort is askin' for trouble with the law."

"Better trouble with the law than you in a hole in the ground, Mo."

Moses chuckled. "I reckon that's the direction things are headed regardless. But, if I don't make it to any help, I at least die without losing the arm." He rolled his head to the side. "Just find us somewhere to start over. Promise I won't complain if I'm around long enough to see it."

Elijah closed his eyes momentarily, unable to process it all. He forced Moses to drink more water, made him comfortable in his bedroll, and climbed into his own. He watched Moses for a long while, not turning away until he saw he was comfortably asleep.

Elijah made a silent vow, there under the vastness of the night sky – he would get Moses through this, no matter what it took. They had been through too much suffering and supported each other through too many hardships not to see this through.

As he closed his eyes, he remembered Maggie's letter and removed it from his coat. Sighing deeply, he ran his hand across the staining, then stared at his name on the envelope before opening it.

Union Pacific end of track
June 9, 1866

Dear Elijah,

I find myself at a loss for words, yet compelled to write this letter at the urging of Mr. Hobbs, who assures me he will ensure its delivery.

First and foremost, I wish to express my deepest gratitude for all that you and Moses have done. Your actions have brought a measure of justice for my father and our town and given me a chance to begin rebuilding our livery. The share of the bounty money will be instrumental in this endeavor.

When we first met, I confess, I was uncertain what to think of you. Your world seemed so far removed from the life I knew. But over time, I have realized that beneath the actions that some may judge harshly lies a man driven by a profound sense of duty to his brother and those he cares for. Your strength and resolve, though born from tribulation and loss, have not gone unnoticed.

I am aware that your path may not lead you back to Omaha. Mr. Hobbs thinks this unlikely. While I do not know what the future holds, my hope for you is simple – that you find success in your mission, safety in your endeavors, and the peace you seek.

Please write when you can, though I am unsure how or if you even have the means to send a letter. Know that my thoughts, hopes, and prayers are with you and that a part of me will always wait for our paths to cross again.

With all sincerity and hope,

Maggie

Elijah refolded the letter, replaced it, and made a second silent vow before falling into a fitful sleep.

ELIJAH'S SLEEP WAS FRAUGHT with the sounds of war—a relentless echo of hooves pounding the earth, the metallic clatter of weaponry, and the cries of the unknown that had become all too familiar during his time in the war. In his dream, he was guiding men through an ambush, the noise growing louder and now accompanied by the boom of artillery.

Awakening from the vivid nightmare, Elijah blinked against the sparse morning light that filtered through dark clouds and the trees. He lay still for a moment, disoriented, the remnants of the dream clinging to him like a shroud. The dark clouds above him were on the move, and a stiff breeze carried a chill.

He turned to look at Moses, lying still in his bedroll. Elijah held his breath, watching until he saw Moses's chest rise and fall in a slow, steady rhythm. Relief washed over him, but a lingering dread tempered it. He couldn't shake the feeling that he was still trapped in the dream; the lines between reality and the horrors of his mind blurred.

Pushing himself to his feet, Elijah pulled on his boots and strapped on his gun belt. His movements were mechanical, his mind still foggy with sleep and the remnants of his dream. He settled his hat onto his head and stepped out of the shelter of the trees.

A flash of lightning and a loud crack of thunder caused him to duck and made him realize it wasn't his dream. Panic gripped him as he stepped into the open, scanning the horizon to the west.

In the distance, he could see a black wall of clouds, rain pouring out of them accompanied by thunder and lightning. Turning his head to the east, he saw a cloud of dust rising where the ground was still dry. The pounding sound of what experience told him was countless hooves and their low rumble of movement carried across the air.

Rushing back to Moses, Elijah gently shook his brother awake. Moses's eyes flickered open, his face flushed with fever. "Mo, we've got to move," Elijah urged.

Moses mumbled something incoherent, his consciousness wavering. Elijah saddled and loaded the horses; his movements were hurried but precise. He carefully helped Moses onto Copper, considering for a moment whether he needed to secure him to the saddle.

Deciding against it, Elijah chose to ride beside him instead, ready to support him if necessary. With one last look toward the source of the dust and noise, Elijah set off, moving at a slow but necessary pace for Moses's condition.

The dust cloud grew more prominent as they rode, and the sounds became more distinct.

"Sounds like those damn herds of cattle they made us babysit in the war," Moses struggled to say. The statement might have been dismissed as the delusions of a fevered and dying man by others, but Elijah leaned forward in his saddle and squinted, then looked to the sky with a sigh. *Thank you.*

His gratitude was short-lived, however. The cloud of dust was indeed a cattle drive, but the animals, likely spooked by the thunder and lightning, were stampeding. Elijah picked up the pace as much as he dared, constantly gauging Moses's ability to stay in the saddle. The cloud of dust grew larger and more defined, and the cacophony of a stampeding herd filled the air.

Moses slumped in his saddle. "Eli..." he murmured weakly, his voice lost in the tumult.

Elijah, gritting his teeth, made a swift decision. "Hold on, Mo. Just hold on. They can help us if we don't get tromped down." He urged their horses outside the path of the stampede, riding perilously close to the frenzied animals. The ground shook under the relentless pounding of hooves, the air thick with dust and the overpowering smell of cattle.

Elijah's horse, sensing the danger, balked, but with a firm hand, he urged the animal forward. They wove through the stampede, narrowly avoiding the panicked beasts that surged like a living tide. His heart raced as he expertly guided them through the melee, his instincts as a horseman coming to the fore.

Cowboys emerged like ghosts, desperately trying to circle the herd to halt its deadly run. With Moses in tow, Elijah joined their efforts, his shouts merging with theirs as they worked to turn the cattle. Elijah mimicked their efforts, helping to circle up the cattle as the cowboys looked on with astonishment.

The wind suddenly picked up, dark clouds roiling overhead. Then, as if by some divine intervention, the worst of the storm moved past them, leaving only rain that began to pour, a deluge that seemed to wash the madness from the earth. The cattle gradually calmed, their circling slowing in the developing mud pit.

Elijah guided Moses away from the cattle, turning in his saddle to search for their pack horse. He spotted it wandering nearby and looked to Moses, who held up a knife. "Cut him loose," Moses managed. He then reached down shakily to replace the knife and fell to the wet ground on his bad shoulder, eliciting a howl.

Two cowboys approached them, their faces streaked with dust turning to mud. The rain continued to fall, heavy and cleansing, as the danger passed, leaving a sense of peace in its wake. "Where the hell did you two come from?" The older of the two asked.

Elijah gestured around with a blank look on his face, unsure where even to start. "We're in a bad way," Elijah said.

"Appears so." said the older of the two riders.

Elijah moved to his brother's side, and the two cowboys dismounted, inspecting Elijah, Moses, and their horses.

The more senior of the two cowboys, a weathered man with a broad-brimmed hat and a dripping rain slicker, stepped forward. His sharp and assessing eyes took in every detail of the scene. "What happened?" he asked in a gruff, no-nonsense tone. Elijah noticed the man kept a hand near his revolver and kept his hands away from his own.

"He was shot almost a week ago. It reopened in another fight. I think it's infected now." He gestured to Moses, who was barely conscious. "He's burning up."

The other cowboy, a younger man with a lean build and an air of cocky confidence, was still holding his rifle. "Sounds like y'all had quite the exciting week," came a deep Texan drawl. Elijah saw him staring at his cavalry hat.

Elijah met the junior cowboy's stare and looked back at the other man. "Please, if you have any supplies or a doctor, I can pay a little. I'll work to earn whatever is required. Just help us."

The senior cowboy knelt beside Moses, pulling his coat aside to inspect the wound. With a quick motion, he cut open Moses's shirt, revealing the wound. It was a ghastly sight—bruised, discolored, and oozing signs of infection. The man's expression turned grim as he stood up.

"I can tell you right now what our old sawbones is gonna do," he said bluntly.

"But maybe we can save him," Elijah said, more to himself than to the cowboys.

The Texan then noticed the bullet hole in the crown of Moses's hat lying on the ground and whistled. "Appears lady luck is 'bout out of cards to deal him."

A silence fell over them. The senior cowboy eyed Elijah for a long moment before asking, "Which side of the law you fellas on?"

Elijah hesitated a second. "Mostly the right, somewhat recently the wrong. . . depending on who you ask."

The cowboy sized him up once more, then mounted his horse. Looking toward the cattle, he saw Brutus running full speed, weaving through the animals. "Dog yours too?"

Elijah followed Brutus's movements momentarily, thinking of how the dog had saved him in Julesburg. "He is."

The cowboy gave an approving look. "We could use a good hound." He looked back to Elijah. "We'll ride you in; see what Mr. Stratton has to say about all this." He reached his arm down to Elijah. "Name's Hank."

"Elijah, my brother Moses."

Hank clicked his tongue. "We'll see what we can do for your brother, Elijah." He looked at his partner. "Travis, help him get situated and make sure his brother stays in the saddle; I'll go ahead and pass the word you're comin' in."

"Thank you," Elijah called out. He looked up to the sky, the rain cleansing him, then turned and watched the man ride off.

Hank chuckled. "And thank you for the help," he called back.

Travis helped Elijah get Moses back in the saddle, then situated his own horse near Copper as Elijah mounted. As they set off, Hank looked across at Elijah. "Y'all must have one hell of a tale to tell," he said, a note of curiosity in his voice.

"We do," Elijah answered.

EPILOGUE

— ⋅ —

Dakota Territory - September 1866

E lijah Barber rode along the rugged expanse of the Bozeman Trail, the fading light of the setting sun casting shadows across the undulating landscape. The terrain was a stark mosaic of rolling hills and rocky outcrops, interspersed with open prairie that stretched into the horizon.

The mountains, awash in the fiery hues of the dying day, stood as silent sentinels overlooking the trail. The peaks, dusted with early fall snows, glowed a reddish-golden hue, reflecting the sun's final rays. The sky above was a canvas of deepening blues and purples streaked with the vibrant oranges and pinks of the sunset.

Elijah's new horse, a sturdy, calm, blood bay with a resilient gait, moved beneath him. The horse was not Bear, but this new mount proved reliable and steadfast, becoming Elijah's regular choice from the remuda. Being told the mount didn't have a name, Elijah had named the horse 'Drifter,' a tribute to their shared destiny of moving across the vast landscapes of the West.

The rhythmic sound of Drifter's hooves on the hard-packed earth was a steady, comforting beat in the otherwise now quiet world. The air was crisp, carrying the scents of sagebrush and the distant pine forests.

As Elijah crested a slight rise, he paused to survey the scene before him. In the valley below, a stampede's aftermath was under control. They were in Crow Territory, caught up in Red Cloud's war of his aligned Lakota, Northern Cheyenne, and Northern Arapaho against the Crow and the increasing intrusion of the United States and the White man. The stampede was an attempt by hostile Sioux to rustle cattle or continue to inflict loss on the intruders. A few shots were fired, and perhaps a few cattle lost, but otherwise, all was now well.

The sinking sun bathed the valley in a melancholy light, the scene's beauty at odds with the violence it witnessed. Elijah nudged Drifter forward, descending into the valley where drovers had begun circling the stampeded cattle, occasionally breaking off to bring stragglers back into the fray.

As Elijah rode into the camp, the atmosphere was filled with relief. The camp, usually lively around chow time, was quieter tonight. Injured men were being tended to around fires that flickered like beacons in the growing darkness. Elijah could hear soft murmurs of conversation, the clang of cooking utensils, and the occasional lowing of the last straggling cattle being pushed back in – a soothing backdrop to the evening's tense undercurrent.

The chuck wagon was a hub of activity, with men queuing for a hot meal. Their quiet voices carried stories of the day as night riders, and guards were posted around the perimeter, vigilant against further surprises. The reclaimed herd, now somewhat calmer, spread out across the nearby grazing land, their silhouettes visible against the faint glow of the horizon.

Elijah dismounted from Drifter, his muscles aching from the long day in the saddle. He took his time unloading his gear, patting Drifter's neck in gratitude. The horse had become his steadfast partner, and he ensured Drifter was well cared for, handing him off to a nearby hand who promised to see to the horse's needs.

As he headed towards the chuckwagon, a figure emerged from the shadows, approaching him with a purposeful stride. This was Jonathan Stratton, the man who had organized this ambitious cattle drive. Stratton was an imposing figure, tall and broad-shouldered, with a weathered face that spoke of years spent under the harsh sun of the open range. His eyes were sharp and observant, missing nothing that happened in his camp.

His dark hair was peppered with gray, and his neatly trimmed beard added to his commanding presence. He wore a wide-brimmed hat that cast his face in shadow, but his eyes were piercing as they fixed on Elijah.

"Barber," he said, his voice deep and resonant. "I heard about the rustlers and stampede. You did well out there. You kept a lot of my men and our herd safe."

Elijah nodded, his fatigue forgotten in the presence of this man. "It was rough going for a spell, but luckily we're alright."

"Luck had little to do with it," Stratton replied. "It takes skill and guts to stay calm like that. A stampede is one thing, a stampede while being attacked. . . We are grateful to have happened upon you."

The compliment gave Elijah a sense of pride. Stratton's acknowledgment meant a lot in this world where respect was hard-earned. "Well, sir, we're the ones who are grateful."

Stratton scoffed. "Good Lord Barber, I'm not that old. Drop the sir business."

"Well, Mr. Stratton. . ." Elijah chuckled, and Stratton just shook his head. "I best be gettin' some chow and shut-eye before it's my turn to ride the herd."

"Before you go. . ." Stratton grabbed Elijah by the arm. "Got two things for you: A request and an offer."

Elijah narrowed his eyes, attempting to study the man's face in the darkness. "Alright, then."

"We're coming up on Fort Phil Kearny. They sent out a rider earlier; they must have caught wind of the skirmish. The colonel at the fort says we can't continue up the trail with fewer than fifty men but that he can't spare any. Also said that we can't come any closer because he needs the remaining grass for his own stock."

Elijah scratched at the thin brown beard he'd been growing since the summer. "Ain't the whole point of these forts to protect folks headin' up the trail?"

Stratton spit and kicked at the dirt. "Don't I know it? They got their hands full with Red Cloud, though. He's been wearing down all three garrisons through Powder River country all summer. I reckon I'd do the same if this were my land." He studied Elijah for a moment. "Anyhow, thought as an army man, you could talk to the Colonel and say we're willing to fend for ourselves?"

"Oh, I dunno, I—"

Stratton held up a hand. "Not gonna make you promise any results, and odds are we'll just decide to sneak by in the night anyhow."

Elijah snorted, a thin grin on his face. "Alright then. What's the offer?"

Elijah made out a smile on Stratton's face in the dim light of a nearby fire. "I didn't bring these beeves all the way from Texas just to make a one-time profit and call it a day."

"I wouldn't think so." Elijah was unsure where the conversation was headed.

"When I came through Alder Gulch and made my fortune a few years back, I realized two things: There's going to be a whole bunch of folks looking for beef, and there is more grazing land and access to water than anywhere else you could imagine. I intend to use the money I got and the money from selling these critters to start an enormous operation, and I want you to be part of it."

Elijah's eyes opened wide. He had assumed this drive was just a way to try and save Moses and put food in his stomach while earning a living on the way to a fresh start. "What role could I have in that?"

"I don't know what I'll call it yet, but I'll need a foreman of some kind. Someone to run operations, protect my land and assets, and so on." Stratton grinned broadly. You'll be rewarded handsomely."

"Mr. Stratton, I'm no cattle foreman, I—"

"Nonsense. You know how to lead men, and you know how to keep troublemakers in line. Hank and Travis can help you with the particulars. They aren't leaders or businessmen and don't want to be. From what you tell me, anyhow, before those bastards burnt it down, you were running a successful business you'd only just learned back in Omaha."

"I'm flattered. . . but I'd have to ask my brother."

Stratton laughed. "I knew you wouldn't go without him, so I gave him the grand scheme and ensured he'd be willing. He didn't even think twice. Said he'd be dead without all of us and that he was in if you were."

"Sounds like Mo," Elijah said, sticking his hand out. "We're in then, Mr. Stratton. And if you're going to be the boss, that's what I'll be calling you."

Stratton clapped Elijah on the back as he shook his hand. "Alright then. Go get some chow."

The man disappeared into the dark, and Elijah wandered to the chuck wagon, hoping he'd not missed his tin plate of biscuits and beans. He had just accepted a plate from the cook when he heard a voice behind him.

"He ask ya yet?"

Elijah whirled and shook his head at his brother. "Can't believe you kept that to yourself." He looked down, saw Brutus at Moses's side, and knelt to scratch the dog behind the ears to great acclaim.

Moses laughed. "Well, you were still off ensuring his fortune was safe when he found me." He rubbed his slinged left arm near the shoulder. "Told him I had plenty to thank him for anyhow, 'specially after he kept that sawbones they ride with from taking the arm off straight away."

Elijah began to eat while looking around the camp, a sense of peace coming to him. "Alright, then. We'll work for Mr. Stratton in Montana Territory. Really start over this time."

"We always said we should just head west up the Missouri and start farming in a new and interesting place." Moses made a show of looking around their surroundings, then grinned. "Guess we just took the long route."

Elijah snorted. "That we did. But I think it'll stick this time, brother."

Moses bent and gave Brutus some attention. "Hobbs would have hated this," he said. Elijah raised an eyebrow, and Moses laughed. "Just the lack of civilization, I mean. I know he'd like being with us." He stared into the distance. "Sam woulda loved both."

Elijah sighed. "I miss them."

They were both silent a moment, and then Moses looked at Elijah. "You're not gonna miss anything back in settled and civilized America, though?"

"I don't believe I will," Elijah replied. He took a bite of food, then nodded as if convincing himself. "I'm sure about that."

"You won't miss any*thing*," Moses said, giving the dog a final pat. He then stood and looked at Elijah. "But how about any*one?*"

Elijah looked east toward Omaha. Of that, he was not so sure.

⚓

Gallatin Valley, near Bozeman, Montana Territory
December 9, 1866

My Dear Maggie,

As the year draws to a close and winter grips the Montana Territory, I find myself in a winter camp nestled in Gallatin Valley, not far from a budding place called Bozeman. The snow blankets the vast, open landscapes here, turning the rugged wilderness into a white expanse. The towering mountains that encircle us are now majestic peaks capped with glistening snow, standing guard over our new home.

I hesitate to provide you with much of the details between when we last spoke and our arrival in this place. Our quest was successful but cost Matt Hobbs his life and almost cost Moses his. Matt was a good man who didn't have to come back, and it pains me that he is gone because he did so.

When I thought all was lost, we happened upon a man trailing cattle all the way from Texas to Montana who gave us work. We earned our keep, and he has offered us work to help run an operation we will establish in the spring. He has already sold some cattle for ten times the Texas prices, and I am embarrassed to admit we are being rewarded handsomely.

We are working hard for it, however. Life here is both challenging and rewarding in equal measure. The days are filled with the hard work of preparing for the harsh winter ahead, but a sense of camaraderie and purpose binds us all. Moses, Brutus, and I have settled into this life with surprising ease. The land is untamed, and each day brings a new adventure.

Despite the beauty and tranquility of this place, my thoughts often wander back to Omaha and you. The memory of our last conversation lingers with me, and I wonder how you fare in the city we left behind. I hope your father is well and you found comfort in life together.

Here, under the endless skies and amidst the quiet beauty of winter, there's a peace I've never known. However, I spend many hours lying awake at night, wondering if I should have returned with you. I fear the decision to keep us, and the rest of you, safe was the one that kept me from you forever.

I hope this letter finds you well and that life in Omaha treats you kindly. Should you wish to correspond, or if the winds of change ever carry you towards the west, please send word care of Summit Valley Ranch. Until then, you remain in my thoughts.

Thinking of you, I remain,

Elijah

PS: I am thinking they could use a livery and freight operation here as well.

THANK YOU

— • —

T hank you for reading! If you enjoyed the book, please consider leaving a review on Amazon and Goodreads. Reviewing is the most powerful way to support the authors you love and help others discover this captivating story. Furthermore, it's an invaluable way to connect with YOU, the reader, and ensure I continue delivering books that resonate with you.

Speaking of writing and reading, if the two Barber Brother novels are the first of mine you've read, you may be interested in a prequel titled *The Sheriff's Pursuit: A Vermilion County Mystery*. Taking place a decade before the Barber novels, it is told from the perspective of Sheriff Talbot Jones as he solves mysteries—with appearances by the Barbers. If you cherish the characters of Elijah and Moses Barber and wonder where their journey goes from here—book three, *The Legacy Stand*, is available now!

Be sure to check out JasonBakerAuthor.com to learn how to follow me on social media and Book Bub or sign up for my Substack newsletter to stay aware of future release dates.

As always, I owe a huge debt of gratitude to my developmental editor, Matt Henderson-Ellis. His exceptional work goes beyond providing guidance, critiques, feedback, and assessments on my drafts; he has been instrumental in shaping me into a better writer and has been a steadfast supporter. His contributions have elevated my work with every draft, and my success wouldn't be the same without him. In fact, his expertise is so in demand that aligning our schedules for this novel was a challenging task, but the results were well worth the effort.

I am deeply grateful to my family, relatives, friends, and acquaintances who have not only purchased my books but also shared their feedback, offered encouragement, spread the word on social media, and recommended my work to others. Your support has been invaluable in reaching readers who may not have otherwise discovered my books, and I owe much of my success to your loyalty and advocacy.

Finally, as always, I'm eternally grateful to my wife. Her partnership in my life genuinely humbles me. Despite Western Adventures not being her preferred genre, I can't express enough gratitude for her unwavering support of my writing (and patience while I recount the historical rabbit holes I go down while doing research). She's a fantastic friend, partner, and mother—and I couldn't do this without her.

-JBB

ABOUT THE AUTHOR

Jason Baker is a career military officer and celebrated author deeply immersed in the Civil War era. His non-fiction book *Chicago To Appomattox* and his fiction series *The Barber Brothers' Adventures* and *The Vengeance of Reed Caine* are full of meticulous research and classic Western adventure, capturing the tumultuous period of American history.

An Illinois native, Jason resides in Northern Virginia with his wife and two young sons. He is a member of the Western Writers of America, Western Fictioneers, and a Color Bearer Donor to the American Battlefield Trust. Jason dedicates his work to preserving and exploring America's historical landscapes and battlefields. When he's not writing or hiking battlefields, he enjoys following Illinois and Chicago sports teams, waterfowl hunting, and traveling with his family.

Learn more at JasonBakerAuthor.com, or you can also sign up for Jason's Substack newsletter.